Hatchir

Hatching Love

Hatching Love

Heidi Matonis

Blue Wren Publishing

Blue Wren Publishing

Hatching Love: a novel / Heidi Matonis / First edition.

Blue Wren Publishing Trade Paperback ISBN: 9798378732210
eBook ISBN: 9798378732210

www.heidimatonis.com

DEDICATION

To Alwyn Wils, my muse and fellow animal lover.

Hatching Love

CHAPTER 1

Beth made some nice improvements to the house this winter – painting the walls, I believe she called it Modern Eggshell. She had some furniture reupholstered, including my favorite chair, and got rid of the flotsam we've accumulated over... close to 30 years. Ghosts, I always thought, are supposed to like old, decrepit places with dust balls and creaky stairs, but I prefer this: a fresh, clean, contemporary look. I plan to stay.

I'm most excited about the yard, now that "spring has sprung" – excuse the tired expression but it describes the setting perfectly. Before I died, my amigo Miguel and I planted bulbs. Daffodils were everywhere last month, and now the tulips are riotous.

During my all-too-brief retirement, I enjoyed having an interest that gave me license to wander outside and tinker around the yard. I never knew I was so interested in botany because I never had time to foster a hobby. I moved from one scheduled appointment to the next. My whole life was a grid of time slots that were filled in by other people and their needs. I just obeyed my office manager, iPad, phone and wife.

At my Celebration of Life, Pierce, the president of the hospital, said what a talented surgeon I was. And I really was. I performed at the highest level. Then Beth spoke. She called me a "devoted father and great husband". Again, true. I never wavered in my duties, a stark contrast to my own father. Sure, he provided a roof and food but that's about it. He failed particularly fabulously as a husband to my ever-suffering mother. So I made it a point of pride that in addition to being Dr. Thomas Paradise – Maestro of the OR, I would also be Dr. Tom Paradise – The Greatest Husband.

It was smart to marry later in life. Any marriage can turn into a train wreck after you drag a woman through med. school and residency. Even I, Mr. Overachiever, knew that one more scheduled time slot – "8:00 - 9:00 p.m. Spend time with wife. Reminder: be affectionate, engaged, caring, concerned, humorous" – would have been too much. I waited until I was a full-fledged heart surgeon. Until I had a touch of distinguished grey just above my ears. Then, and only then, I sent a message to the universe: "Send me The Perfect Wife and I will be The Greatest Husband."

Voilá! Just a week later, I was invited to a dinner party. I had never been to a dinner party, nor had my parents. I was unapologetically breaking a family tradition. I arrived without the prerequisite bottle of wine and had no clever table topics top-of-mind. Everything I had learned about casual conversation was from eating fast food with my mom and later, at all-night hospital cafeterias with half-asleep colleagues.

I never imagined people did such silly, mindless things when they walked out of the hospital or drove home from the office: A group of people, the men with tan faces and the women with fresh makeup, sitting around a polished wood table talking about things, idle things that served no immediate purpose. It blew my mind. I thought, *Is this for real? Is this what success looks like? Is this what I've worked so hard for?* I pinched myself, a reminder to laugh when the others laughed, or at least smile.

The chair next to me remained empty until dessert, which made my social awkwardness even more apparent. I could only turn to the

2

woman on my left to engage in conversation. She wore a fuchsia dress that hurt my eyes and had hyperpigmentation along her jawline, an indicator that she had had some pregnancies. I tried to eavesdrop on other conversations, to literally fish for topics that might be appropriate. *Relaxing* was proving to be more work than open heart surgery.

Then Beth entered the room.

She apologized to the group, slipped into the empty chair on my right and gave me the most dazzling smile that beamed a message to my amygdala: *I'm here for you and only you.* I think I remembered to smile back but I can't be sure because I was transfixed by her chest. She had on a flesh-colored sleeveless blouse that draped very low and made a swag like a hammock.

I hadn't thought of a hammock in years, I don't think I've ever had a reason to say the word *hammock* out loud. But now I saw one, in miniature, right in front of me, and all I wanted was to lie in that hammock beside this angel's heart. I gazed at that creamy expanse of exposed sternum and focused approximately 30 degrees superior and 7 centimeters lateral from where her cleavage started and thought, *You, My Darling, must have a perfectly working heart with clean arteries, elastic valves and synchronized myocardium.*

Thank god I had the presence of mind not to say it.

Later that night, when I found myself in her bed and she had fallen asleep, I let my hand rest on her chest, like I was just casually holding her but, really, I was checking to make sure my professional intuition was right. I felt the steady beat and could imagine the tired blue blood leaving the right ventricle through the pulmonary artery and returning, fully oxygenated, to the left atrium and then pouring into the left ventricle to whoosh out the aorta to the rest of her body. I was sure, without any diagnostic equipment, that her heart worked perfectly.

And time has proven me right. Because even though my heart decided to stop suddenly, *catastrophically*, I'm still here, in our house, a ghostly presence beside her. That beautiful, strong heart of hers won't let me go.

CHAPTER 2

The eggs are here!

I chuckle. My Darling will be flustered that they came so quickly. She'll be even more rattled when she opens the box. I looked over her sweet shoulder as she placed the order to Strohman's Eggs & Hatchery. I saw her make the mistake of putting "1" in the shopping cart. I knew My Darling didn't read the fine print; I'm the meticulous one. I knew she didn't see the notation at the bottom: "one unit consists of 12 eggs."

I saw her pause, reassess, do the math, before she put in the credit card information. She was thinking, *$71.25 seems expensive for just one duck egg and an instruction guide,* but My Darling hit "Pay Now". We were committed.

When we ordered the eggs, I asked myself, "Why eggs? What's the objective? What's the optimum outcome of this human-avian experiment?" These are questions that a scientist asks. And any doctor worthy of his or her degree, remains a scientist at heart, always questioning, analyzing, developing hypotheses to solve potential problems. What's the objective?

Money is no object for us. Among my sterling qualities was the ability to provide my family a more than comfortable lifestyle. Beth will never need to worry about money. Tyler and Evie (our grown children) will have nest eggs (excuse the egg idiom but that's where my head is), money for a house or to help with their future children's education, *my* grandchildren. I'm sure Boring Jim (that's what I call our lawyer) will discuss with Beth the advantages to setting up trusts. I could kick myself for not doing it before dying, but how could I know my time was so near at hand?

The irony that I died from a heart problem, a thing I was so expert in, is not lost on me. I heard my lazy neighbor, Ray, blabbing at my Celebration of Life, "Well, you know what they say, 'the cobbler's children have no shoes' but in this case, it was the cobbler." Guffaw. I wanted to hit him. Beth always told me that I was too harsh for referring to him as lazy, that he was actually a good, hardworking guy. And yet, he never trimmed his bushes and I, and everyone else, had to detour off the sidewalk as we walked by. When I heard him make that quip about me, I realized I underestimated him, I should've called him Ray-the-Jerk.

Let me tell you, it's surreal to look down on your own departure, euphemistically called a *celebration of life*. No one attends dreary funerals any more but they flock to lively celebrations. I didn't find my own celebration that uplifting. I dropped dead right before the holidays, so my celebration was delayed until January 2nd, vax cards optional.

Being a doctor, not a psychic, I never expected to come back. I always assumed that when the heart, the most important organ in the body, stops, it's the end, *fini*. But I was wrong, dead wrong. The delay in my celebration gave me time to change into my comfortable shoes, favorite khakis, a blue button-down and my starchy, stiff doctor's coat. When I dropped dead, I had been shoveling snow in wool pants and a ski jacket.

Does everyone get to choose what they wear for eternity? Or am I an exception? Regardless, I'm perfectly comfortable with my choice.

So my event was actually a collection of people, tired from holiday merriment and leery of large gatherings. The people were there to support Beth, Tyler and Evie. Because, realistically, what could anyone do for me? What had they ever done? What had I done for them?

Beth's two best friends, Stick-Your-Nose-In-Everyone's-Business-Sandy and Drunk Emily, were standouts in their zest for social interaction and ability to deflect attention from me, the person being honored. Sandy worked the crowd like a seasoned politician. Meaning she was looking to connect home buyers to home sellers. Emily, reliably got drunk and loud and was driven home by Tyler. Only my amigo Miguel (and of course Beth) really exhibited the proper amount of grief. All in all, I'd say it was a pretty pathetic celebration of life or death.

I digress, but that's how it is – as a ghost. There are no schedules to hold me to a plan, to focus my attention, to remind me to stay on track. I just sort of float through the day, and the night, for that matter. It's very liberating and I'm enjoying the experience immensely.

I can't read Beth's mind. Trixie, our geriatric dog and I are alike in a lot of ways, we both watch and wait. We're here to serve our Darling, the mistress of our heart. We listen to her voice, watch her movements and facial expressions and then we act. When Beth is sad and lonely which, let's be frank, is a lot, Trixie puts her grizzled head on our Darling's knee and I tuck in right beside her. We can usually evoke a smile; it's not perfect but it's the best that we can do.

Beth seems happier since she ordered the eggs, I mean, since *we* ordered the eggs. Personally, I'm fine but Beth tells our children and her friends that she's "mired in misery" and "suffers from loneliness". I've been gone for seven months, and she's not getting better, she's getting worse – deteriorating. If I sound judgmental, I'm not. The pandemic was hard on everyone and just when the coast was clearing, her beloved drops dead. Everyone tells her, "Time. Time will cure all heartache." Time, as a cure, is a worn cliché. Ask any doctor. We all know time is the ultimate killer – dodge a bullet today, time takes you down eventually.

Anyone can play doctor and prescribe a remedy but I'm not sure even *I* know the cure. I suspect my existence is dependent on Beth's sorrow. Her longing and pining for her lost love allows me a second chance. I'd like her to be happy, I truly would. If she can just sit tight, until we're ready to move to Paris and start our lives over with a touch of culture and romance, we'll both be better off. *Paris* is the cure. Paris is where we honeymooned, Paris is where we'll find love again.

Speaking of Paris, we're learning French!

We started before I died, during the thick of the pandemic. The plan was to practice every day using Duolingo and then we were going to live in Paris, at least for a while. Why not? We had money and time, the world was our playground! When I died, Beth grieved so deeply, she forgot to do her Duolingo and was demoted to the Bronze League. They call it Bronze but it's the rock bottom. We had to battle our way back to the top – Silver! Gold! Sapphire! Ruby! Emerald! Amethyst! Pearl! Obsidian! Diamond! Diamond is where we belong. I really missed it. Doctors know the easiest way to grow old is to stop learning. I don't want to grow old; I want to stay sharp. I think we'll be fluent by winter. *"Nous allons habiter à Paris!"*

Meanwhile Beth's friend, Drunk Emily, a new convert to cognitive therapy, insisted Beth go. She recommended a newly-minted, full-of-herself cognitive therapist. Emily kept saying, "She's the absolute best, Beth, the *best*." Vomit. "She'll help you get a new perspective, *forget* Tom and move on with your life. *Guaranteed*."

So we went to the best cognitive therapist together, couples therapy, if you will. I left Beth's side and wandered over to look closely at her credentials. Public institutions, all of them. I went back to My Darling and whispered one word: "Bush league." Well, two words.

Our appointment was for 45 minutes, but we were out in 32.

Beth's other friend, Stick-Your-Nose-In-Everyone's-Business Sandy, suggested Beth sell the house. "Move on, you don't need the worry and expense, make space in your life, open yourself to a fresh start. " Blah blah blah…

Tyler and Evie, although they don't visit often, like coming back to this house full of happy memories. Beth had my amigo Miguel – Beth's go-to-helper now – do some painting and sprucing up this winter so we would have the *option* of putting the house on the market, but now we like it better than ever.

"Thank you very much, Stick-Your-Nose-In-Everyone's-Business Sandy, we're good. In fact we're *nesting*. Ha!"

I knew selling the house was off the table when Beth ordered the eggs. The eggs were 100% Beth's idea. I would have never thought of it. I sat beside her when she watched the YouTube video, "Incubating an Egg with my Body". I heard My Darling actually giggle at the end. The idea: an Average Joe with a scruffy beard and soft belly decides to incubate an egg. He makes a hatching belt, using a plastic cup and some foam rubber. He wears an unfertilized chicken egg around for a while, blabbing to the camera about feelings of "hope" and "love".

He fancies himself a scientist as he drills a hole and inserts a thermometer, "Don't worry, no chick was harmed!" Gag. He's shooting for 37.5 degrees Celsius and "gets close enough". Then he puts the fertilized duck egg in the belt and wears it around for 30 days. He takes goofy footage of him trying to sleep and him sneaking peeks of his fat abdomen. On day 30, the egg hatches and, I will be the first to admit, the duckling is pretty cute. It's yellow and downy and he puts it in a bowl of water and feeds it dead flies. Children's music plays and the viewer feels good, successful, fulfilled.

Beth even leaned down and showed Trixie the duckling in the bowl. Trixie was mildly interested in the peeping coming from the iPad but overall unimpressed with the science. Like me.

Beth researched where to buy fertilized duck eggs and ordered *one* egg. What's the objective? After two sleepless nights (they're all sleepless) and an afternoon spent entirely by myself, while Beth was out buying supplies to make a hatching belt, I have concluded My Darling wants to finally make use of our pond out back.

It's brilliant!

CHAPTER 3

When I started dabbling in botany. I became very interested in dwarf fruit trees. The process of raising fruit is really the study of genetics. My amigo Miguel was cavalier about the undertaking. He said his family had grown fruit down in Mexico for generations. I did all the research and purchasing, he did the digging. He planted three apples, two pears, two plums and one peach. This is one reason Beth and I can't move to France yet; we need to stay and see all my hard work come to fruition. Haha, literally!

Now the eggs have arrived, and they'll be an interesting project and I will add Aviculturist to my list of accomplishments. I've been waiting quite a while, sitting on the front step beside the delivered eggs, like a child eager to open gifts on Christmas morning, when My Darling finally walks up the driveway with Trixie, her signature ponytail swinging. She walks up to the box and actually looks miffed. Just wait until she opens the box and finds not one egg but twelve!

My Darling is no procrastinator. She bought the supplies needed to make a hatching belt and there's plenty to spare. My amigo Miguel saw her struggling with the drill, making a hole in the chicken egg. The drill bit had already slipped, injuring her index finger (phalange D2). She made a makeshift bandage and let Miguel take charge. We tested the temperature – 37.3 C – .3 degrees better than Average Joe's results. We have our belt and are ready to go!

Beth carries the egg box in and puts it on the kitchen counter. She gets scissors and very carefully slits the packing tape. There's a box inside a box... the suspense builds! She opens the second box and there, before us, are a dozen, smooth, fertilized duck eggs! They're not pure white like chicken eggs; they're the color of old people's teeth that have been stained by nicotine and coffee.

My Darling takes her adorable hand, the one with the makeshift bandage, and puts it to her mouth in surprise. It's an exaggerated gesture, perfect for the cinema. The plot: lonely woman seeks baby, places order, gets way more than she bargained for, kooky chaos ensues. Do ghosts laugh? I say *yes*! Beth doesn't hear me but most definitely, my laughter adds to the laugh track of life and I'm trying to do more of it these days.

My Darling is so disconcerted by the abundance of our package, our hatching cup *literally* runneth over, that she just stands and stares. Ha! I knew this was going to happen and have hatched (excuse the pun) a few ideas of my own for dealing with the duplicates. Remember, Beth is the initial mastermind. That being said, I am a committed partner. I'm ready to pull my weight to hatch an egg and populate our pond.

Beth sits down, paging through the hatching handbook. The author is Mary Strohman, probably the matriarch of Strohman's Eggs & Hatchery. It's obviously self-published and I've found two typos already.

Beth's engrossed. I'm bored. I've read more clever stethoscope manuals than this hatching handbook. She gets a highlighter and underlines, "Eggs which have been in transit should be stored in a cool place (40-60F) 12-24 hours prior to incubation." That's a surprise; I would have skipped over that bit of information. She walks over and looks at the gauge on our wine cooler, it's 55 F on the dot. She moves some bottles around and puts the tray of eggs in and walks outside. Trixie and I follow.

It's approximately noon on Friday. My Darling just bought us 24 hours to solve the problem of 12 eggs. (Potentially 12 babies!)

After a few strolls around the yard, we go back into the house and My Darling sits down at her laptop, and goes to her Facebook page, which seems like a typical teen procrastination tactic, but then she types:

Friends, join me in an experiment to hatch happiness! Please watch this video (hyperlink). If this idea delights you and you want to join me, I have a hatching belt and egg ready to deliver to you today! I have a pond on my property and can take any ducklings that need a home when your job as a mother duck is done. Please reach out in messenger: time is of essence.

She takes a photo of the tray of eggs and the hatching belt that Miguel helped her make and adds it to the post. It's positively brilliant!

However, I'm bothered by the description: *an experiment to hatch happiness*. I realize she had to give *some* motivation to prospective participants to go through 30 days of inconvenience, yet it hurts my pride – I'm happy and content and realize Beth isn't. But for once, just once, I'm going deep within myself, I'm learning about me, Tom the human, not Tom the doctor. I'm confident that after the fruit trees bear fruit, and we move to Paris, she'll be happy, too.

I really like how she says, *I have a pond on my property and can take any ducklings that need a home.* More ducks for our pond! That was very clever. Beth is like Tom Sawyer getting Huck Finn to whitewash the picket fence, but instead of whitewashing, its hatching eggs, even more laborious.

I must admit, my solution to 12 vs.1 egg was a little less involved. I thought we should make a second hatching belt – have a control and a variable – in case egg A wasn't fertilized or got damaged, we'd have egg B. Beth would wear two belts and we'd throw the other 10 eggs away. Problem solved!

We're reading peacefully when Trixie barks. Beth and I get up and go outside, where my amigo Miguel is taking a bag of fertilizer out of his truck. It's fun to listen to Beth tell Miguel of her surprise that 12 eggs came. He exclaims, *"Ay caramba!"* We all laugh. Then

Beth takes him inside and shows him her Facebook post. They bend over the tray of eggs, like they are gemologists accessing the value of a tray of diamonds. They find one egg with a tiny crack.

Frankly, I'm relieved. That brings us down to 11. We all walk out to the back yard and Beth gently lays the egg in the compost pile. They both look so sad. I want to yell, "It's not a living thing! There's no blastoderm! I'm more alive than that cracked egg!"

Of course, I can't yell, so I just watch. Beth thinks every soul is worth saving and I think it's this sterling quality in her that gives me this second chance. I think Trixie understands. She cocks her head, looks right at me and wags her tail. She never lived in the true animal kingdom, kill or be killed, but she understands the weak don't survive.

Trixie is old now and only hunts in her dreams, just like I only do surgery in mine. I miss that satisfying crack of the sternum and all the sharp, shiny tools. I miss being called "Dr. Paradise". I miss the relatives thanking me effusively for saving their loved one. Some of my ghost days lack... adrenaline, but it's okay.

Beth and Miguel walk away while I stand lost in thought. When Beth calls, "Trixie Girl, come!" We both lift our heads. Trixie trots and I walk to the garage. Beth is telling Miguel to make as many hatching belts as he can with the supplies we have. I mentally access that there is enough foam rubber for 40 hatching belts, maybe enough rolled Velcro for 10 hatching belts and Beth carries out six more deli containers.

Miguel goes to work while Beth and I walk inside to check our Facebook post. We have no messages but Beth has a "Friends request." It's from my amigo. Beth laughs, he's right on the other side of the door, in the garage. She "accepts", which, I guess, is the gracious thing to do.

I'm not sure if Beth and I were ever Facebook friends. I always thought Facebook was a waste of time. I begrudgingly had an account for my patients to feel connected to me. But, in reality, the only thing that interested me was their malfunctioning heart. That's just the plain truth.

After she accepts Miguel as a "friend" she gets a "ding!" and a "wave" in Messenger. It's Miguel again, waving. She "waves" back. This is even more absurd than I realized. Then, and only then, she gets a message from Miguel: *"Quiero un huevo."*

Beth goes out to the garage. Miguel is grinning at the workbench with his white teeth and porcupine hair, holding his phone. "Yes, of course you can have an egg, Miguel! How about ten!" They both laugh.

"No, no, no, just *uno*."

When Beth closes the door, she's still smiling. They both found the exchange entertaining, funny, fulfilling. As living, breathing Dr. Paradise, I would have found it wasteful, cumbersome, ridiculous. But as Ghost Paradise, I'm trying to be a little more light-hearted and frivolous.

There were times, when I was living, when I tried, I really tried to enjoy pointless interactions, but my resolve had limits. The truth is, I never even enjoyed interacting with my own children all that much. Don't get me wrong, I loved them and I certainly provided for them. In hindsight, I can say with a degree of certainty, the only person I truly enjoyed, day in and day out, was My Darling. She was everything the doctor ordered.

As a ghost, I vow to work on myself. I will be more tolerant, if not for me, than for Beth. A string of *happy* little interactions like this will get us through to the fall. If Beth stays happy *enough*, I'm sure the natural course of events will lead her... *us*... to our new life in Paris.

CHAPTER 4

I've accepted the notion that electronic friendship can bring moments of happiness, when we get a second "ding!" (*not* from Miguel). Now that I know how this works, the "ding!" is actually a little exciting, like that first spontaneous heartbeat off bypass. *This* "ding" is from a woman named Jessica Kline. I don't recognize her name and I don't think Beth does either, because she furrows her brow as she reads the simple message: "I need 3 eggs." Right below, a separate message bubble: "Please."

I'm terrible with names. I'm sure if I was young today, some doctor would place me on a spectrum of some kind, which is totally fine. Some of our most brilliant minds, Sir Isaac Newton, Albert Einstein, Paul Dirac, and even Steve Jobs were on the spectrum. Excellent company.

It was Beth who suggested I remember names by adding descriptors. The descriptors made people come alive. Beth said it was unfortunate that most of my monikers had a negative bent, but how else could I remember if I didn't join them to their identifying truth?

Beth goes to her Facebook home page and searches Jessica Kline. She scans the woman's gallery of pictures. There are many photos with small girls in them. Beth studies one picture that shows Jessica on a yoga mat doing a twisty pose. She reminds me of Beth, long legs, brown ponytail, coordinated exercise outfits. My guess is that she knows this woman casually from yoga class.

"What is your address? I will deliver them."

"Five-thirty Round House Road."

I whistle under my breath. Round House Road is swanky. It's the tornadoes cut in our tenderloin town. I could've bought a house on Round House Road years ago but Beth liked where we were. With the addition of the fruit trees, I was beginning to think of it as my gentleman's farm. But seeing that coveted address rankles my pride a bit.

I remind myself, who cares about addresses? Addresses and social status are for the living. My job now is to stop and smell the flowers, laugh more and support Beth 'til we pull up stakes and move to France!

Miguel taps on the door and steps into the mudroom. I'm not sure when this started but it seems a little overfamiliar. Trixie doesn't even bother barking. He tells Beth he's all done. We all step out to the garage and survey the seven hatching belts. It doesn't take a math wizard to know that would be the output of this pile of supplies. She asks him if he wants to take his egg now and he says, "*Sí*."

Beth gets the tray and holds it for Miguel like it's a box of artisanal chocolates. He contemplates and picks an egg from the center, which strikes me as greedy and presumptuous. I don't like his choice. It might have been the best egg in the bunch, the dark chocolate covered caramel egg, so to speak. Beth just laughs and reminds him to keep it cool and start wearing it tomorrow.

Beth carries the tray and three hatching belts into the house. She lays the belts on the counter, selects three eggs and gently pushes them into their foam rubber nests. She puts the tray with the remaining seven eggs back into the wine cooler, carries the eggs out to the car and arranges them on the passenger seat. Trixie and I have both followed her out to the garage. Beth bends down and pats Trixie's head, "Come on, girl, you have to stay here." She takes Trixie back in and I'm left... torn.

Part of me knows it's more prudent to stay home, on my gentleman's farm, but part of me really wants to see this palatial house

(I'm assuming it's palatial) at 530 Round House Road. It's a calculated risk; I don't know if this woman has dogs, or if that even matters. I don't know if this woman is clairvoyant, or if such a thing even exists. I'm still not sure how my vapor-self interacts with the outside environment. My thinking goes: I seem to exist very well in my home beside my loving wife, or should I say, possibly *because* of my loving wife. I am perfectly safe here…

…but I want to see why this smiling, well-kept woman wants three eggs! She has a small torso which will be hard pressed to accommodate three hatching belts. Plus, Beth has sold this as a "happiness experiment"; what does she need that she can't buy? How much happiness does this woman *have* to hatch?

I'm going. It's just *too* mysterious!

Beth drags Trixie back into the house. Trixie gives me an accusatory look, like, "Why do *you* get to go?" Ha! Being a ghost has its privileges... but sometimes so does being a dog.

I climb in the open driver's door and work my way into the back seat. Sitting in the backseat is annoying. First, there's dog hair, second, there's no leg room. Neither should bother me, but they do. I much prefer the front passenger seat but I very well couldn't *sit o*n the eggs.

The drive out Round House Road is lovely; tulips and dogwood are blooming, splashing the landscape with color. Majestic houses sit in the middle of emerald lawns, like ladies sitting on picnic blankets. The *créme de la créme* live in our town and, specifically, on Round House Road. In fact, the hospital's number one donor has a house out here. We'll probably drive right by it. He's some sort of hedge fund manager who thinks, because he shits money, he's king. But those are no longer my concerns, it's a beautiful spring afternoon and I'm out for a ride with My Darling.

When we see 500s on the mailboxes, Beth starts to slow down. It will be on our right, an even number. There! The big gate is Tudor style.

I'm so glad I came; this will be worth the risk of admission. Beth inches the car forward, giving the gate time to open. The long driveway, lined with beautiful old trees, curves extravagantly. The last bend, reveals a house that looks like a castle made of old field stones, with one rounded corner like a miniature turret. It's obviously very old and is probably a replica of some ancient estate in Ireland or England. Is it possible I'll see a fellow ghost?

The grounds are well kept, edged and mulched, and the driveway makes a circle in front of the house, with tulips blooming in the center. But the front of the house is a mess, with toys scattered around the granite steps: small bikes, roller skates, scooters and even large empty boxes. At first I think the boxes were thrown out the door because some large appliances were just delivered and unpacked but then I see little squares cut out and drawings on the sides. They're being used to make forts or houses or whatever kids make.

There's a big rainbow drawn on the driveway with sidewalk chalk. Beth is careful to stop short of driving over it. It looks like this old manor cannot contain youthful exuberance and it spills out the door.

While I'm admiring, observing and speculating on this new environment (This is only my second car ride!), Beth gets out and closes her driver's door. Bam!

I'm getting ready to worm my way from the backseat into the front seat and make my way out the passenger door but two young girls burst out of the house and I freeze. I've not laid eyes on a child in almost a year and I am startled, maybe even intimidated. Beth walks around the car, opens the passenger door, takes all three hatching belts off the seat and Bam! Slams the door.

In a blink, I've lost my chance to exit and I'm trapped in the car like a goldfish in a bowl. The two little girls are both talking to Beth, jumping up and down. They seem to have no inhibitions when it comes to strangers. Now Beth is talking to them but I can't hear what she's saying.

A third girl, the tallest, comes out of the door. She slowly descends the few granite steps while holding on to the banister. The younger two girls have crazy frizzy blond hair, falling down their backs like fairy nymphs. The taller girl has short hair and is more delicate in her features and more reserved with her movements. The mother, I assume Jessica, steps out; I gasp. She's wearing white jeans, a navy tee and her hair is in a swinging ponytail and could be Beth's younger sister or her grown daughter.

They talk, laugh and gesticulate. Jessica touches each of the girls' heads, probably introducing them. Then Beth touches each of their heads with the same gesture.

I've moved up to my rightful spot in the passenger seat and have my face pressed against the window but the thick glass and the quick conversation, layered with the chatter of children's voices, makes it impossible to understand a word.

The busy scene takes a crazy twist when Jessica kneels down, lifts the smallest girl's dress and straps one of the hatching belts around her middle. When the mother drops the dress back in place, there's a long tail of Velcro hanging down. I can tell Beth doesn't like this. Jessica runs up the stone steps and returns with scissors. She kneels again, lifts the dress and trims the extra Velcro. I can see the child's belly; it's a white orb. As her mother fiddles with the fit and where the hatching belt should sit, the child's thumb finds her mouth. She smiles the entire time.

This tot is way too young to take on 30 days of the rigorous responsibility of hatching an egg. She can't possibly understand how her actions will affect this other living thing, be it a duck, which I don't really care about, but still...

Jessica calls the second child over, lifts her dress and fits her like the first. Maybe she's eight years old. It's so hard to guess and I forget all the milestones of juvenile development. She, too, smiles; this child seems just as pleased with her strapped-on obligation as the youngest.

Then Jessica rises and goes to the tallest, I assume the eldest. I'm not sure if this child is more leery of the 30 days of difficulties ahead or why the mother seems to approach her with hesitation. This girl is wearing pants and the mother only lifts her shirt. Instead of an orb, there's a rib cage with protruding bones, as delicate as any fledgling bird.

This girl never actually smiles but she doesn't frown, either. I can't read her mood from behind the car window but I can definitely read Beth's; her posture is stiff and her mouth rigid. She's uncomfortable with the mother bestowing these eggs on these children. My guess is that Beth feels like a co-conspirator and she blames herself for not asking more questions before agreeing to giving them the eggs.

Beth starts talking emphatically to Jessica and the girls but only Jessica listens. Poor Beth is doing her best but the two youngest have started to ride circles around her on their tiny pink bikes. Beth does a forced smile, waves and gets in the car. I look over at her and I can tell by Beth's frown that she just plain disapproves.

I'm a naturally curious person, a problem solver, so this will be fodder for my active intellect, but right now, my role is supportive spouse. I'm not sure my whispering is heard on any level, but I'd like to think I can influence, guide, support My Darling with my murmurs. Otherwise, what good am I? So I try to reassure her by whispering, "It's not our problem. We needed to get rid of the eggs anyway."

The two littlest girls ride their bikes after us as we make our way down the loopy driveway to the gate. Beth keeps looking in her rearview mirror to make sure they're a safe distance behind us. The gate opens and we head toward home as I wonder why Jessica thinks her girls need to participate in a happiness experiment? They look plenty happy to me.

Even though I was inhumanely trapped in the car, it had its rewards: the house was magnificent, the woman captivating and the children were fascinating. I found the whole pantomimed scenario mesmerizing.

Being the ever-so-helpful husband, I whisper, "Motown," into Beth's ear, hoping she turns on music and cheers up but she doesn't seem to hear me. Or chooses to ignore me.

CHAPTER 5

By the time we get home, Beth seems calmer and happier. Once inside, she turns on some 80s rock, we swing to the beat and she decides to treat herself to a glass of wine. When she opens the wine cooler we check the remaining seven eggs. They're fine, nothing new to report.

While she eats dinner, I lean over and whisper my master plan: "Don't stress, we'll just throw *all* the extra eggs away." Beth frowns. I don't know if it's dinner or my plan. We watch one show and do Duolingo in bed. It's a perfect Friday evening, cozy *and* productive. Lights out, night-night.

But nights can be odious for me. As a ghost, I don't need sleep *per se*, at least not REM. Don't get me wrong, I love lying down beside My Darling, putting my feet up, but I don't actually sleep. It's not that peaceful. I usually start the night next to Beth but end it beside Trixie.

Once My Darling is deeply asleep, I put my ear to her chest and check that fantastic heart of hers. Most people think the heart sound is a simple lub-dub, but that's completely wrong. There are actually five points of auscultation. The aortic, pulmonic, tricuspid, and mitral valves make four sounds and the fifth sound is Erb's point, located left of the sternal border in the third intercostal space.

I must check them all because, as Ray-the-Jerk, pointed out at *my* Celebration of Life, the cobbler died *without* shoes. I swear, this cobbler's wife won't die without shoes! So, each night, I eventually rise from my unruffled side of the bed, lay my ear against My

Darling's chest and listen for the five sounds of coronary health and then I spend a few moments whispering in her ear.

What do I whisper?

I usually start with, "I love Tom. He's The Greatest Husband. He's everything I need. I'm so happy." Then I think about our day, maybe there was something we could improve upon. For instance, today it was being part of that obscenity of strapping those eggs to those tots. To address this discomfort, I whisper, "It's okay, we would've thrown those eggs away anyway. This debacle is Jessica's problem, not ours."

I usually add something I'd like to accomplish the next day, sort of plant my to-do list, so to speak. Tonight, I whisper, "We need to do more Duolingo tomorrow. We're not at the top of the leaderboard and it'll be time to move to Paris before we know it. We also need to double check that Miguel gave each of the fruit trees a boost of fertilizer." And of course, being thorough, I whisper, "We'll need to strap our egg on, the 24 hours will be up." I'm really indifferent to the eggs and I know Beth won't forget, but I feel it's my job to support her in this venture. Afterall, I *am* The Greatest Husband.

Tonight, my whispers circle back to how much she loves me. I think seeing Jessica reminded me of all the tenderness in our early courtship and how "I love you" wasn't just meagerly parsed out at the end of the day. So I lean close and murmur, "I love you, Tom. You're handsome and strong and I burn for your touch. I'll never let you go." And I add, "I love you too, My Darling. You are my life. You are everything to me and without you I'm *nothing*."

My work is done and I go downstairs and join Trixie beside her dog bed.

Trixie is a stupendous dog. I neither really appreciated nor loved her when I was alive. She always seemed dirty and obsequious and I didn't understand why Beth and the kids fussed and fawned over her.

24

But once I was retired, I had the time to notice the nuances of her stellar character and her charms grew on me.

The first year of my retirement, I must admit, I was depressed. The days seemed to stretch forever and I dragged through them but I wasn't alone; the pandemic brought everyone down. Trixie never left me or gave up on me. She just stayed beside me, concerned and encouraging.

When I marked my second year of retirement, I got the spring back in my step. I began to see each empty day as a great opportunity that *I* got to fill with whatever *I* wanted. Trixie enjoyed the new me and accompanied me while I walked around the yard finding little projects and improvements for my amigo Miguel.

Being a ghost has made me appreciate man's best friend, namely Trixie. Throughout the day, she gives me quizzical looks that amuse me. We're teammates in our efforts to help, support and love Beth all day, every day. But at night, Trixie suffers and I assume the role of the doctor and healer. Trixie is old. She used to sleep up in our room, on the floor, on Beth's side of the bed, but now the stairs are too much for her arthritic old legs. If I were alive, I'd carry her up those steps, but she's too heavy for Beth. So each night, My Darling puts Trixie in her dog bed, pats her head and walks upstairs.

Little does Beth know, Trixie whines all night long. She feels all the pains she suppresses during the day, it's a very common phenomenon, even in people. Most likely it's the drop in cortisol, which acts as an anti-inflammatory. I like to sit beside Trixie and try to soothe her with Spatula. I should say, *Beth's spatula*, but now it's mine.

Beth has... *had* a very old rubber spatula, a relic that needed to be replaced. It was probably in the boxes we unpacked when we moved into this house. It has scraped untold numbers of mixing bowls filled with cake or cookie batter. The rubber has turned yellow and there are little shards missing from a nip of the mixing paddle or just

25

from brittle old age. The wooden handle has been chewed by a teething child, or maybe Trixie.

The first month after I died, Beth made a cake for her friend Emily. She had gone to rehab and was coming home, freshly sober and self-aware. When I was alive I called her Drunk Emily but after *my* death and *her* rehab, I changed her name to Self-Aware-Emily.

I digress. Beth is alighting around the kitchen like a beautiful pink butterfly. The spatula is on the counter with the chewed wooden handle jutting over the edge. Beth turns, bumps it with her hip, feels nothing and I watch the spatula start to slide down over the edge of the counter. The only thing that slows it is the sticky cake mix adhering to the marble. It's tortuous to watch its slow descent, inevitable fall and contamination. So, without really thinking, I reach out and grab it. And you know what? *I'm actually able to hold it!*

My ghost self is able to physically interact with this lowly spatula. I can think of many more instruments that I'd rather be able to interact with such as: clamps, forceps and scalpel, the common work horses in cardiothoracic surgery but instead, I am handed a spatula, a common workhorse in the kitchen. I can almost hear Ray-the-Jerk quip, "Beggars can't be choosers!" (which does have a ring of truth). And even though I was initially irked by the indignity of this lowly utensil, I have grown to depend and love Spatula and have no plans to give her back.

Occasionally, I see Beth bend over and paw through the utensil drawer, thinking that somehow she's overlooked it. Nope. I've got Spatula stashed under the cushion of my favorite chair. I hide Spatula there until I need her. If I want to carry Spatula during the day, I can tuck her under my arm, inserting the rubber end in my armpit. Spatula has proven indispensable over and over and it's nice to have one possession I can call my own.

At night I use Spatula to soothe Trixie. I sit beside her and stroke her, trying to ease away her pain. She seems to appreciate it and occasionally thumps her tail. I've put my head to Trixie's rib cage and listened to her heart. It's my clinical opinion that her heart is fine but her body is riddled with cancer. Cancer is an insidious slow death but a catastrophic heart attack sneaks up on you and catches you by complete surprise. As a human I never liked surprises, good or bad, but as a ghost I like them even less.

So morning finally comes and I tuck Spatula under the chair cushion. Beth comes down and takes the eggs out of the wine cooler. The self-published hatching handbook says to let the eggs gradually come to room temperature before beginning the incubation process. Beth runs her hand over the cool surface of the eggs and leaves the tray out to begin warming.

She makes coffee and checks her Facebook post; we have messages. Most just say, "Fun!" But Stick-Your-Nose-Everyone's-Business-Sandy's says, "Good Luck. Let me know how that goes!" I read it imagining a snide tone of voice: "how *that* goes". Beth replies, "I will!" I've always thought of Sandy as just plain rude but Beth says Sandy is "fun and kinetic".

Beth checks her Facebook messenger. Nothing.

We have seven eggs reaching room temperature and a ticking clock. I can tell Beth is agitated when she decides to take Trixie for a walk. Good ol' Trixie gives me a backward glance like, "I'll do my best to make her happy."

I let my mind wander. If Beth had left the door open, I would have enjoyed strolling out in the yard and fussing over my dwarf fruit trees with Spatula in hand. I'm not sure what I could accomplish but it would be nice to be outside. Instead, I'm left staring at the eggs, contemplating if I should crush a few to make Beth's life easier, her conscience clearer. I am pressing Spatula against the cool shell of an egg when a "ding!" stops me. I know that "ding!" It's Beth's Facebook messenger. We just got a message; maybe our overabundance problem is taken care of!

27

CHAPTER 6

When Beth and Trixie get home, Beth fusses around the kitchen.

"Check your messenger! We're on egg time here, we only have a few more hours to get rid of these extra eggs!" It's not so much my concern for the eggs, I really only care about one egg, our egg, the egg My Darling chooses and we hatch and nurture together. But a message is a message and I'm actually tempted to get Spatula, tap Beth and point to the laptop, but I know that would be... problematic.

It's getting close to noon when Beth finally flips open the laptop. Her eyes track to the upper right and she clicks on the corner icon. Together, our eyes devour the message. It's from Jessica and merely says, "We need 3 more eggs." In a separate bubble, "Please."

Beth's brow is furrowed in a most unbecoming way. Dare I say a scowl? I'm as annoyed as Beth by the carelessness, the lack of responsibility, the disregard for life... but then I realize – I'm not annoyed at all. This is actually the best message we could've received.

Beth's fingers hesitate over the keyboard. Is she going to type NO? I whisper in her ear, "Yes, say yes, please, please."

Her fingers levitate... she taps, "OK."

She takes a tea towel and carefully wraps three eggs in it. While I'm trying to guess which ones will be the leftovers, rubbish, unloved, she goes out to the garage and brings in three hatching belts. I'm confused because the girls already have belts with custom-cut Velcro straps. My Darling runs her hands over the four remaining eggs, picks three and pushes them into their foam rubber nests. Then, to my astonishment, she straps all three to her thin torso.

She stares at the last egg, the reject. I can tell she's reluctant to give up on it and she's ticking through all the possibilities. I whisper, "Compost pile." But Beth brushes off my idea and she opens the range warming drawer. She touches the stainless steel with her hand and feels a slight warmth. Our kitchen floor has radiant heat and one of the pipes runs behind this drawer, keeping it continually warm, without actually having to turn it on.

Beth takes the last egg, makes a nest out of a dish towel and puts it in the warming drawer. It's a good solution but completely unscientific and unproven. She runs upstairs and comes down wearing a blouse printed with flowers, I think it must be new. She's wearing it untucked so it can drape over the three belts.

Poor Trixie has to stay. I jump in the passenger seat when Beth opens the driver's door. She puts the sachet of three eggs in the cup holder and we're off, with *six* eggs. The day was bright and clear but now it's getting dim. The clouds heading our way are deep gray and look like they're full of rain.

By the time we're in front of the Kline's gate, there are fat raindrops intermittently hitting the windshield. The front of the house is arranged with the same tableau of pink toys scattered around the front door. The boxes, still strewn around, are starting to absorb the rain. The chalk rainbow is dissolving bleeding colored rivulets of water.

I'm careful to get out of the car with Beth and not get trapped this time. Before we can ring the doorbell, Jessica comes to the door and invites us in. Her ponytail swings as she walks through the grand foyer into the kitchen-living area.

The house does not disappoint, it's as magnificent on the inside as the outside. There are a few really old heavy wooden pieces, namely a dining room table and a huge wall cupboard that look original to the house, but the rest of the furniture is contemporary, light, airy, and expensive.

The inside is cluttered, strewn with toys and girls' things. I see a pink tutu on the sofa and a coffee table piled with dress-up clothes. There's a hairbrush and ribbons on the kitchen counter. Jessica makes no apologies, or pretenses that this degree of chaos is exceptional.

She calls, "Girls!"

The two youngest come running into the kitchen, screaming. They're wearing nothing but little girls' underwear with Disney princesses on them. A nanny comes running after them, brandishing two tee shirts.

I decide to stand on a kitchen chair that's against the wall and away from all the action. I don't trust the two young girls' erratic movements. I don't know what will happen if one of them bumps into me or decides to walk right through me. It's all a little precarious and unpredictable.

The smallest is holding her hatching belt, yelling, "I want an egg! I want an egg!"

"Charlotte. *Stop!* Please!" Jessica says,

The second girl has quietly untied the tea towel and is touching the three eggs. I think she's trying to figure out which egg is the best.

"Sophia, let me see!" Charlotte screams.

Then the third girl walks in. She's dressed in pants and a fleece top even though it's quite warm inside. Because her hair is short, it doesn't tumble down her back in a wild mess. She's as neat and delicate as the day before.

Jessica moves over to this girl and gently lays her hand on the girl's tidy hair. She says in a low voice, almost more to the girl than to the rest of us, "Margaret had a bad night last night, didn't we?" She looks the girl in the eye and this girl looks truly mournful. She nods in agreement with her mother. It's hard to believe she's involved in the breaking of all three eggs.

I don't understand this intimate scene between mother and daughter. I'm having a hard time giving context to the excessive wealth, the chaos and mess and the general mood of rambunctiousness, dampened by regret? Melancholy? Sadness?

Meanwhile I'm ignominiously standing on a kitchen chair looking down on all of them. I watch Beth for clues. Her eyes are narrowed and I can tell she's as disoriented as I am. Jessica is not fleshing out any scenario in which all three eggs break, so Beth brilliantly takes matters into her own hands and they all watch the Average Joe hatch the egg video together.

Beth asks for a piece of paper and a pen. The middle sized girl, Sophia, brings her a pile of paper and eight markers. Beth makes a simple grid with three rows of ten squares. In the third square, first row she writes, "Veins."

"Veins," Sophia reads.

Beth explains how on day three they'll hold their eggs to the light and look for veins, just like Average Joe did.

In the last square she draws a little duck outline. She asks Charlotte, "What's that?"

Charlotte says, "Duck!" But then she pouts and says, "I can read, too!"

There are twenty-seven squares between "veins" and the duck drawing, a virtual eternity for young children. Beth hesitates, she needs to give more structure to this calendar. Eighteen squares after "veins" she writes, "tea party" and then one square over she adds "rain date".

Margaret chuckles. "So, guys, we're going to have a tea party this day but if it rains, it will be the next day, just like in *Mosey Posey and the Tea Party*."

Beth smiles. "That's right, and I'll come over, if it's okay with your mom." Jessica nods. "And we'll let our eggs get to know each other and see how they're doing. " Beth has masterfully brought order to the dysfunction. She's given these girls a schedule with clearly defined goals. "This is a big job and we're doing this together." She lifts her flowery blouse and shows them her three hatching belts.

Jessica says the tutor will incorporate egg development into their curriculum, "They're still being homeschooled." They exchange cell phone numbers and Beth promises to check in regularly. They've each chosen a new egg, pressed it into its foam rubber nest and strapped on the hatching belt. Everyone is smiling. But then Margaret softly says, "Thirty days is a long time. What if I can't make it?"

Charlotte looks at Margaret, pops her thumb in her mouth, hits Sophia with her free hand, laughs and runs. Sophia runs after her. Jessica doesn't react at all, her eyes don't leave Margaret, but Margaret has dropped her gaze to the floor. Jessica bursts into tears.

Margaret mumbles, "Never mind," and walks toward the door to let us out. On her way to the foyer, she walks right by my safe-perch chair and I'm able to look down onto the top of her head. I see how sparse her short curly hair is. I recognize it – it's chemo hair.

I climb down and hurry out the front door to get into the car with Beth. We drive down the loopy driveway, watching the windshield wipers as we pause to let the gate open. We're both alone, deep in thought. I hone the complexity of the domestic scene down to one question: What kind of cancer does Margaret have?

But then I realize I have a nagging question: Where is Mr. Kline, husband and father?

It's Saturday.

CHAPTER 7

Visiting bewitching Jessica Kline, her two unruly children and one sick child was unsettling.

I'm not sure Beth got why Jessica became so emotional at the end. She definitely understood that it was time to make our exit when Jessica started crying and Margaret walked us to the door.

I feel like asking Beth, "How's this happiness experiment going? Maybe bees would have been better?" But, of course, I don't. Can't. The windshield wiper blades go *rub*, reset, *rub*, reset. It's not turning out to be a promising day.

I'm jarred out of my contemplation by tick… tick… tick. Beth has turned on her turn signal one street early. I have no idea where we're going and if it will be safe for me. Suddenly, going to Kline's seems like a foolish choice. I should've just stayed home with Trixie. I remind myself that I can always opt to stay in the car. The car is a safe place for me.

To my delight, we turn into our favorite gourmet shop, Bon Vivant. The day I had my catastrophic heart attack, I went out the door joking, "Stay put, My Darling. Your man is going to clear the way to the road and then saddle up and resupply at Bon Vivant."

I haven't been in Bon Vivant for ages. I haven't seen the beautiful, imported bottles with their colorful labels or smelled the strong cheeses competing for olfactory receptors. It's truly a magical marketplace. Oh, and the service! Gentle Ben works behind the prepared foods counter. He's a maestro in his own right. He can smooth talk any customer into doubling, tripling what they came in to buy.

Sly Sydney, who works the cash register, is the brains behind the operation. She's the consummate professional who doesn't blink when she hands you your tiny bag of food and tells you your total is $86.57.

When Beth parks, I act quickly and climb out. I'm still standing flat-footed as she sprints for the front door, so I have to jog to catch up. It's not hard rain, just big steady drops. When a customer comes out, I am able to slip in. The shop is small, plus it's Saturday around lunch time so it's extra bustling.

Beth has already made it to the back, where Ben reigns over prepared foods. Some pompous jerk wearing tennis whites smiles at Beth as we wait. She smiles back, just to be polite. His match was undoubtedly cut short by the rain but he couldn't be bothered to change. We used to play tennis, doubles until my right shoulder got... shall we say cranky? That's when I started to notice how obnoxious it was to *wear* your tennis clothes around town.

I'm glaring at the guy when Ben asks Beth what she would like. She says, "A half a pound of lobster salad and a half a pound of citrus roasted potatoes, please." When he hands her the two containers, he doesn't try to upsell her. I'm a little surprised. I watch as Mr. Tennis Player steps up and listen to him order and I observe Ben closely. He smiles and chats and describes a few things that perfectly complement the sliced filet. Mr. Tennis Player falls right into Gentle Ben's trap.

This sounds very familiar and jogs my memory. Ben used to call me "Doc". I'm watching, thinking, remembering when I realize Beth has walked away! In a panic, I hurry down an aisle, almost bump into a woman with a child in tow, trying to get to the front of the store. Beth is nowhere to be seen. She's left me!

I rush out the door and am walking, looking across the small parking lot to see if our car is still where we parked it, when I almost step on Beth! She's sprawled on her back on the wet asphalt. I'm shocked. How did I let this happen? There's a scooter lying askew and I imagine she must have not seen it and tripped.

Worst of all, there's a man crouched over her. His back is broad and strains the seams of his suit. I can see his shoes sticking out from his folded knees. They have ridiculously pointed toes. I haven't seen shoes like that in years; as medical residents, we called them "roach killers". I wish I had Spatula. I'd pound him on the back and tell him, "This is a job for a doctor, you Lug!"

But I can't do anything but crouch on the other side of her and watch The Lug ask if she's hurt. He has some sort of accent. Beth is actually laughing. She's embarrassed. She's telling The Lug how she did not see the scooter (just as I thought) and she feels fine. The Lug is nodding but he's staring at her torso. Her thin, flowered blouse is beginning to cling and the shapes of the three hatching belts form three alien mounds. How I wish I had Spatula! I'd smack him across his broadside.

Beth follows his gaze. "Oh, no!" she gasps. She sits up and ever-so-coquettishly lifts the hem of her blouse, exposing the tiniest crescent of her abdomen to The Lug.

This time, it is *I* who gasp.

To his credit, The Lug rocks back, away from My Darling. He looks startled, actually alarmed. But Beth is so breezy and amiable that he rocks back for only a moment. Then, *not* to his credit, he leans forward for a closer look as Beth describes how she's hatching eggs using her own body temperature. She pulls the hatching belt ever so slightly away from her body and turns it to a 30 degree angle so he can see the smooth off-white egg. His shaggy head is practically under the tent of My Darling's blouse.

Beth comes to her senses and puts the hatching belt back in place and straightens her blouse. The Lug stands and Beth holds up her willowy arm. He grasps her hand and gently pulls her to her feet in an arc. It's like they've choreographed this lift for years and have been waiting to perform it.

They both walk to the overhang of the store where there's a dry bench and sit down. Beth pulls out her phone and they sit shoulder to shoulder watching Average Joe hatch his egg. When was this tête à tête verbally agreed upon? Did I miss an exchange when Beth was on the ground?

I'm still feeling left out when the woman I nearly bumped into comes out with her child. She pops her umbrella and walks off, with her kid riding his scooter. Everyone seems to think everything is fine and I'm left sputtering in the rain trying to figure out if I'm more angry at the careless woman and child or at the chummy Lug.

I only have a moment to fume when I see Beth raise her blouse (again!), un-Velcro one hatching belt and hand it to The Lug. He gives her a big smile. It's the same kind of smile I used to give my fellow surgeons when they congratulated me after a successful surgery that defied all odds. My smile would transmit, "Thank you. My win is your loss. I'm still the best."

Beth is typing in something into her phone. I think he is spelling his name but he's speaking too low for me to hear. I hurry over. If I had Spatula, I wouldn't be able to control myself. I would risk it all to stop this exchange now.

But then I hear Beth, My Darling, say quite firmly, "I'm hatching two eggs." She touches her right side and says, "This one's for me." Then she touches her left side and says, "This one's for my husband Tom. He died last winter. I know, if he were alive, he'd want to hatch his own egg."

She says it so sincerely, even The Lug is embarrassed and gazes across the parking lot. I'm moved by her genuine emotion but the truth is, I would *not* be hatching an egg – neither of us would be. I'd be researching where we were going to live in Paris. There'd be no need for this preposterous hatching experiment.

Beth stands up, takes our shopping bag of delicacies and we walk to the car.

"*Au revoir*!" calls The Lug and waves.

It hits me – The Lug has a French accent.

CHAPTER 8

Sunday is my favorite day of the week. Beth usually stays home and we spend the entire day together. My amigo Miguel doesn't even stop by. Sunday is "family day", which is great if you have a family. Sometimes I think Beth is especially lonely on Sundays but she has me and Trixie. And Tyler and Evie usually FaceTime on Sundays.

Last night was a little difficult for Beth, since it was the first night wearing the hatching belts. She had to lie flat on her back and be careful not to roll too much onto one side or the other. I spent the night shuttling up and down the steps with Spatula. I'd sit a while stroking and soothing Trixie and then I'd run upstairs to check Beth's position in bed. At one point, I had to use Spatula to roll her off her left side because I was worried about her crushing my egg. It sounds stressful and tiring but I actually enjoyed it because it reminded me of being on call at the hospital.

This morning Beth looks a little tired. It's slightly cool and she's just put on yoga pants and my old Johns Hopkins sweatshirt. It's baggy on her and you can't see the hatching belts at all.

At 8:00 a.m. sharp, Beth's phone rings. It's Tyler calling FaceTime from Thailand. It's exactly 8:00 p.m. there. He usually calls Beth as he heads out to dinner and tells her about the past week and then previews the week coming up. I know exactly how his mind works. He's organizing his grids of time and making his to-do list as he talks to her. He's cementing his goals and holding himself accountable to accomplish them. Tyler is brilliant and ambitious; he's a chip off the old block. He's working on his PhD in marine biology. His thesis has to do with cryogenic freezing and reanimation of coral egg and sperm. He says it's a critical step in preserving biodiversity in ocean reefs.

I'm, of course, proud of him but I think his skeletal coral creatures lack the true complexities of the human heart. When I was alive, Beth would say, "Tyler is not you. He isn't interested in human biology. He wants to solve more complex problems and save an entire ecosystem."

This struck me as naïve and ignorant. The human body *is* the ultimate ecosystem and nothing is more complicated than the human heart, except, perhaps, the human brain. But the brain is a gelatinous mess that lacks the fortitude and resolve of the heart. Have you heard the joke, what's the difference between god and a brain surgeon? God doesn't think he's a brain surgeon.

I bend over Beth's shoulder so I can see Tyler on the screen. He looks tan and healthy. There's a pause in conversation as he takes his phone and gives us a street view.

"Mom, are you sure you don't want to put the house on the market? You could sell it and come to Thailand for a while. You'd love it here."

Beth shifts the phone to her left hand so she can adjust a hatching belt. "Tyler, I can't. I have Trixie and I'm working on a spring project."

She does not tell him about the eggs. I'm not sure why. I feel he'd embrace the experimental nature of the endeavor but he also might try to dominate, dictate, direct. This is Beth's *happiness experiment* and I guess she's going to keep it that way.

He gives us a big smile. "Okay, Mom, but Trixie isn't going to be around much longer. Maybe in the fall. Bye. Love you!"

When his image disappears, Beth just sits, one leg tucked up and one leg curled under. She looks sad and small in my old sweatshirt. She stares at Trixie and Trixie wags her tail once and pulls herself up from her bed to lay her head on Beth's knee. Trixie knows when our

Darling needs comfort. The three of us make a sad triptych. The thought of Trixie dying is unbearable, especially to me. In some ways she's the glue between Beth and me. Her intuitive nature allows her to straddle my ghost world and Beth's physical world.

If a ghost cries and no one hear him, is he really crying? The day has only started and we're all so low.

Beth keeps her phone beside her all day because Evie isn't like Tyler, predictable. Evie will call but you never know when. She's in California, the three hour difference is harder to coordinate than the twelve hour difference of Thailand. Evie has a job in tech sales that doesn't seem to leave her very satisfied or at least doesn't consume her passionately, the way Tyler's research consumes him.

Evie volunteers, she exercises, she has a big network of friends and she dates... *beaucoup*. I don't approve of all her dating and when I was her living father, there were a lot of other things I didn't approve of. Evie feels the rules don't apply to her but she's wrong. The rules apply to everyone.

Beth used to say, "Stop judging Evie for being happy." I thought this was very unfair. I wasn't judging Evie based on her happiness, I was *protecting* her

Beth would mollify me by citing examples of friends whose children made even "freer" choices. Beth called Evie a free spirit, which strikes me as an oxymoron, now that I *am* one. Even spirits must follow rules and restrictions. Life is work, work is life; you show up and *do* the work. Only now I see there can be light-hearted moments where one can laugh or enjoy the whimsy of something small and beautiful.

So the three of us (Beth, Trixie and me) mope around most of the day waiting for Evie's call. It's so ludicrous she has that power over us.

She finally FaceTimes at 7:00 p.m. Beth is eating dinner with her laptop open. It's nice because we can see Evie on a bigger screen.

She is walking across Golden Gate Park, the sun is shining, it's 4:00 p.m. there. Her blonde hair blows and she definitely looks happy. Beth asks, "Where are you going?"

She says to watch friends jam. There'll be dancing on the grass and everyone is bringing a dish. Beth asks Evie what she's bringing. She says, "Tequila!" I think, *of course you are.*

But Beth laughs. She suddenly seems as free and easy as Evie. Their conversation zigzags, touching on a million subjects with no transitions. There's mention of a cute outfit, a recommendation of a podcast, followed closely by a reference to a completely unrelated newspaper article about the criminal justice system. Evie mentions a date she had and they both have a good giggle. They seem desperate to squeeze a week into that 20 minute walk across the park.

"I see the group, Mom." Suddenly she gets more serious. "How *were* you this week? I just hate to think of you bumping around that big house alone. Mom, you and Trixie should just move out here. We could be roomies. There's *tons* of single men!"

Beth laughs, it's hearty and youthful. "Bye sweetheart!" she yells into the computer, "I love you!"

Evie never ceases to find new ways to irritate me. Don't get me wrong, I love her but her cavalier attitude about life, love, and responsibility embarrasses me. I take a deep breath and remember the joy she brings My Darling.

I note that Beth didn't share the hatching experiment with Evie, either. I have no doubt that Evie would embrace the serendipitous nature of the experiment. If she were here, she'd ask for a belt and egg, strap it on, walk out the door and proceed to break it.

The eggs are our secret and if it's successful we'll become parents of two little ducklings. I've already named them: Little Leftie (mine) and Rightie. They are just one more reason not to sell the house. I'm thinking that when we go to France, it will be fall, the fruit trees will have borne fruit and Little Leftie and Rightie will be getting ready to fly south.

The timing will be perfect.

CHAPTER 9

Last night was another busy night of running up and down the stairs. At one point, I thought for sure Beth had crushed Little Leftie. I came into the room and she was in a fetal tuck completely on the left side. With the help of Spatula, I was able to ease her back flat.

When I was done flattening Beth, I ran downstairs, where poor Trixie was whining in obvious distress. It's a good thing I've such great endurance and need so little sleep. Beth and Trixie would be in trouble without me!

When I was living, I'd go into the office extra early on Mondays, making it a point to always be the first one in. I'd go over my patient files and the surgeries I was scheduled to perform that week. I envisioned myself like a steam engine stoking up. By the time the other doctors arrived, I was full speed ahead, my mind focused, my body a blur of movement but my hands as steady as a statue. I used to fill my coffee cup to the tip-top just to prove to myself, and anyone watching me, that I could carry it without spilling a drop.

Monday mornings aren't quite as exciting on my gentleman's farm, but I like them. Beth sits at the counter with a pen and paper and thinks. Then she writes: "Text Jessica, Talk to Miguel, Trixie Vet." She turns the page over on the planner that she leaves sitting open on her desk. There are seven completely empty squares. This is kind of a letdown for me. There is no laser focus needed.

Beth checks her watch and texts Jessica, "How's it going? All good?"

Jessica immediately texts back the thumbs up emoji.

Both Beth and I are pleasantly surprised that the Kline clan seems to have gotten the hang of the hatching belts. Then Beth walks to the back door and calls Trixie to go on a walk. Trixie is slightly reluctant to walk out the door. I'm not sure if she wants to stay with me or if her old joints just ache too much.

I'm left sitting in my favorite chair with Spatula safely tucked under the cushion. I wish I could go online and order some bees and hives (wouldn't Beth be surprised!). There are a lot of things I *can't* do but I need to remember to feel gratitude. Beth has these sticky notes on her bathroom mirror and the coffeemaker. "What am I grateful for?" "What am I letting go of?" "What is my focus?" I like these reminders. They would have irritated Dr. Paradise but they are helpful to Ghost Tom.

Beth returns sooner than I expected. She actually startles me as she comes in and immediately calls the vet to make an appointment. She must have noticed how really unhappy Trixie is. Trixie goes and lies down in her bed, looking dejected, like she failed at the most basic task of walking with her mistress. I wish I could pull Spatula out and stroke her. She looks at me sitting on my chair and can't figure out why I don't come and soothe her. If I had a heart, it would break.

Beth makes a vet appointment for 2:00 p.m. this afternoon. I don't need to check my calendar to know I'm free but I definitely don't think the vet is a place for me. I've never been to the vet; Beth always took Trixie. I have no idea of its layout and if the waiting room is packed with dogs. Can other dogs sense me like Trixie does? I still have no idea and certainly don't want to find out in this high stakes situation.

My Darling sits down to read and I watch her. She's reading *Eat, Pray, Love* and I don't like it. Self-Aware-Emily gave it to her and said it was some nonsense about a woman who travels around eating and praying and then falling in love. Self-Aware-Emily even had the audacity to say, "This could be *you*, Beth!" Gag.

When I was alive, there was always a book on Beth's nightstand. Usually it was something weighty, like a biography of Abraham Lincoln. I've noticed, since the pandemic and my catastrophic death, her reading material has become more abundant and less curated. She consumes books, many that serve no purpose. We should be spending our time practicing our French or researching places to live.

I am sitting watching Beth smile and read, when there's a tap-tap. Trixie's tail does one up-down thud in her bed and Miguel walks in. Beth doesn't seem surprised in the least. Perhaps their relationship is on a whole new level now that they're Facebook friends. I feel My amigo Miguel is becoming a little too comfortable in my house with my wife. Miguel's wife died years ago and, technically, he's a single guy. All the rooms are painted and it's spring, there's plenty of work outside.

"How's it going, Miguel?"

"*Muy, muy bien, Señora Beth*!" He grins with his white teeth and lifts his tee shirt to show Beth the hatching belt.

Miguel is not a young guy, I think he has kids as old or older than ours but his abdomen is smooth and I can literally see the classic 6-pack – external and internal obliques and rectus and transversus abdominis. I guess doing physical labor six days a week has its benefits.

Beth lifts her tee shirt. Her abdomen is smooth but doesn't have the definition. She shows him the two belts.

"No trouble sleeping?" asks Beth.

"No, no," he chuckles and runs his hands through his already standing up hair. "I sleep like *los muertos*!"

"Me too!" Beth laughs.

This makes me grind my teeth thinking how Little Leftie would be cracked and leaking yolk if it weren't for me and trusty Spatula, but there's nothing I can do, I just have to listen to this nonsense.

Beth confirms with Miguel that he fertilized my dwarf fruit trees. She sweetly adds, "Tom would have loved to see them bloom, and the fruit, this fall."

"*Sí, sí,*" says Miguel but he doesn't look very wistful or sad. He tells her how he'll tidy up the work bench and start edging and mulching. "It's a big job, I'll have to spread it out over the next few weeks while trying to keep up with my other clients."

Beth tells him that she's not worried. It will get done. She trusts him. Yadda, yadda, yadda. But then she says, "Miguel, you're so busy. Why do you want to hatch an egg?"

It's a very good question and I hadn't really thought of it. We both look at him. Even Trixie raises her head.

Miguel hesitates. He seems to like to pepper his English with common Spanish words that we all should know. When we discussed yard projects I found it annoying, not knowing if he was dumbing himself down or trying to smarten me up. We wait for his answer.

"Señora Beth, I have *una hija*, Fernanda."

"Yes, I know," Beth smiles. Sometimes when Miguel used to stop by, he had Fernanda with him. She's younger than Evie.

"Ever since her mother died... six years already, we have been like this." Miguel takes his two fists and bumps the knuckles against each other.

I understand this gesture very well. I think if I'd been doing the talking I would've said, "Ever since Evie was born, we have been like this," and bumped my knuckles together.

"She lives with me and is a good girl. She has a job and goes to college. She will be someone! But she has gotten pregnant. She doesn't want to marry the father he's no *bueno*." Miguel sighs and moves one hand to the mound of the hatching belt. "I wear the egg to show support. I want to show her that her Papa loves her unconditionally. We're a team." But then Miguel looks down at his work boots, "I haven't said these words to her yet. But the egg is softening me. I'll tell her soon."

Beth looks glassy eyed. She takes two steps and hugs Miguel, careful so their belts don't collide. She says, "You're a good man, Miguel. Let me know if I can help in any way."

I didn't like the start of the conversation when Miguel showed off his abs and I definitely don't like the end with the hug, but the middle, the part about his daughter, captivated me. I would've liked to hear more.

When Miguel goes out, I slip out and follow him. It's a lovely day and I know Beth will come in and out several times and I'll have plenty of opportunities to go back in the house before she takes Trixie to the vet. I feel like getting some exercise by following Miguel around the yard.

My amigo Miguel has just become more complex and definitely more intriguing. I never really thought of him much but now I realize we're both men in conflict with our willful daughters. He's seeking acceptance, a state of peace, where I accepted and fostered a state of perpetual irritation. It's only now that I'm contemplating compromises.

We work hard for a few hours and then Miguel goes to his pickup truck, opens the door and gets his lunch and a thermos. He sits on the running board and eats a couple rolled tortillas and drinks what smells like coffee out of the thermos. There's a photo taped to the dashboard of his truck. I've noticed the photo before but it's a little faded and hard to see from outside the truck. With the door open, I'm able to gingerly climb over Miguel and sit in the passenger seat. There are some gloves and receipts on the seat but that's okay. I really want to look closely at this photo of his headstrong daughter, Fernanda, who sounds so much like Evie.

The faded photo has three young adults, two young men and one young woman. They all have big smiles, like their father. Fernanda wears a lacy blouse and her long dark hair hangs over her shoulders. Her lips are full and her lashes are like brushes. She's the crown jewel in this composition.

Suddenly, I hear a dog bark, mean and insistent. It startles me and I freeze.

It's only the ring tone on Miguel's phone. I almost laugh... almost.

Miguel answers, says, "*Sí*" tosses his thermos and empty lunch bag, on my lap, climbs in, slams the door and backs down the driveway with *me* in the passenger seat.

How do you say *Holy Shit!* in Spanish?

CHAPTER 10

I'm kidnapped!

This is what you call it, no? If the police pulled us over right now, and if I could explain, it would most definitely be kidnapping.

I think of Beth's little sticky notes. The new me takes a few deep breaths. I start with *gratitude*. Honestly, I can't think of anything about this situation to be grateful for. Skip. *"Letting go*. I will let go of my stress as the kidnapped victim... not easy but I will try. *Focus*. I will focus on getting back to Beth. And Trixie.

The emergency is a leak in some lady's irrigation system. I don't get out of the pickup, I stay put and watch water spraying where no sprinkler head exists. Miguel nods and looks very grave, like this is a ruptured artery. He walks back to the truck and rummages around his tool box. He replaces a segment of underground hose, and checks the system.

When he gets in, he reaches down by my feet and picks up a battered spiral notebook that's open to a page. He takes the pen that's slid into the spiral binding, looks at his watch, jots a number and tosses it onto my lap, not the floor. I can see there are about 50 names that run down the first page. "Señora Paradise" is at the top. We have the most numbers on our line. I realize this rudimentary notebook and pen is how Miguel does his billing. I never saw billing for my surgeries.

But every month I saw a bill from Miguel. "Paradise" on the top of a piece of paper, the number of hours x $20, the total circled. He used to fold it and put it in a note-sized envelope in our mailbox. Since working in the house over the winter, I notice he just comes in and lays it on our counter. There's no address and he now writes "Señora Beth" at the top.

Even though I could find a hundred ways to improve on Miguel's billing system, starting with the crappy pen and greasy notebook, I admire how it's forthright, factual. I like how "Paradise" is at the top. We're obviously the most valuable customer.

None of the houses that Miguel stops at intrigue me. I wait patiently in the truck as we do the rounds. The most fun I have is trying to guess which name in the notebook we're visiting. When Miguel gets in and takes the notebook to make a notation, I think, "Ah, this was Poverwicz, I guessed it was Acosta." And so the game goes.

Finally, Miguel calls it a day and drives to Little Flower or *Pequeña Fleur,* as its inhabitants call it. It is a tiny community nestled next to our town, where all the nannies, housekeepers, lawn men and drivers live. The makeup of the inhabitants has changed over the last century. I believe it started out more Italian, *Piccolo Fiore*, and now it's firmly Hispanic: Mexican and Central American.

I spent zero time in Little Flower. I'd heard there's some good restaurants but never went. The prospect of spending the night in *Pequeña Fleur* would normally appall me but the possibility of meeting Fernanda, the crown jewel in the photo, quite possibly the crown jewel of all of *Pequeña Fleur,* excites me.

We pull up to a faded green duplex, two front doors side by side. It's an awkward structure and my guess is that it was a single family home that was divided. What was the front yard is now a concrete slab for parking, enclosed by a chain link fence. Miguel noses up to the gate of the fence, but no electronic sensor or invisible gears grind it open. He has to get out, drag it open and drive through. His truck is now the third vehicle parked on what used to be the front lawn.

I'm ready to make my move and jump out when Miguel opens his driver's door. I have no intention of spending the night locked in the pickup. It turns out I could have relaxed and taken my time because Miguel leaves his door open while he walks back and drags the gate closed. He returns to the passenger side and gets his notebook, thermos and garbage from my seat.

A woman pokes her head out of the second floor window (definitely *not* Fernand-the- Crown-Jewel) and yells, "*Cómo está el huevo?*" Miguel laughs, lifts his shirt, flashing his 6-pack abs and says, "*Muy bien!*"

It seems as though the egg experiment is common knowledge in these parts.

Miguel walks to the left front door, the one that does not correlate with the woman who yelled from the window. I follow, a dutiful kidnapped shadow. I almost step in what appears to be an enormous dog turd but avoid it at the last second. I don't give it much thought because I'm concentrating on staying close and not getting locked out. I don't want to spend the night in this makeshift car lot.

Crossing the threshold, my senses are accosted. I have not been in a house like this for years, not since I grew up. It's the kind of house where everything is just right there, we literally walk into the kitchen. I can see the sofa, the TV, the bathroom door, the kitchen table, and even the stove and counter. I can smell the chili in the pot and hear the Latin beat coming out of the small speaker on the shelf. It's a lot to take in but it all recedes to the background when I see Fernanda.

She's standing by the stove, stirring a pot. She looks up and smiles. "*Hola, Papa.*" It's so sweet and sincere, it would warm the cruelest father's heart. I feel the happiness emanate from Miguel's body. He gives her his biggest smile, and says, "*Hola, mi hija.*" She wipes her hands on a towel and with no accent asks, "How's the egg?" Miguel pats the mound under his shirt. "*Muy bien. Y el tuyo?*"

She laughs and pats her slight belly. "Pretty good!"

They sit and eat together. Some of the conversation I understand but some is in Spanish and spoken too quickly. I gather from the number of boots and shoes lined up against the wall and the size of the pot, one or both of the brothers live here, too.

When they're done eating, Fernanda sighs. "I have to study." That's easy to understand and I can't help but nod in approval. She gets up, turns the music off her phone so the speaker falls silent and walks up the stairs with its worn runner.

Miguel washes the dishes and gets a soda out of the fridge. He pops the can and we sit side by side on the sofa. I don't understand the Spanish language shows we're watching but it doesn't matter. We're both tired from our day. The TV is mindless and soothing and it's definitely more entertaining than watching Beth read mediocre novels. Between sips, Miguel rests his hand on his hatching belt.

I think about what Miguel said regarding Fernanda and how they – and he bumped his knuckles together – clash. This tender Monday evening did not look discordant to me. I try to imagine if Miguel was me and Fernanda was Evie, would I be so... I'm not sure what the word is... accommodating? Would I strap on a hatching belt for 30 days to show solidarity and empathy?

I doubt it.

On one hand, I think Miguel donning the belt is ridiculous because it solves nothing. But on the other hand, if there *was* discord, and now there's peace, the hatching belt seems like a small inconvenience.

Miguel tips to the right and lays his head on a sofa pillow. He lifts his legs up and I have to move off the sofa and sit at the kitchen table. Just after midnight, two young men come in. They're very quiet and slide their shoes off. They put their thermoses on the counter and get a plate of chili from the kettle on the stove. The three of us sit at the kitchen table. They talk a bit in hushed voices and I just nod like I understand. Then they stand, put their dishes in the sink, and walk over to the sofa. One son clicks the TV off and bends over and gives

Miguel a kiss on his head while the other unties his boots and pulls them off. Miguel mumbles, "*Gracias*."

They go upstairs. The house is quiet and I have nothing to do. I don't have Trixie to comfort and don't miss Spatula because Miguel is safely positioned on his right side and his egg is on the left. At one point, he grunts and rolls onto his back which is also safe for the egg, or *el huevo*.

I decide to go upstairs and explore a bit. One door is firmly closed and I hear the active snoring of the two young men, Miguel's sons. One door is wide open, a single bed is neatly made and empty, this must be Miguel's room. On the dresser is a framed photo of a woman in an apron, I assume it's his deceased wife. She's smiling at the camera while Miguel kisses her cheek. It's a happy, spontaneous photo capturing a moment of joy in a hard life.

The last door is Fernanda's, it's slightly ajar and I'm able to slip in. The room looks like Evie's did when she was about six. It's pink, pink, pink and reminds me of Jessica's little girls. There's a little white desk with a thick book open. It's organic chemistry. A philosophy book is closed beside it. Fernanda is lying under a pink cover, breathing softly. I'm concerned that her mother died relatively young and wonder if there could be any hereditary factors. I need to check Fernanda's heart.

It's easy enough. I lay my ear against the coverlet, and listen. The beat is steady and slow and I'm reassured that Fernanda is healthy and strong. Then I gently lay my hand on her belly. She's probably about five months pregnant and can still hide her condition with a loose blouse. I immediately feel movement. Not big waves, just flutters. The baby is probably healthy and strong, too. I wish I could tell my amigo the good news.

The night passes slowly, but thankfully Miguel rises with the first light. He carefully takes off his hatching belt and lays it across the toilet seat while he showers and puts on clean clothes. He straps the belt back on and we quietly leave while the rest of the house sleeps.

We make a lot of stops, one includes a big cup of creamy looking coffee and eggs wrapped in a tortilla. We pull into a lawn supply business and I watch Miguel shovel mulch into the back of his truck. It seems like a lot of work and I am just hoping and praying this mulch is for Señora Beth. I'm anxious to get home and help Beth with our eggs and comfort Trixie.

As we drive down my road, I think, "I'm grateful for that new experience." It's funny. It just sort of pops in my head. I'm honestly grateful for spending the night in *Pequeña Fleur*, seeing how my amigo lives his honest life and watching Miguel and Fernanda interact.

Being kidnapped wasn't so terrible.

CHAPTER 11

Trixie greets us, tail wagging, and Beth greets us, eyes red, balled tissues in hand.

"*Señora, que pasa?*" Miquel says and touches his hatching belt. His first thought is the eggs.

"No, not the eggs, Miguel." She touches both Little Leftie and Rightie, "It's Trixie, she's gone."

I want to laugh and say in my ghost voice, "Beth, My Darling, she's right here." Literally, she's right at my knee, looking up at me with adoring eyes, the consummate good girl.

Beth looks so miserable as she explains, "I took her to the vet yesterday. I knew she was old but she was always so happy."

"*Sí,*" Miguel nods in sad agreement.

"But yesterday she was different, unhappy, no joy, the vet said 'pain.'" When Beth says *pain*, her voice cracks. "The vet said her body was riddled with cancer, it was even in her bones. He said it was lucky she was pain free for as long as she was. Basically, she was good until she wasn't."

Miguel is looking very grave. "It's just like my wife and Señor Paradise, good until they're not."

This is nonsensical. Comparing my catastrophic heart attack to an old dog's cancer and Miguel's wife's... I don't know what. It's absurd! Unbelievably, Beth nods in agreement.

I reach down and pat Trixie's head with my ghost hand because trusty Spatula is inside, under the chair cushion. She wags her tail fervently. I cup her under her muzzle and stare into her eyes. Her tongue drops out of her mouth and she plainly smiles at me with a twinkle in her eyes.

Because of Beth's lioness heart, we live on, both of us. I am actually slightly abashed as a medical professional. I may have underestimated the loyalty, the tenacity, the sheer power of My Darling's heart. She will never let us go.

The rest of the day is one of contradictions. Beth stays inside, sad, even though it is a glorious 72 degrees and sunny. Trixie and I stay in the yard watching Miguel edge and mulch. On days like this, Beth is in the habit of keeping the back French doors open onto the veranda. Trixie and I can come and go at will. Part of me feels like I should go, sit inside next to Beth and comfort her, but the other part is enjoying the activity in the yard. Trixie seems jubilant not to be burdened by her decrepit body.

I watch Miguel take a simple spade tool and cut a neat edge around each bed. He alternates between edging and hauling mulch. It's all hard physical work. We have just over two acres, most of it landscaped and groomed. There's a little wild fringe around the pond and the back left corner, but otherwise it's all planted and must be edged, mulched, mowed, trimmed and fertilized.

Miguel works from roughly 8:30 am until 6:00 pm. He takes two breaks, one to eat lunch and one to drink cold, creamy coffee. He only finishes about a third of the job. I can see why Señora Beth is at the top of his accounting system.

I idly think of Jessica Kline's yard at 530 Round House Road. She probably has close to five acres of groomed lawn that demands weekly attention. I picture a truck pulling up to the gate, dispersing an army of Miguels to accomplish the spring work. I imagine Mr. Kline coming home, driving up his loopy driveway, enjoying the vista that all his hard work can buy.

After surveying the perfection of the grounds, I wonder how he feels when he walks into the mayhem at the front door? Is he disappointed in Jessica, or does he embrace her *laissez faire* attitude? Who makes sure the children do their homeschooling lessons? Does he worry about Margaret and is he involved in her care? Who's Margaret's medical advocate? Everyone, young and old, needs an advocate, I could tell you hospital horror stories about who and what can drop through the cracks. I am not saying one child's life is *more* precious than another's, but I am saying the system is messed up.

Miguel pops his head in the open veranda door. "*Mañana*," he says. "*Mañana*," Beth replies. Trixie and I don't really want to go in but there's no telling when Beth   might close the French doors. I had an uncomfortable night last night and I don't want another one, so we both go into the house.

Beth is busy on her laptop. I look over her shoulder and see she has posted on Facebook about "my dear Trixie going to happier fields". This post has garnered 56 comments. Beth is scrolling through them, even Tyler and Evie have commented. Tyler's says, "Best dog ever." Evie comments, "Loyal friend, always supportive, taught me the meaning of unconditional love."

This seems a little extreme. I think, "Really, Miss-Free-Love-In-San Francisco, a dog taught you that?" But then I remember when Evie was younger, Trixie always slept in her room, on her bed. There were many nights when Evie would be distressed, maybe she got a bad grade or wasn't included in some girl thing, I don't know. Beth would say it was just typical "teen angst" and take it in stride, but it seemed like her habit to drop the drama down in the midst of the family. I would've had a stressful day (opening chest cavities can be like that) and I didn't need or want to come home to this vortex of agitation.

Inevitably, my annoyance would turn to anger, which caused Evie's maelstrom of feelings to crystalize into animosity. Which she directed solely at me. We would actually yell. Yes, she was capable of making the venerable Dr. Paradise lose his cool. Then she would simply take whatever she needed and stomp upstairs for the night with Trixie faithfully following her.

Beth would tell me, "Don't play her game, be the adult," but I always did. Maybe it felt good to dive into the deep pool of emotion and feel its extremes.

It's all conjecture at this point. Water under the bridge. History. But I feel time and distance have given me some clarity. Maybe I should have just listened instead of reacting? Maybe I learned something from those 32 minutes with The-Absolute-Best-Cognitive-Therapist?

As Beth scrolls through the comments of condolences, I notice Stick-Your-Nose-In-Everyone's-Business-Sandy has written: "I have a friend with puppies! Call me!!!"

It's just like the real estate pimp to not even mention Trixie and her years of loyalty and love. I bet Sandy barely remembers that I was a devoted partner to Beth, or as some might say, The Greatest Husband. Sandy is the type to slam the door on the past and only live in the present. She sees Beth living in a house that she, Sandy, deems too big and now she sees an empty space where a dog should be. Sandy is toxic.

Beth gets to the bottom of the feed and then goes back to the top and clicks on a tab she keeps open. It's Average Joe hatching his egg. On day three, about two minutes into the video, he lays his egg on his phone with the flashlight app turned on. he is able to see little veins threading through the egg, proving the egg is viable. I had forgotten about this milestone.

Beth jumps up and lays her phone face up on the counter with the light shining brightly. She very gently works Rightie out of his hatching cup and lays the egg on the screen. She bends closer. Her long hair almost blocks my view but we can both see tiny thready veins! Beth carefully puts Rightie back and lays Little Leftie, my baby, on the light. We both hold our breath.-Little Leftie has thready veins too! We have two viable babies – big hats off to our parenting!

I'd like to remind Beth of the egg she left in the warming drawer and see if we are 3 for 3 but I'm pretty sure Beth has forgotten it is there. As a scientist, I am curious about the random test versus the controls A and B.

Beth takes her phone and texts Jessica. "Lay your phone down with the light on. Put each of the eggs on it. Do you see threads? Those are veins. Let me know! Watch the hatching video for reference." She copies the text and sends it to Miguel.

Jessica gives her a thumbs up emoji.

A few minutes later, Miguel sends, "*Si*!! *Muy bien*!"

Beth looks happy for the first time today. She smiles as she moves around the kitchen, emptying the dishwasher and taking some cheese and vegetables out to make a late meal. Trixie and I are tickled to have Beth do more than just mope. The house is big and empty for a ghost man and his ghost dog, especially if the only human just sits quietly. It definitely lacks all the action and commotion of the Kline mansion and the comings and goings of Miguel's duplex. Beth pours a glass of wine and even turns on some music. I sit on my favorite stool at the counter and enjoy watching her.

But then My Darling reaches for her phone again. She narrows her eyes, like she's thinking as she scrolls through her contacts and she starts typing. I move closer but she hits *send* before I can read over her shoulder. Thankfully she puts the phone down and the screen stays lit for a few moments. The text reads, "Put a strong light behind your egg, see if veins are forming. Beth."

Beth's phone immediately buzzes back.

Beth texted The Lug! I can see his name is Friedrich. It's like he's been holding his phone, waiting for My Darling to text him. He texts, "Yes, I have checked. Life is forming."

It's an odd text. I can tell Beth thinks so too. It doesn't leave room to continue a dialogue. Dare I say, it's the *opposite* of flirty. Beth hesitates, holds down the text bubble and gives him the clapping hands emoji, which seems pretty harmless. She goes back to cutting up vegetables for a salad. Just as she sits down to eat, he texts back, "Is life forming for you?"

Another odd text. It's safe to assume he means in the eggs but still, it makes one ponder. Beth texts, "Yes! Both eggs are forming veins!!"

This response seems excessive, over the top. She's reminding him that she has *two* eggs and she seems to be begging for attention with her use of exclamation points. There is nothing modest about it. Frankly, I'm disgusted.

Here's where I give The Lug some credit – he doesn't take the bait. He merely responds with a smiley face. Bravo for The Lug, he showed dignity and self-restraint.

Beth looks slightly disappointed as she eats her salad. She scrolls through headline news and we both read together. I'm not as interested in current events as I used to be. They seem irrelevant to my situation but I still feel it's my civic duty to stay informed.

Beth's phone goes "ding!" and she switches to her texting screen. It's Jessica, not The Lug, which is fantastic. "Yes! All 3 eggs have veins!! The girls are so happy!!!"

This text is effusive but I don't mind. I find it sweet. She has done one "!" for each of the girls, the two rambunctious ones and Margaret, the well-mannered but sick one. Holding back nothing, Beth gives her a heart emoji. I fully support this choice. I don't think Beth is yet aware that Margaret is sick.

The rest of the evening is pretty uneventful. We do our Duolingo in bed and turn out the lights. Nights will be duller for me now that I don't have to shuttle up and down the stairs soothing Trixie while watching out for Little Leftie and Rightie. Trixie is, actually, as good as new. She can easily climb the stairs and we can all be together in the bedroom.

I experiment. I pat the side of the bed like I used to see Evie do. Trixie, with no hesitation, easily jumps up and settles next to me. I probably shouldn't let her on the bed, it's a bad habit, but it feels right. It's nice to have her beside me, warm and breathing. Being the only ghost in the house made me feel like the odd man out. Now Beth is the odd man out.

With Trixie tucked beside me, maybe I'll sleep peacefully and the nights will pass without boredom. I close my eyes but then I feel Beth rustling on the other side. She picks her phone up, goes to the texting screen, clicks on The Lug's thread and types, "My dog died."

"My dog died" is such a cheap call for help, a cry for attention, I can't stand it. Here we all are, together on the bed. We couldn't be cozier and then Beth goes and brings The Lug into our lives. It's wanton and completely inappropriate, given the intimate context.

I'm positively smug as I see Beth stare at the screen, expecting a response. Poor helpless, beautiful Beth, with a dead dog on top of a dead husband. My Darling is usually amazing and wondrous, but every once in a while she manages to piss me off. It seems to be happening more often, which begs the question: Are you still The Perfect Wife?

I'm most definitely still The Greatest Husband. I'm supportive, protective and omnipresent. That being said, I decide to go downstairs and sleep on the sofa. I need my space and some time to cool off.

CHAPTER 12

In the morning, my temper has dampened to match the weather, cool and rainy. Trixie sits beside me on the sofa and I'm able to pet her, no Spatula needed. With Ghost Dog Trixie, Spatula is superfluous. Part of me wants to play a trick on Beth and put her back in the utensil drawer. It would be fun to see her expression, "Oh! There you are! I've been looking all over for you!"

Of course, it's just a fleeting thought. Spatula is dear to me and I'm sure she'll prove useful when we move to Paris. I have no idea what foreign situations I'll find myself in. It's nice to think Trixie will be able to go to Paris. I don't see why not. We could take any seat on the plane, even the dreaded middle and be perfectly fine. Trixie is such a well-behaved dog, she can sit at our feet while we sip coffee at outdoor cafes. No leash needed.

Beth looks decidedly unhappy this morning. She keeps looking at her phone and I get a certain satisfaction that The Lug hasn't responded. Why should he? How does one respond to such a desperate text from a female stranger?

My Darling sighs and calls Stick-Your-Nose-In-Everyone's-Business-Sandy, which she hasn't done in a very long time. Their friendship cooled when Beth didn't take her advice and put the house on the market. Of course, it was very convenient that Sandy's advice and professional needs aligned. They decide on lunch at a cozy creperie and I would love to go. It's the perfect place to dream of Paris and use some of our Duolingo French, but it's probably not safe. The interior is small, it's always busy and noisy with tables the size of large plates. I think Trixie and I will sit this one out.

When Beth leaves, she has on the coat that we bought in Milan. No one will be able to see her hatching belts and I wonder if she'll even remind Sandy of her experiment. Sandy has the attention span of a goldfish, she probably already forgot her snide Facebook post: "Good luck! Let me know how *that* goes!"

The more I think about Sandy and her self-serving ways, the more I'm fine with staying home with Trixie. But I have second thoughts when, at the last minute, Beth tucks her laptop under her arm. Why should she bring her computer for lunch with Sandy?

I am already snuggled in with Trixie on the sofa and shrug off my fears. We watch Beth leave. Sitting on the sofa with a faithful ghost dog on a rainy day might sound very boring, especially after being a life and death, world-renowned heart surgeon, but it's not.

My thoughts are wispy and travel easily. In quiet moments like this, I enjoy seeing where they take me. I guess you could call it day dreaming. I never thought in a million years I'd call myself Dr. Day Dreamer. Sometimes I get marvelous solutions to complicated problems but other times I ruminate on the past. Today is one of those days I ruminate.

I think about the hospital's biggest donor, Gunther Schlitz, Jr. He was nobody to me, a name on a wing of the hospital. He supported the institution that supported me, so he was in my Good Guy column. One day, his father, Gunther, Senior. needs open heart surgery.

It's assigned to me: perform open heart surgery on Gunther Schlitz Sr. I'm 71 at the time. I've done this procedure a thousand times. My hands are still as steady as a rock. Yet, I don't want to do it.

I know I'm being handed a live grenade by Pierce Wilson, president of the hospital. There are up and coming surgeons itching to take my number one alpha surgeon place, but all of them are quietly waiting out this operation. No one is clamoring to save our sacred donor's father. I'm virtually forced into my scrubs, pushed into the OR and handed my instruments. President Pierce probably sat in his office drinking scotch and sweating while I performed eight hours of open heart surgery.

It was a cage match. Two men went in. One came out – forced into retirement and the other came out... a vegetable.

With one slice, I created hypoxia, triggering a stroke and simultaneously going from the institution's asset column to the liability column. Of course, I was able to save face by retiring but everyone knew my last operation was botched.

It was not the hero's end I deserved.

CHAPTER 13

Beth comes home looking much happier than when she left. She lifts her shirt, adjusts Little Leftie and Rightie and puts the laptop down on the counter, where it sits, a slim vault of secrets. I still have no idea why the laptop was the right accessory to bring for lunch with Stick-Your-Nose-In-Everyone's-Business-Sandy It's vexing.

Even more vexing is when Beth unwinds the grubby bandage she has wrapped around her index finger. She hasn't changed the bandage since the accident and, frankly, I've forgotten about it, being so busy with the eggs. The tip is swollen and inflamed. The wound where the drill slipped off the egg is oozing and the sides are pulling apart instead of coming together. Sandy probably made some comment about the grubby bandage. In my defense, hands notoriously get infected. They are bacteria magnets that often get inflamed before they heal. That's my professional opinion.

My Darling goes to the medicine cabinet and finds pretty much nothing: no Band-aids, no gauze, no tape, no anti-bacterial spray. I think of Ray-the-Jerk and his "cobbler's children have no shoes comment" and I grind my teeth. Ideally, if I knew my shitty heart was going to fail, I'd have stocked the medicine cabinet, called Boring Jim, our accountant, set up trusts, and ordered bees and hives. But no one had written "drop dead" on my calendar, so how was I to know?

Beth carefully washes her finger, dries it, wraps it with paper towel, and picks up her purse. I am 95% sure she's driving to the pharmacy to buy some first aid supplies. It's a dull afternoon and Trixie and I would really like to get out. I'll be antsy and ill content when night falls if I don't *accomplish* something today. Also, I long to see the pharmacy, walk up and down the aisles of medical supplies, examine items, read ingredients, and have a chance to practice medicine again. So I say, "Come on, girl, let's go!" Trixie knows those words well and we both swoosh out the door and into the car with Beth. Trixie knows her place and climbs into the backseat.

My intuition is dead on. We drive straight to the pharmacy and park right in front. When Beth opens the door, I tell Trixie, "Stay." She's happy to be along for the ride and will wait while Beth and I go in.

The first aid section is in the back of the store, where the pharmacist fills prescriptions. It's neat and orderly and I'm extremely pleased I decided to come. The pharmacy is just the kind of experience I am looking for on this gloomy day. My only disappointment is how fast Beth throws supplies in her basket. I'd like to dawdle.

We're finishing up, when Jessica rushes to the back of the store and hands the pharmacist a prescription. Beth and I almost don't recognize her. She's in a large, oversized jacket with a baseball cap for the rain. Her hair is down and she looks disheveled and tired. I'm not well versed when it comes to women and all they do to look presentable but, as a man, I *do* know Jessica is not "putting her best foot forward". As a doctor, I can feel the physical agitation emanating from her.

Beth says, "Hi, Jessica, nice to see you."

It's said gently so that she doesn't startle Jessica, I don't think Jessica has even noticed us standing nearby in the first aid aisle.

"Oh. Hi, Beth. I didn't see you." (Just as I suspected.)

"How are the girls doing with the eggs?"

"Fine, fine. They seem to have gotten the hang of it."

"I'm so glad. Please tell them I look forward to our tea party."

Jessica looks confused and then nods. Beth can sense all this is horribly awkward and the very last thing on Jessica's mind is polite chit-chat. Beth does a little wave and drifts over to the rack of greeting

66

cards. I am bored to tears as she picks up one stupid card after another. One card has a practically naked man with a bow tie opening a bottle of wine. Inside it says, "Thank you for your service." What occasion could possibly call for a card like this? Cards are verbal pablum for idiots and I've always despised the convention of giving them and, even worse, receiving them.

I hear the pharmacist call Jessica's name and hurry back to the pick-up counter. I want to see what prescription she's getting filled. It's Zofran.

Zofran is an anti-nausea drug given after chemo. Chemotherapy is so brutal on the body that the expression, "What doesn't kill you makes you stronger," describes it perfectly. I think of Margaret with her bird-like rib cage and I imagine her retching with nothing to offer up to the relentlessly demands of chemo.

I see Beth pop a card into her basket and head to the checkout in the front of the store, meanwhile Jessica is putting her credit card in the pharmacist's terminal. I'm standing flat-footed, looking from one to the other.

Jessica pays, "No receipt, thank you," turns and briskly walks to the front of the store. I follow right behind her. She actually overtakes Beth when the wide automated doors slide open. She says a clipped, "Bye." It's not rude, just all business. Our two cars are side by side right out front, our navy Lexus and Jessica's white Range Rover. I see Trixie looking at me from the backseat, her tongue is out and she's smiling. Such a good dog.

As a surgeon, I always had to make split-second, life and death decisions. My decision I must make right now is whether to walk 30 degrees to the right, with Beth, or walk 30 degrees to the left, with Jessica.

Trixie puts her nose against the window.

I make a professional decision and jump into the Land Rover. I'm needed more somewhere else and I still a doctor, just not a *practicing* one. Trixie looks confused but she'll be fine. Beth will be fine, too. She'll bandage her finger and probably spend the rest of the day reading with Trixie beside her. My skills will be of much greater value at Jessica's house. I'm a chivalrous man by nature; it comes part and parcel with being The Greatest Husband.

I wish I could put my seatbelt on because Jessica drives like a bat out of hell. We literally fly up Round House Road. I forget to look at the tulips and dogwood and just hang on. When we get to her gate and it slowly opens, she almost rams it.

I look back and watch the gate close. I wish I could go back and get Spatula. I fancy myself a miracle worker but even miracle workers need tools.

CHAPTER 14

The front of the stone mansion has a different mood on this rainy day. All the pink toys look like their sulking in despondent neglect. The cardboard boxes are long past serving any purpose and lie like giant, misshapen toadstools, no doubt killing the grass under them. The sidewalk chalk rainbow ceases to exist and if it did, Jessica just parked over the top of it.

I barely make it out of the car alive. Jessica's hurried exit from the car is my cue to stay very close; Jessica waits for no man or ghost. There are some little girls' costumes scattered in the large foyer and even two pink bikes lying on their sides.

I hear cartoons and someone speaking in Spanish coming from the kitchen-living area. Jessica bounds up the stairs. At the top we make a right, which takes us through an arch into a whole suite of rooms. It's the master suite. There are mirror images of each of the rooms within the suite: his closet and dressing room are on the right, her's on the left. His bathroom with a glass shower on the right, her's with a clawfoot tub on the left.

At the end of the hall, there's another arch and we step into the master bedroom. It's a glorious room with windows looking out onto the lush green backyard, a swimming pool and tennis court. There are heavy silk drapes with blue tassels, a fireplace, two club chairs facing a coffee table and an enormous bed with a tall headboard. Tucked in that bed, barely visible, is Margaret. She's lying on the side closest to the windows. There's a towel on the pillow and a towel on the floor, where an old plastic mixing bowl sits.

Margaret, the sweetest child I've ever met, has dark circles under her eyes. She looks like an exhausted princess lying amidst all this luxury. Jessica sits on the edge of the bed and smooths Margaret's hair back even though it's perfectly in place. "I'm here, my angel. Mommy's here. I have your medicine." She gives Margaret the medicine, chased with a sip of Sprite. "That's good, Mommy," Margaret says. Jessica kisses her forehead. "I'll be right back."

Jessica runs back downstairs and I follow. She throws the hat and jacket on a bench in the foyer. I now notice the hat has a tiny squash racquet and logo on it and the jacket has some tiny golf flag and logo. I am not versed in these elite athletic enclaves, I never had the time or interest, so the nuances of the logos are lost on me.

Jessica goes into the living area which is sunken two steps below the kitchen and has rows of glass doors that look out back. She surprises me and speaks Spanish fluently. I catch exactly two words, *Carmen* and *gracias*. The middle aged woman gets up from the sofa; she was the one holding the tee shirts the other day. She says, "*Vengo en un rato,*" as she heads to a small door next to the utility closet. When she opens it, I see a narrow set of steps ascending to her room over the garage, or perhaps a room in the turret.

There are school workbooks open on the coffee table, lots of markers, snacks and drinks.

Sophia and Charlotte are snuggled up, staring at an animated show. "*Adiós*, Carmen." They barely look up. Carmen must get a break before preparing dinner and the evening duties.

"Did you do all your homework?"

Without taking her eyes off the TV, Sophia, my little reader says, "It's so easy, I could do it in five minutes, Mom."

Charlotte pulls her thumb out and echoes, "It's so easy, I could do it in five minutes." She reaches down to her middle and adjusts her hatching belt before putting her thumb back in her mouth.

"Okay," Jessica says, "Then just *do* it!" She turns and we stomp back upstairs.

The rest of the afternoon passes uneventfully. We spend most of the time at Margaret's side. We read to her. We hold her forehead when she leans over to retch, then we cool her head with ice. Essentially, we try to comfort a very sick child.

There is a tenderness between mother and daughter that I've never witnessed so intimately. Maybe Beth had it with Evie but I was never there to see it. I think how hardy and hale our Evie was and still is. She was never so soft and vulnerable, like this dove. At one point, Margaret asks, "How's my egg, Mommy?" Jessica smiles and lifts her own shirt, "Snug as a bug in a rug." I must admit, I've forgotten about Margaret's belt and find it poignant her mother has taken on the burden.

When dinner time comes, Carmen reappears and makes macaroni and cheese. I haven't seen plain old macaroni and cheese out of the box in years. It actually looks pretty good and Sophia, Charlotte and Carmen enjoy it immensely in front of the TV. Jessica carries a small bowl up for Margaret but she shakes her head, she doesn't even want it in the room.

I stop following Jessica and just sit beside Margaret. We can see the horizon turning pink through the trees. It's sunset and the bedside clock says 7:57. It's very peaceful in the luxurious room with a bed like a silken cocoon. There's been no mention of Daddy. No macaroni and cheese was kept on the stove for him, like the pot of chili at Miguel's. The only way I know he exists is evidenced by his closet filled with clothes and the shaving supplies next to his sink. I plan to take a closer look at them later but at the moment I'm content sitting quietly, a doctor who makes house calls.

Jessica comes back to the bedroom at 9:00 and peels her clothes off. In med school, we'd occasionally debate the beauty of the male anatomy versus the female. I thought it was such a ridiculous argument and always kept my thoughts to myself. There's no contest.

The male body is engineered for strength and endurance. It's a stripped down biological entity that is economically functional. The female body is something else altogether. It's extravagant; meant to attract, reproduce, sustain and then wither. It's a flower not evolved to endure the test of time. It's meant to be enjoyed fully while it blossoms, every man knows this on an instinctual basis, whether they admit it or not. Granted, it was my body that failed and Beth's that endured but this was just a statistical outlier.

Wearing just her underwear and the hatching belt, she walks over to Margaret and lets her peek at the egg. Margaret gently turns the egg in its foam rubber nest, just like Average Joe shows you how to do in the video. She says, "Night-night, duckie."

Jessica puts on a silky gray nightgown, climbs into bed and lies next to Margaret. I sit on the edge of the bed next to Margaret in case she needs me. I think we are all settled for the night but then in about fifteen minutes, Sophia and Charlotte show up beside Jessica's side of the bed. Sophia is the spokeswoman: "We want to sleep here, too."

Jessica sighs and moves closer to Margaret and the other two climb in. Charlotte yelps, "Sophia, don't squish my egg!" Then my nest of females is silent. A few minutes pass and I can hear the rhythmic noise of Charlotte sucking her thumb.

These females, one woman and three girls, have this whole huge mansion but they prefer to pile into this one bed. One exhales and the other breathes in the used, moist air. They're crowded into the warmth and security of this human hatching belt called a bed. There's no male to protect them and I feel needed, alert to danger. I vow not to roam for the entire night. I lay myself across the foot of the bed like a faithful dog and there I lie, their defender.

I just wish Trixie was here to keep me company.

CHAPTER 15

Jessica left the drapes open and I watch the light slowly fill the room. It's still dreary, with heavy skies and spitting rain, but it's well past sunrise and no one has moved. I kept my vow to defend my damsels through the night but now I'm itching to move and explore. I get up off the foot of the bed and allow myself to wander.

There's a framed family photo on the dresser that I missed because there's a stack of folded clothes sitting in front of it. In the photo, Charlotte is half her current size and held on Jessica's hip, so she's probably two. Sophia is in the center, holding Margaret's hand. Margaret has a beautiful smile with full cheeks and long hair in pigtails. Mr. Kline is standing beside Jessica. One arm is draped over her shoulder while the other hand reaches down and touches Margaret's shoulder. They're on some beach, judging from the turquoise water, probably the Carribean.

I am reluctant to admit but it's a nice family photo, even *with* Mr. Kline in it. Mr. Kline is undeniably handsome. He has brown wavy hair that he wears longish, blue eyes and an athletic build. Everyone looks happy, relaxed and very healthy. If they all crowded into one bed that night, it was out of love and not because the world seemed dangerous and unpredictable.

Where are you, Mr. Kline?

It's time to get some answers and I start with his dressing room, where there are three walls of clothing, drawers and cubbies. There's a rack with the prerequisite men's suits, plus a black tux but the theme that strikes me, as I survey his belongings, is sporty. There are cubbies with hats with logos of different golf courses, there's one rack with nothing but garishly colored polo shirts, and shelves piled with every type of athletic shoe possible. There's no question about it, Mr. Kline is a playboy and I don't mean it in the Hugh Heffner sense of the brand Playboy, I simply mean he enjoys playing games.

I never had time to play; I worked. In high school, I needed money to go to college. When I was In college, I needed money to go to med school. I always just worked, worked, worked and it all turned out great, good, fine. I found The Perfect Wife, had my two kids, boy girl, got a dog and bought my gentleman's farm. How is it Mr. Kline has all this time to play but has managed to acquire so much more than I did? He appears to have captured The Perfect Wife, has *three* children and a historic estate on five acres. What are the rules to the game *he's* playing? I didn't know there was a game where you get to win at everything.

My thoughts are disrupted by giggling. I rush back to see what I've missed. Margaret, Jessica and Sophia are all sitting up in bed. Sophia is gently pulling Charlotte's thumb out of her mouth and Charlotte keeps grunting in her sleep and putting it back.

Jessica glances at Charlotte but she can't take her eyes off Margaret, who looks so much better. Margaret says, "Mom, can I have my egg?" Jessica smiles, lifts her nightgown and unstraps it. Margaret lifts her pajama top and Velcros it on. The two girls and Jessica get out of bed, leaving Charlotte sleeping. I go downstairs with Margaret and Sophia and leave Jessica to do her morning absolutions in privacy. Jessica comes down a few minutes later wearing yoga clothes and her hair in a swingy ponytail.

Carmen makes pancakes from scratch and Sophia chatters to her in Spanish. Margaret is already at the counter with a school book open. Jessica tells her don't worry, Mr. Smith won't care, she has all day to catch up on her homework. I can't imagine Evie being so sick and then jumping up and being so concerned about her homework. It would've been a battle royale to get her to open her books and being sick would've been her defense. I would be the bad cop and Beth would've taken her side and coddled her. Just thinking of the possible scenario irritates me. Of course, thank god, Evie was never this sick and getting chemo.

Charlotte comes down looking sleepy, her thumb in her mouth. Carmen sweeps her up, carries her to the sofa, turns on cartoons and cuddles her. She yells over to Jessica, "Don't worry about those pans, I'll get to them later."

Jessica doesn't seem the least bit concerned about the bowl of pancake batter and the greasy skillet. Beth would never tolerate this clutter and mess. I don't have a ton of experience with women and domestic chores but my guess is that Jessica is a woman who is used to things being done for her. Whether those things happen now or later is no concern of hers.

I find the inner workings of this all female household fascinating and enchanting. There's a lack of urgency, competitiveness and conflict that I find charming. These (now) two women and three girls seem perfectly happy to love, support, and nurture each other all day long. They're content to live and let live, behind their gate, in their mansion. The thought of wicked cancer worming its way into this Eden angers me. I feel it's up to me, Dr. Paradise, and my male energy to slay Corrupt Cancer in this house of love. Mr. Kline certainly doesn't seem to be doing anything about it!

All three girls go snuggle with Carmen on the sofa. Jessica wipes her hands on a towel and walks purposefully through the foyer to the front door. I have no idea where we're going or what the rhythm of Jessica's day is. I follow her closely through the foyer to the front door. I'm eager to go outside, feel the temperature, maybe get a ride back to town in the Land Rover.

Jessica opens the front door and I step out, waiting for her to follow. She hesitates and calls back, "Carmen, *trajiste el correo?*"

Carmen yells, "*Si!*" With no warning, Jessica takes a step back and slams the door!

It's late morning with a steady drizzle and I am stuck outside like a dog with mange. There's absolutely nothing I can do to change my situation. I can think of nothing but to sit down on the stone front steps and wait. Time passes.

Lesson #1: people who don't have dogs, don't open their doors as often as people who do.

Beth and I were always opening the doors for Trixie. It was a necessity of her bladder but it was also an exercise to prove our love over and over. Clever Trixie would stand by the French doors, look out, look at us, wag her tail and smile. Did we love her enough to get off the sofa and open the door? Yes we did!

Two minutes later, after she sniffed where a squirrel once was and did a piddle, she'd stand at the French doors again, look at us, wag her tail and smile. Did we love her enough to get off the sofa *again* and let her in? Yes we did!

That's why, weather allowing, we always just left the French doors open.

That's not the case with the Klines. The oversized front door is tightly closed and every window is sealed. I can't get back to my charges. I wander around to the back and examine the pool and hot tub that has a fence around it. It's all very neat and the pool toys are orderly, I'm pretty sure the pool maintenance crew tidied up. There's a service driveway out past the tennis court that I didn't know existed which enters the back of the property. The asphalt strip is straight and functional. It doesn't bother to loop and bend like the front driveway. At the end, there's a utilitarian gate, higher, less inviting than the front gate but definitely capable of doing its job to keep people out. An older yellow car is parked in the back, that must be Carmen's. She must come and go from the back while Jessica and people like Beth loop through the front.

I'm torn. Should I sit on the back stoop and see if the lawn crew or pool maintenance drive in the service entrance? Or should I sit in front and wait for the girls to come out and play or Jessica, ideally, to get in her Land Rover and drive to town? I alternate, walking front to back, back to front. During one shift in front, I hear the girls squealing behind the door. I peek in the small window and see Sophia and Charlotte riding their pink bikes around the foyer. When I sit in the back, I hear the constant drone of cartoon voices coming from the TV.

The day crawls by.

No lawn crew descends. No pool maintenance arrives. Carmen doesn't go. Jessica chooses not to leave. Mr. Smith, the alleged tutor, doesn't even make an appearance. It's just me, myself and I and I'm getting anxious. I'm anxious because I'm needed in two places at once and I can't get to either one. I should either be *inside* watching over Margaret and supporting Jessica or I should be at *home*, with Beth and Trixie. I've been away much longer than I planned when I made the snap decision to jump into Jessica's car at the pharmacy.

The clouds have finally cleared and the sun is an orange lozenge dipping below the horizon. It must be about 8:00 p.m. I see the lights come on in the master bedroom and imagine my tribe of women getting ready for bed in Jessica's luxurious bedroom. I see Carmen's light blink on under the eaves – so cliché! The thought of my damsels cozy without me, Beth completely alone not knowing faithful Trixie is beside her and me, sitting trapped all night, makes me a little crazy. I *should* be able to figure out a solution, I'm a thoracic surgeon!

I walk down the service drive to examine the gate more closely. The gate is solid and at least 6' tall with an electric sensor. If I had Spatula, I could wave it in front of the sensor and be out lickety split. There are some scrubby pine trees near this gate, which I could possibly climb, stand on the wall and then jump down.

Compared to the rest of the property, this area is slightly neglected, the trash and recycling bins are lined up here and there's an old stone shed that is probably original to the property. I'm weighing my choices of climbing a pine tree or scrambling on top of a recycling bin, relishing neither. I am almost 74 years old in human years and the thought of an inevitable 6' drop on the other side of the wall doesn't excite me.

Just when I have calculated that the pines, with their nicely spaced branches, are the better option than the tippy recycling bins, I hear an engine purr. I stand to the side like a toy soldier at attention. I don't want to get hit in my eagerness to exit. The purr comes from a sleek black Porsche. I can clearly see the man behind the wheel because he's holding his phone in his hand and the light from the screen is shining back up into his face. He looks up, straight at me, when the gate is fully open.

There's no doubt, it's Playboy Kline, I'd recognize him anywhere.

He isn't wearing a suit, he's wearing one of those ridiculously bright polo shirts. His hair is just as long and wavy as in the photograph taken on vacation. He doesn't look stressed or exhausted, like he just spent eight hours in life and death surgery. The fact is, he looks like he doesn't have a care in the world.

Once again, I have to make a snap decision. I would like to see this male walk into that house of love and see what happens. Where does this male energy belong? Why hasn't he been here helping sweet Margaret through the night? Will he sleep in the bed with Jessica? Will the three girls in their hatching belts join them? Will they reunite to be the happy family in the photograph?

These are big, unanswered questions but I've been yearning to escape all day and feel I must follow through with my plan to return to Beth and Trixie. So I make the committed decision to walk out as the Porsche drives in. I watch the gate close behind me.

I take a deep breath to begin my walk home and another question pops in my head, *"Why does Playboy Kline use the service entrance? Is he a thief in the night?"*

CHAPTER 16

I estimate it's a four to five mile walk home. The road is scenic in the moonlight. The air is cool and damp. It's not what I had in mind but the exercise won't kill me. (Shoveling snow already did that!)

As I walk, I can't help but think about Mr. Kline and how he's a breed apart from me and my brethren at the hospital. I don't really have experience with these sorts of men in my life. Quite frankly, I'm more comfortable with someone like my amigo Miguel. We share the same work ethic and the same sense of purpose. We approach each day with a yeoman's pledge of duty and place one foot in front of the other. We're grounded. Now we're both working on finding compromises with our daughters. Miguel might be working slightly harder at it than me.

Maybe Ray-the-Jerk is a little like Playboy Kline? I've seen Ray taking his golf clubs in and out of his car on Sundays when he should be trimming his hedges or at least *paying* someone to trim his hedges. That's just a fact. I know he's a jerk for what he said about me being "the cobbler with no shoes" at my celebration of life. That's also a fact.

Maybe Playboy Kline is just a fancier version of Ray-the-Jerk? It's an interesting thought. I never really had male friends; I don't really understand them. I liked them fine when we were all in work mode. I knew what to say, how to act. But when the situation was relaxed, social, I was lost. The conversation always drifted to sports or finance, neither of which interested me.

As I walk, I feel all the tender feelings that I experienced in that nest of women and girls, fall away. Thinking of Playboy Kline and

Ray-the-Jerk has put me in a toxic stew of masculinity. I don't *want* to feel this way, I'd prefer to remain calm, peaceful, noble but competitive, combative masculinity has always been part of my world and I can't help myself. On a positive note, it definitely makes me walk faster.

I'm walking next to a high stone wall for a few minutes before I reach its entry gate. It's a huge piece of property that I've always noted while driving up Round House Road. Big boulders have been ominously placed along the edge of the road to keep drivers from pulling over and parking along the roadside. The person who lives in this estate cares about every inch of his property, even the part outside the wall. I respect that.

The mailbox is shiny black and has a large 221 painted on it. The address is 221 Round House Road, but why state the obvious? The whole set up, mailbox, brace, post is new because you can see where the old one broke off and how this new one is 12" to the right and set in fresh concrete.

I'd like to have a new mailbox like this one and I bend down to look closely at the little tag. It says Mr. Postbox, but I'm also able to read "Schlitz 221 Round House Rd" written in pencil on the wooden post. The workers who arrived with a whole load of posts and boxes, dug a hole, poured concrete and installed the best quality post and mailbox money can buy, made a big mistake; they forgot to clean off the customer's name penciled on the post.

Now I know where Gunther-Schlitz-Who-Shits-Money lives.

Revenge has never been part of my psyche but when I think of the stress and my ignominious retirement, it crosses my mind. Tonight will be a night of reconnaissance. I survey the stone wall, the gate and the sensor. It's so simple, it's laughable. The gate has an intercom but all I have to do is stand here and wait for someone to drive in or out and then I can just stroll in. I'll bring Spatula, enter the property, exact my revenge and then just wave Spatula in front of the gate sensor and

81

stroll back out. I'm not sure what form my revenge will take, maybe I'll merely give him the fright of his life. I think, TBD and am giddy with the simplicity of it.

The walk down Round House Road to my home, my gentleman's farm, takes a few hours. Having to walk it has proven to be a blessing in disguise for two reasons:

1. I have discovered where my nemesis Gunther-Schlitz-Who-Shits-Money lives.

2. I have confirmed that I'm still in pretty good shape.

Overall, the night has been a great success and I am content, sitting on my back veranda, in my preferred chair. The sun is coming up and it looks like it's going to be a fabulous day. It's Beth's habit to make a cup of coffee, open the French doors, and sit outside to drink it when the weather is nice. We used to do it together while Trixie sniffed around and did her morning constitution. I feel positively ebullient, waiting to see My Darling and Trixie.

I don't have to wait long; there are no sleepy heads at this house!

I see Beth walk up to the glass door. She looks lovely with her hair hanging down, wearing a mauve and blue kimono we bought in Japan. She's holding a cup of coffee, laughing as she opens the door.

I smile. Yes, My Darling, I'm home!

Out of the door, tumbles... not Trixie, but a preposterously fat puppy. It's a yellow Lab. It's wagging its stumpy tail at Beth, but then it sees me and charges, barking! I'm so startled that I leap up on the chair like an elephant spying a mouse. It's outrageous.

Beth is still laughing as she floats down the stone steps, cup of coffee and phone in hand, taking the seat opposite me. The French doors are wide open. As I stand on my chair and listen to the incessant yapping, I watch the doors.

Trixie never comes out. Trixie is no more.

CHAPTER 17

Beth has killed our beloved Trixie and gotten this insult of a canine – this juvenile whelp that does not recognize me as the master of the house and now barks at my feet while I stand on a chair opposite of my laughing wife. If Beth can dispense with Trixie and be charmed by this peewee distraction, how does that bode for me?

As Beth sips her coffee, she watches the pup with amusement. After about a minute, he stops his barking, trots over to the grass, spreads his back legs wide and pees, looking very serious. Beth laughs again. Then, either because the pup is so young or, because the pup is so stupid, he forgets about me, the ghost, standing on the chair.

I'm able to sit down, which is a relief.

Beth picks up her phone, looks at the screen and calls Stick-Your-Nose-In-Everyone's-Business-Sandy. To paraphrase the long, inane conversation, it goes something like this: I can't thank you enough. Yes, I love him. No, no name yet. Thank you again for encouraging me. Yes, I feel much better.

I don't need to hear Sandy's end of the conversation. I've heard plenty. The irrefutable conclusion is: this is all Sandy's fault. I remember her insensitive comment on Facebook when Beth posted about Trixie's passing: "I have a friend with puppies! Call me!!!" I recall how Beth went to lunch with Sandy and brought her laptop. They weren't looking at real estate, they were looking at *puppies*. It is all abundantly clear. It makes perfect sense now.

Beth was deceived, hoodwinked, bamboozled.

It's unfair to blame her when it's Sandy's doing. I will still call Beth The Perfect Wife but Sandy's need to get involved, manipulate, run the show has taken my closest companion and replaced her with an adversary. She has brought undue stress into my after life when I was just beginning to enjoy each day and appreciate small wonders.

Stick-Your-Nose-In-Everyone's-Business-Sandy is officially downgraded, if that's even possible to Stay-The-Hell-Away-Sandy.

Beth, pup and I go inside. And even though my home has been invaded by this ball of pudge, it feels great to be within its four Modern Eggshell walls and I plop down on my favorite chair, knowing trusty Spatula is just below me.

Pup doesn't pay me any attention because Beth is giving it a scoop of puppy chow served disrespectfully in Trixie's bowl. She's taken chairs and blocked off the kitchen-family room area so the dog has limited space and only hardwood floors in case he has an accident. She's also left the French doors wide open for easy in-out access.

I barely close my eyes when the little varmint starts to yap. Miguel is here.

I feel like I haven't seen my amigo in ages. I feel a sense of satisfaction saying that we're truly amigos now. I've met his daughter, we've had coffee and tortillas, and I've even decoded his billing system. That's *much* more intimate than I ever was with any of my co-workers at the hospital.

"Look, Miguel!" Beth says as the three of us walk out.

Miguel gives Beth his classic smile, bends down to pet the irritant who wriggles with happiness from this stranger's attention.

"*Qué guapo!*" He cocks his head, "And how is *el huevo?*"

"*Está muy bien.*" She cracks her kimono open slightly so he can see her hatching belt.

"El *mio tambíen.*" He stands straight and lifts the edge of his tee-shirt. "Do you have a name for this *campeón* yet?"

"No. What's '*campeón?*'"

And then it occurs to me. In this gentle, sneaky way, Miguel is teaching Beth Spanish. I'm not sure if she agreed to this or if this is subtle manipulation with a bigger plan, but I'm too tired to think it through. I just take mental note that it's just one more thing I need to keep an eye on.

"Champion," Miguel says, "*Campeón* is champion." Then he adds, "He'll be the great *Aquiles* and protect *todos nuestros patitos*

Beth laughs. "*Patitos*?"

"Ducklings" says Miguel, pointing to her belts.

"I like the name Achilles a lot... *mucho*. Let me give it some thought." She pets the pup. "I picked up Trixie's ashes yesterday. I thought maybe you could dig a little hole under Tom's dwarf peach tree. Do you think it was her favorite?"

"*No, Señora,*" he frowns. "She liked lying by the big rock overlooking the pond. She should go there. She'll be able to watch over our babies when they hatch."

It's a sweet image: Trixie as the eternal guardian. I smile.

"But I could dig a hole for *El Jefé's* ashes under the dwarf peach tree. I think it was *his* árbol *favorito*."

"I think one burial is enough for the day," Beth laughs.

Laughs.

My ashes are in a beautiful vase on the mantel in the family room, where Beth can glance at me when she cooks or reads her book. We bought the vase in Venice and paid more to have it shipped home than the purchase price. I love my dwarf fruit trees but I don't want to be mingled with their roots in dark oblivion and, god forbid, Beth sells the house one day...

I almost faint at the thought.

We go inside, Beth, pup and I, and leave Miguel to his work. Beth sits down and calls Tyler. It's not the scheduled day or time. It's a Friday at 9:00 a.m. We usually call on Sunday mornings. Tyler picks up immediately, it's 9:00 p.m in Thailand and asks if everything is okay. He's a good and dutiful son.

Beth laughs and holds the phone in front of the fat pup and says, "Look what I have!"

Tyler grins and tells her how great that is yadda, yadda. Then she asks him what he thinks of the name Achilles. Tyler smiles broader and says, "It's heroic." They hang up.

It's only morning and so much has already happened. I'm tired from all the uncertainty locked outside Jessica's house, plus the long walk home. Just sitting on my chair and watching Beth constantly move around the kitchen-family room area is plenty of activity for me. I marvel at how one small pup can demand so much attention. At about 3:00 p.m, Beth looks at her watch and FaceTimes Evie. This is very unusual. It rings and rings and Evie doesn't pick up. Beth looks disappointed. But about five seconds later, Evie calls back. "Oh my gosh mom, are you okay?" She sounds out of breath.

"Yes, fine," Beth chuckles, "Look at your baby brother!" She holds the phone to the annoyance's face. Evie gushes about how "delicious" he is. She approves of the name Achilles. But then Beth adds more to the story, a narrative side-story that she didn't share with Tyler. She tells Evie how she went to pick the pup out. All the puppies were in a barn and there were 14. "Just imagine!" She said this pup was the fattest and strongest. It crawled over its brothers and sisters to get in her lap. Stay-The-Hell-Away-Sandy's friend had said, "That one is greedy for life."

Beth says it definitively and Evie looks attentive, like she's actually giving Beth her full attention.

"And so I picked this one." She holds him up and kisses him on the nose, "To remind me to be greedy for life. I'm *ready* to be greedy for life."

Evie's face lights up and she claps her hands in front of her face. "That's great, Mom! Really!"

I look at this little ball of organs, entrails and fur that has been given the heroic name Achilles and I think, *you're nothing more than a little sausage.*

CHAPTER 18

Before going up to bed, Beth rubs Little Sausage's velvety ears, kisses his nose and puts him in the crate.

I spend the night contemplating man's nature. *If it's a woman's to nurture, what is man's?* I keep equating *maleness* with the desire to dominate. My deep thoughts make the sunrise come quickly. The day starts normally enough, Beth gets up, opens the French doors, lifts Little Sausage out of the crate and carries him to the lawn.

He pees.

Then he follows her inside. She feeds him puppy chow from Trixie's bowl, he eats and drinks greedily. Then Beth calls him outside and walks around the yard.

He poos.

He doesn't give me hateful looks or loving looks, he just casts questioning glances my way, like a child when a wayward uncle drops by for dinner.

We sit outside. After Beth drinks her coffee and reads the paper on her iPad, she watches the video of Average Joe hatching the eggs *again*. It's redundant, repetitive, ridiculous. I've no idea why she needs to keep watching it. Little Sausage and I follow her into the house. He keeps his eyes on me the entire time. Beth goes into the powder room, which Miguel painted Chelsea gray for a "little drama". There are no windows and when you close the door, it's dark and moody inside. I slip in with her but Little Sausage doesn't make the cut and is left on the other side of the door, whining.

Beth puts her phone on the counter, turns on the flashlight app and gently removes Rightie from the belt. She sets it on the light and we both lean forward to look. Her hair brushes my face like a memory. The egg appears to have a dark oval inside, and the dark oval moves!

Beth smiles and places the egg back in the belt. She then reaches in and pulls out Little Leftie, *my* chick. I hold my breath as she puts it on the phone screen. I wonder if she cares as much about Little Leftie as she does Rightie. It's like children, can a parent really control how they feel about one child compared to the other? Can I help it if Tyler was always easier?

We peer down. Little Leftie lives!

Despite my limited participation and the fact I can't actually carry the burden of the belt, Leftie seems to be thriving against Beth's body. Once again, proving Beth is The Perfect Wife.

Meanwhile, Little Sausage is yapping outside the door like he's being tortured. When we come out of the powder room, we all go back outside because, guess who needs to poo?

Beth texts Jessica, "How's it going? Put the eggs on the phone light and check if you can see an embryo moving." Jessica gives her a thumbs up.

Then Beth narrows her eyes and stares at the pond, looking for the answer to a question. She goes to the top of her text messages and hits the little *write* icon. She starts to type in "Fri" and I see the space populate with the name "Friedrich," aka The Lug. It's as though she texts him all the time. She starts to tap out words very slowly.

"Good morning!" (Sounds too friendly.) "Your chick should be moving by now. Mine are!" (Correction, Leftie is mine.) "We can check together, if you want. I'll be at the store at 11:30 today."

What does *that* mean? When did Beth get on such personal terms to know that The Lug will be at Bon Vivant around noon on Saturday? Did I miss something? Apparently, he's a regular. Or maybe he works there? Is this considered a *rendez-vous?*

I watch Beth tidy the kitchen, then go up and get dressed. She comes down wearing white jeans, a blue untucked blouse and sandals. She looks fresh and pretty. That's it, I'm going with.

Beth gets her reusable shopping bag, "I'm trusting you, Achilles," she says, and without putting Little Sausage in the crate, just walks out the door. Click. The mudroom door closes. I hear the garage door open and close, while I'm left still fumbling for Spatula.

I wish I could yell after her, *And I'm trusting you, my Perfect Wife.*

I figure she'll be gone forty-five minutes tops. Beth won't linger, even if she plans to make goo-goo eyes at The Lug, she knows that Little Sausage's bladder waits for no man.

Little Sausage wanders around the family room rug, weaving like a fat, drunken sailor, then he just tilts over and falls sound asleep. He's about the size of a shoe box. I don't know much about dogs, but he acts like an infant with all his peeing and pooing and now this deep sleep.

I sit on my favorite chair and watch him. His breath comes in and out, little sighs of air, not unlike Evie when she was a baby or little Charlotte now. I am reluctant to admit, but it is sweet to see Beth have something to love so tenderly, even if it's just Little Sausage. Beth is following her nature. It's not that Little Sausage is such an extraordinary pup.

Perhaps the female nature to nurture helpless beings is superior to the dominance of man? Perhaps these helpless creatures are coveted by women for just this reason – they're helpless? I wonder if anything has ever been written on this topic?

Looking down on this defenseless little being, I realize that I can't hear his sleep sodden breath. Little Sausage isn't moving – not his sides – nothing. I panic. Will I have to resuscitate this pup? This is *one* skill out of my area of expertise. I lean down, thinking of how to seal his mouth while I blow into his nose. It will be awkward but miraculous. Then I'll be the hero!

But when I lean down to place my lips on his moist snout, he lets out a tremendous nasally snore, like he was saving it up just for me.

I laugh and eye what Beth calls her *fancy pillows,* large corner pillows with luxurious Tibetan lamb fur. They sit in each corner with long silky hair and give the pillow arrangement *texture.*

Knowing it's not my nature to nuture, is it a quality I can cultivate? I flick one of these hirsute squares to the floor and pat it with Spatula. When Little Sausage doesn't respond, I tap him on the rear and then tap the pillow again. He gets up dully, wanders to the silky oasis laid before him and flops down on it. Surely this exotic fur feels better than even his own mother. He sighs and goes back to sleep.

I sit in my chair, watching Little Sausage sleep on the fancy pillow, waiting for Beth. Forty-five minutes comes and goes. I try not to stew about Beth's tardiness and try to focus on the sweet contentment of sleeping Little Sausage. Bottom line, Little Sausage *is* greedy for life, there's no doubt about *that.* He was born in a barn competing with 13 brothers and sisters. His presence will remind us all, Beth *and* me, to live each day fully.

We are a matrimonial team and each of us has a part in a life of future happiness.

I start doing my part by renaming Little Sausage "Saucisson", it's diminutive in French for sausage, the *opposite* of heroic Achilles. I chuckle at my cleverness. It will remind me that he, will be joining us in Paris. If I soften towards Saucisson today, perhaps I can soften towards Evie tomorrow. I'm a work in progress.

I start thinking about how Saturdays are awkward days in the week that serve no clear purpose. They are unpredictable and this one is no different.

I always scheduled at least one surgery on Friday. I'd frame it as a positive to the patient, "You'll miss less work that way," but really, I did it for me. I wanted the freedom to say to Beth on Saturday, "Sorry, My Darling, I have to make rounds, there's Mrs. Such and Such." Beth would look at me sadly and take Evie to a birthday party or Tyler to one of his baseball games.

Since I died, Saturday nights haven't been so bad, but before that, they were *the worst*. Saturday nights I was required to socialize. I define "socialize" as: coming together in a common location with amiable intentions.

Parties were the absolute worst. Once a party was put on the calendar, sometimes weeks in advance, I would dread it, each and every day. Put a bunch of adults in a large room, give them all the alcohol they can consume, stir them around so they mix and mingle, it's a sure fire recipe for disaster. Things happen at Saturday night parties that would never happen on any other day of the week.

Once, one of those unfortunate events happened to me. Once.

It happened at a party with Beth's friend Self-Aware-Emily. She had kids Tyler's and Evie's age and she and Beth's paths crossed frequently. When Beth realized her proclivity for alcohol, she pitied Emily, and heaped most of the blame on Emily's husband.

I don't know the root of Emily's problem and I don't care. I just know her problem became my problem the night she sprayed herself with Beth's signature perfume and wore some beguiling pushup bra that made her look much more scrumptious than she was. It was my first month of forced retirement and I was feeling pretty low, hung out to dry, victimized for turning Schlitz Sr. into a cabbage. I'm not using that as a justification for my actions; it just shows where I was... mentally.

That Saturday night, Beth dragged me to the party, insisting it would be "good for you". She packed me in the car and drove there, like I was some sort of child going on a playdate, tousling my hair, saying, "Don't be a grumpy old man." There, now you've got the context in which my misstep took place.

I found the bar and as the evening went on, I found myself in a narrow hall with Drunk Emily. Together, we found a secret door that was flush with the wainscot paneling on the walls. It was the china closet, just outside the butler's pantry. We giggled, like children playing hide and seek, and pushed ourselves into it. We had to be very careful because there were shelves with stacks of dishes, platters and gravy boats. I don't remember much, but I *do* remember Emily picking up a gravy boat with a big turkey painted on it, the kind you'd use on Thanksgiving and saying, "Let's just sail away," and she bobbed the gravy boat in the air. Sailing away that night seemed like a very good idea.

In the morning, I wasn't sure how far my play with my playmate had gone in the secret china closet. I had just turned 71, how much defilement was I capable of? While I was looking for clues, Beth actually complimented me on "letting loose for once". She didn't know the full extent to which I let loose and my lips were and are *forever* sealed. I'm not about to abdicate my standing as The Greatest Husband for one indiscretion. And let's be frank, I don't even know if anything happened.

Overall, it was a terrible blunder and I deeply regretted anything I did or didn't do that night in the china closet but in a twist of irony, it jarred me from my torpor, from my *deterioration*.

I woke up that Sunday morning with a pounding headache and as I slowly found my footing. The gravy boat became my metaphor for embarking on adventure. My plan was that we would move to France! I shared my vision with Beth and we started doing Duolingo that very night and pouring over street maps of Paris, but, of course, the pandemic postponed my plan.

Most people would say my catastrophic heart attack and subsequent death was the turning point to my life but I would say it was really the china closet. The china closet and gravy boat made me greedy for life and I've proven that not even death can stop me from living it!

I had a nagging dread that Drunk Emily would let the story of our china closet liaison slip but the moment for confession never came, thank god,

After a full two hours, Beth walks through the door, smiling ear to ear. My reverie dissipates. I need to stay present, it's abundantly clear that there is a larger threat for Beth's affection than Saucisson.

None of this is ideal but I know struggle is part of success. I'm greedy and will endure. If there are impediments between My Darling and me, Spatula and I will remove them.

CHAPTER 19

As if I could forget, it's an unpredictable Saturday, no one sticks to a plan. Beth's phone rings just as Miguel pulls up in the driveway with lovey Fernanda, the jewel of *Pequeña Fleur*, in the pickup.

Beth waves to Miguel while she talks to Self-Aware-Emily. "Of course you can stop by and see Achilles and yes I'd love to go out for dinner tonight."

Miguel does not look happy. My amigo *always* looks happy. If there was a talking bubble above his head it would say, "Did you say fiesta?" But today there's just a storm cloud.

My Darling doesn't even notice that my amigo is cheerless. Beth is bubbly, effervescent, ebullient. Miguel introduces lovely Fernanda and Beth hugs her, examines her, smiles ear-to-ear. In the old days, Fernanda would occasionally accompany Miguel to work. Beth would give her treats and she would play with Evie, if Evie was home. We haven't seen Fernanda in years; she has grown from a cute girl through adolescence and has arrived on the other side a magnificent young woman. A young Sophia Loren, there I said it. I'm dating myself but you get the point – gorgeous.

Fernanda smiles and asks if "Evie is home to play?" which makes us all laugh. Then Beth takes Miguel by the forearm and kind of drags him inside. Fernanda, Saucisson and I follow. She picks her phone off the counter and pulls him into the dark powder room, Fernanda follows but Saucisson and I are both left on the other side of the door. He looks up at me and wags his tail. I look down and give him the hand signal to sit and he amazingly, he obeys.

From inside I hear Miguel's voice, "Mirá! Mirá!" They all come out of the powder room and Miguel stops and slips his egg back in his belt. Miguel looks so much happier than when he pulled up in the driveway. He says, "See Fernanda. We're *mamás* together!"

Lovely Fernanda laughs like a tinkling bell.

Now that Miguel has said *mamá*, the air is clear. She *knows* that Beth *knows* that she's pregnant. She's no longer the innocent little girl that Beth knew. They've moved on to a new relationship, they're two women.

Miguel becomes serious. He tells Beth how Fernanda's *novio*, Dmitri, won't leave her alone. Dmitri sounds intelligent. Like a-chess player, no problem at all.

But Miguel says, "He's a bad guy," and that Fernanda is trying to break it off with him even though he's the father of her baby. He says, "It's complicated."

Miguel explains that Fernanda needs to study for her college finals, which are this coming week. He's not comfortable leaving her alone in the house, could she study here?

Gracious Beth says of course. There's lots of room. She's welcome to sleep in Evie's room if she wants to stay over. Beth would enjoy the extra person in the house.

I stand back and listen to all this. Naturally, I have no problem with lovely Fernanda staying, I welcome it. I'm just observing the scene. There's a puppy greedy for life at Beth's feet, there's a lovely young woman with child, there's Miguel with a hatching belt and egg in good health, and lastly, there's My Darling, with two hatching belts and two eggs developing: I feel my gentleman's farm has become a cradle of life. I'm proud; a farm *should* be a place of reproduction and growth. I didn't plan it, but it's all good.

Fernanda gets her books and a small duffle bag from the truck. Beth sets her up to study in the sunroom, brings her a glass of juice and tells her to help herself to "absolutely anything" in the kitchen.

She tells her to put her duffle bag in Evie's room. She says, "I'll be as quiet as a church mouse."

Fernanda laughs. "There's nothing quiet about my house or my neighborhood, make as much noise as you want."

The afternoon flies by. I walk between the sunroom, the family area and the veranda. Saucisson keeps Beth moving in and out and I like to take peeks to check on Fernanda and her studies. She's a good student with unwavering concentration. She gets up four times to go to the bathroom. At one point, she walks in the kitchen with her empty juice glass. She waves to Beth, reading on the veranda, fills her glass with water, and returns to the sunroom.

Evie could never sit like this. Tyler could. Don't get me wrong, Evie did everything well, very well, but I know she could've done everything *better*. Nothing deserved 100% of Evie's attention or dedication and nothing still does. She calls it "work-life balance" but I think it's a euphemism for "flakey." I watch Fernanda sit, with her head bowed and her hair hanging forward and I imagine what a wonderful mother she'll be. I can't picture Evie with a baby.

At about 6:00 p.m, Self-Aware-Emily shows up. Beth offers her a seltzer with a splash of juice and they sit outside and play with Achilles. I never liked Drunk Emily, she was erratic (and proved to be a temptress). Self-Aware-Emily comes with different drawbacks, the most dangerous being her possible need to right past wrongs, but it's been a year and a half since my death and Emily's rehab. I feel the zealous moment for confession has come and gone.

Emily loves Achilles and constantly picks him up and kisses his nose. She's thinking about getting a puppy. Beth lifts her blouse and shows Emily her hatching belts. Emily gasps, she forgot about the Facebook post, and questions ensue.

I like listening to their soft conversation but I also like walking back to the sunroom, where Fernanda has switched on a light. She occasionally stares out the window at Beth and Emily, sitting on the veranda. She sees Beth lift her blouse, she witnesses Emily lean forward for a closer look. I wonder if her peers have the same response to her belly. I wonder what Fernanda thinks of the hatching belts and that her father wears one. She's a quiet, beautiful mystery to me.

Before leaving for dinner, Beth and Emily walk to the sunroom. Beth introduces Emily to Fernanda and asks Fernanda if she can keep an eye on Achilles, or should she put him in the crate before going? Fernanda says she's happy to watch him and will walk him around outside every hour. Beth says there are containers of prepared food in the fridge and Fernanda should help herself to anything.

I'm on the fence about whether I should go or stay. I don't know where they're going to eat or which car they're taking. Lovely Fernanda is home and home is always a safe place but going out, for a change, sounds nice too. I'm torn.

I decide, "What the heck, it's Saturday night," and go!

CHAPTER 20

Our town has a picture perfect New England main street. There are expensive boutiques, small restaurants, and coffee shops. In the summer, there's abundant outdoor dining and it feels like you're on vacation. It's a place to stroll, wear finery, be seen, see others, eat a delicious meal and go home. I had just started to enjoy and appreciate all these niceties before I died.

Beth offers to drive, which affirms my decision to go. Since Self-Aware-Emily walks around the car and gets into the passenger seat. I climb in the back. Fernanda comes to the door and waves goodbye. We all wave. It's like we're one big happy family but I'm the child this time around.

After we park, we stroll down the main street. Emily says, "Hi so-and-so" or points, "There's who-ja-ma-call it." Beth comments that Emily knows so many people and Emily laughs and says, "Because I *leave* my house!" It's the sort of chatter that would normally leave me prickly and irritated but on this late spring night, I'm enjoying being one of the girls.

There's an open table outside at the Mediterranean restaurant Eggplant, which is next to our favorite creperie. The restaurant is a good dining choice but it's a difficult space for me to navigate. They get seated at a small table outside that's nestled against the front windows and there's very little room for me to stand. I wander a few yards off and read the large creperie menu practicing my pronunciation, pretending I'm ordering in Paris.

When I check back at the table, Beth is frowning. Self-Aware-Emily has ordered a glass of wine and is telling Beth that she has "everything under control", explaining how she's just a "social drinker now". The air between them is fraught with tension. I am trying to decide where to position myself, between the conversation and the physical space. It's all just awkward.

I'm getting more intuitive from my time with Trixie. Regardless, I can read her mood at a glance and her mood is *not* good.

I don't know much about alcoholism but I do know that's not how it works; it's not so simple. You can't go back and just dabble "socially".

Emily has never exhibited brilliance or grit, so seeing her slip backwards is no great surprise to me, but Beth seems authentically distraught. Emily says, "Let's change the subject," and she begins asking Beth more questions about the eggs: "Can you sleep wearing the belts? What will happen when they hatch?" This animates Beth a bit but then the waiter brings their food, Emily orders another glass of wine and they slip into silence.

I wander over to look in a bookstore window, occasionally glancing to check on Beth's and Emily's progress. I get intrigued by a book cover, *The Next Pandemic*. I think I recognize the author's name as a former classmate. When I glance back, I do a double take: there's a man wedged in between them at their table for two, social distancing forgotten. I rush over like a summoned waiter. It's Ray-the-Jerk, looking absolutely ridiculous, folded into a chair at a table where he does not belong.

I really haven't given Ray much thought since my celebration, only occasionally when I'd watch Beth and Trixie swerve slightly in front of Ray's house, stepping off the sidewalk to avoid the untrimmed hedges. I'd think, *Ray, you are so lazy*, but then I'd have to correct myself and think, *No, you're such a jerk*.

Ray and his wife have been our neighbors for a long time. I think Beth brought them a tray of brownies when they moved in. Their kids have grown up, like ours, and they have cycled through a whole rainbow of labs: yellow, chocolate, black. Beth would occasionally go on dog walks with the wife. We were never super friendly but we've never been unfriendly, either. I kept my vitriol about the bushes to myself and since my demise I've had no way of sharing the indignity of his snide quip.

Beth and Emily both have their faces turned and are completely engrossed by whatever Ray-the-Jerk is saying. The plates are cleared, Emily's wine glass is full, Ray has a martini and Beth has seltzer. I walk up mid-sentence.

"—it was such a shock. I don't know how I didn't see it coming. After thirty years of marriage you think you know someone."

Beth and Emily both nod their heads.

"I'm so sorry Ray," Beth says.

"Wow," Emily says.

Ray looks sad but not too sad and suggests they talk about "happier things".

The best I can figure, his wife skedaddled, bolted, ran for the hills. Good for her. She probably had to ask him to trim the hedges one time too many. If I was going to take sides, I'd take hers. (It doesn't help that he's sitting so close to my wife.)

Emily shifts the conversation to Beth's hatching eggs. Beth is uncomfortable with the attention being diverted to her and having to explain her motivation to hatch eggs against her body, but Ray-the-Jerk sits riveted as Beth tells about finding the video of Average Joe, her sense of loss and loneliness and her grasping for meaning in life. She describes to them her surprise when 12 eggs arrive and recounts how she posted The Happiness Experiment on Facebook to find parents for the eggs. She mentions how Miguel, her "man about the house" took one, how a woman on Round House Road took three and then needed another three. Lastly she tells about the stranger, Friedrich, aka The Lug, who helped her in the parking lot of Bon Vivant.

Ray leans back. "So after he helps you up, you talk this perfect stranger into hatching an egg?"

I must admit, it *does* sound intriguing the way Ray-the-Jerk posits it.

Beth thinks and replies, "Yes, I guess... I guess I did. But there was an openness to him, or perhaps a sadness. It seemed natural that I would give him an egg and that he would accept it."

"Is he still wearing it?" Ray asks.

"Yes, he's proving to be a perfect mother duck!" Beth says and smiles broadly.

"Show him your eggs, Beth," Emily urges.

"Yes, show me your eggs, Beth," Ray repeats with a smile.

Beth hesitates, she obviously doesn't want to lift her blouse up, and I feel it is crass and indelicate for these two to even ask such a thing in public. But Beth, ever obliging, lifts the drape of her untucked blouse so Ray can see the two deli containers.

"Is the experiment working? Do you feel happier?" he asks.

"I am definitely happier than I was a week ago. So, yes, I'd say it's working." She says this firmly, confidently, looks at Emily and says, "Let's go, I want to check on Fernanda and bring her this dessert while she's awake, and check on my new puppy."

"New pup?" Ray asks.

"Yes, poor Trixie passed away last week."

"You found a quick replacement for her. I assume finding a replacement for Tom will be more difficult."

"But that doesn't mean she shouldn't try!" Emily adds cheerily.

Beth stands, the check is paid and Emily's glass is half full. Beth says, "Come on, Emily, if you want a ride," and starts walking. I'm right beside her. We're both outraged. Or at least I am.

When Beth turns down our street, Emily asks where exactly Ray lives. Beth is pointing and turning her head to the left, when a red car, I don't see the make or model, pulls out of our driveway. I don't think we know anyone who drives a red car. I wish Beth had been looking; to take note.

Once home, Beth offers to drive Emily to her house but she insists she's fine to drive. They say goodnight and My Darling and I go inside. Saucisson is waiting for us in the mudroom and pees on the floor with excitement to see Beth, and maybe me, who knows? She laughs, gently reprimands him and then carries him through the kitchen out the veranda doors onto the lawn.

Fernanda is standing in the kitchen by the sink. She looks surprised to see us home so soon. I don't think Beth notices because she is focused on Saucisson, but there are two plates, two forks and two glasses in the sink. As Beth walks out with Saucisson, Fernanda opens the dishwasher and puts them in.

None of this is a big deal, hardly noteworthy, but let's just say, I noticed. When Beth comes in with Saucisson, she gives Fernanda the to-go container with a beautiful piece of baklava swimming in honey. They decide to split it and sit side-by-side at the kitchen counter, like an amiable mother-daughter. Saucisson sits nearby, greedy for a crumb to drop. Beth asks Fernanda about her classes and exams this week. It's a sweet scene, augmented by a sweet dessert and I feel part of something bigger.

We're all here, under this pool of light. Little Leftie and Rightie are warm and moving inside their calcium shells, just like Fernanda's infant moves inside her. Beth kisses Saucisson on the nose and puts him to bed in his crate. He whines. We go upstairs and Beth sighs once as she turns out the light.

Lying in the dark on my side of the bed, I realize we never did Duolingo. There were too many distractions. This Saturday has proven more unpredictable than most.

Tomorrow we'll have to get back to our routine.

CHAPTER 21

Sunday can't be a repeat of Saturday! Who's to say if it will be better or worse? Just more predictable.

I'm already sitting at my preferred place at the counter when Beth comes downstairs in her kimono. I spent the night walking between Beth, Fernanda and Saucisson. They all slept like lumps, hardly moving. Beth is now so used to Little Leftie and Rightie that she barely twists left or turns right in the night. She lies on her back, hands crossed over her heart like she's ready for interment.

Beth takes Saucisson out of the crate and carries him out to the yard; she doesn't want to give him a chance to piddle as he waddles across the floor. And even though it's a little cool (only May) she leaves the French doors open. She's determined nothing comes between Saucisson and his housebreaking success.

She makes coffee and then sits and FaceTimes with Tyler. He catches her up on his past week and the week ahead. It's sort of a one-sided monologue but Beth doesn't care. She holds the phone up to Achilles and tells Tyler he's getting bigger and stronger by the day. She still doesn't mention the eggs. Before they say goodbye, he tells her she should visit Thailand. He always says this and I don't mind. It's just to alleviate his guilt that Beth is alone and to make her feel wanted and welcome. Tyler is a good and dutiful son.

Fernanda comes downstairs in pjs and joins Beth in the kitchen. My Darling offers to make her breakfast but she declines. She says her dad will come by pretty soon and they go to the same place every Sunday for a late breakfast. She says all their friends and family show up at different times and eat at long communal tables. "It's almost everyone's day off, we relax and laugh."

This sounds so foreign to me, to spontaneously come together in a crowded, noisy place to *relax*? Beth cocks her head. I can tell it sounds foreign to her, too. "That sounds lovely," she says.

As they sit at the kitchen island, Beth glances down at her phone. "Oh good!" she says.

Jessica has just texted her, "Sorry for the delay. We checked. Yes, all the eggs have movement. The girls are thrilled!"

Beth texts back, "Fantastic!!!"

Jessica, being uncharacteristically chatty, responds, "The girls are asking when you're coming for the tea party."

Beth pauses. The tea party was an idea devised to get the girls to the halfway point of hatching. I seriously doubt Beth thought they'd get that far. I think she's charmed by these girls but I also think she's uncomfortable with the dysfunction; she knows something is off and can't put her finger on it. I'm sure she noticed the absence of Mr. Kline and had the tack not to inquire, but I doubt she understands yet that Margaret is so sick

My Darling, being ever so polite, texts back, "Soon! Let's pick a nice day."

Jessica seems satisfied with this vague answer and gives her usual thumbs up emoji.

Beth tells Fernanda a little about Jessica and the three girls hatching eggs. Fernanda seems surprised. "So much responsibility for such small children! The egg is hard enough for my dad!"

Both she and Beth laugh. I know Beth and I are thinking the very same thoughts. There are approximately nine or ten years between Margaret and Fernanda. Margaret is hatching a duck egg for 30 days. The duckling can eat and live fairly independently once it's hatched. And Beth has offered to take the ducklings to live in our pond. Fernanda is hatching a human baby, the most demanding of all

babies. It will cry, suck, and cling, requiring all of Fernanda's energy for a very long time. She has no idea what's ahead of her.

Fernanda goes upstairs and dresses and when she comes down, she has her books and her duffle bag. Beth looks surprised and says, "Oh, you're not coming back?"

"I can't stay here forever!" Fernanda laughs.

"It's no trouble, you're more than welcome."

My amigo Miguel does a soft knock and then comes in. There's *holas* and *adioses* and he and Fernanda are gone. The house suddenly seems deathly quiet. Beth gets dressed, she sits, fiddles and appears ill content. She takes Saucisson in and out so many times that even *his* digestive system can't find another drop of urine. Then she puts Saucisson in the crate, grabs her purse and leaves.

Slam!

I have no idea where she's going. This was all done quickly and no invitations were extended. Saucisson and I feel rejected, abandoned, and caged.

I sit in my chair and twirl Spatula. It feels good to have something in my hand. I'm thinking about Drunk Emily vs. Self-Aware-Emily vs. Drunk-Again-Emily. I can't decide which one I prefer (if any) and which one is more dangerous. However Drunk-Again-Emily is a new beast and might let something slip about the china closet and the gravy boat.

I'm pulled out of my speculation when there's a chime. Someone's at the back door. It's Sunday, people just don't drop by on Sunday, it borders on rude. The front door, with its doorbell and foyer, is for formal guests and the back door is for everyone we know and usually like. I can't imagine who it would be on a Sunday, nor can Saucisson. He's in his crate, glaring at the door, barking. I walk to the back door,

It's Ray-the-Jerk.

He's standing at the backdoor with some sort of potted plant. He waits, sounds the chime again and then presses his face against the window to look in. His face is distorted against the glass and I hate him with all my heart. Without thinking, I take Spatula and I smack the window where his ugly face peers in. He jerks his head back and looks very surprised.

Saucisson stops barking and does a low growl. I chuckle to think how Spatula and I startled Ray-the-Jerk. Comical.

Ray hastily leaves and I don't have long to wait for Beth to arrive home. To my surprise, she has a bag from Bon Vivant, which makes no sense; we already have five Bon Vivant deli containers in the fridge and she brings home four more. I wonder if it's Gentle Ben's fault and he's finally started upselling her. I *do* know My Darling doesn't look particularly happy or hungry. And she just puts all the containers in the fridge.

The day drags on. I, admittedly, am slightly bored yet content, but I can see Beth is still agitated despite her brief outing.

At 4:00 p.m, Beth FaceTimes Evie. It's earlier than usual but I can see My Darling is antsy and doesn't want to wait for Evie's call any longer. Evie actually answers the phone on the third ring, laughing, "You caught me still in bed!" It's 1:00 p.m on the West Coast. She tells Beth what an incredible night she had dancing, coming home in the morning light, she hasn't done that "in ages". It's rainy and gloomy in "San Fran", Evie says she might stay in bed until she has to get ready for a different date that night.

Beth laughs and laughs. She tells Evie, "Enjoy it while you can." When she has children, *if* she has children, she won't be able to do things like that. Beth tells Evie about Fernanda, Evie was always the big girl, five years older, but now it's Fernanda that's going to be the mother. "Ugh," is all Evie can say.

The conversation is winding down. Evie starts her usual pitch for Beth to move out there and they'll be "roomies and have so much fun". She always adds, as a bonus, "There's tons of single guys out here." My Darling laughs. I think Evie's closing pitch makes Beth feel loved, wanted and desirable. I allow myself a chuckle to prove that I can play along with this vision, even though Evie pushes my buttons like no one else.

I think we're coming to a closure when My Darling lowers her voice and moves the phone a little closer to her face, like she and Evie are conspirators. "Evie," she whispers, "I may have found someone that I could love."

Evie gasps. *"Already? Who?"*

"No one you would imagine and it'll probably come to nothing. I'm just throwing it out to the universe."

I feel like a knife is being inserted into my gut.

"Good for you, Mom! I'll keep my fingers crossed. Be bold, not passive. *Be greedy!*" Beth nods in acknowledgement. They say I love yous and hang up.

I stare at Beth. *Do I really know you?*

She looks directly at me, sitting in my preferred stool at the counter, but without seeing me, of course, and texts: "I have a new puppy! Stop by if you're on my street, 22 Woodhill Road."

She's texting Friedrich, aka The Lug.

Not three minutes later, there is a knock at the backdoor. Beth jumps off of her stool and hustles to answer it. Saucisson is yelping and I arm myself with the Spatula.

We all go to the back door. Who are we expecting...The Lug?

It's just Ray-the-Jerk again, standing there with his dumb potted plant. Beth and Saucisson look disappointed but I'm actually pleasantly surprised. I now know there are worse threats than Ray.

Beth opens the door and lets him in. Ray-the-Jerk tells her some lame story about how he had this potted hydrangea and he thought she might want to plant it in the yard since he "sees her planting bushes all the time".

Beth laughs, "Are you sure you're not mixing me up with Miguel?"

Ray fusses over Achilles. He compliments the little tub of lard on his athletic ability, which makes Beth laugh again. He says he's thinking about getting a puppy too, since his wife took their dog with her.

Beth advises him to wait. "Linda and Bongo will probably come home soon."

Ray doesn't seem convinced and I get the feeling that Ray doesn't want them back, at least not Linda. When he leaves, Beth closes the door and ruffles Saucisson on his head. I think she feels grateful that she's not completely alone, like Ray; she has Achilles, the eggs and me.

Although Beth keeps checking her phone for texts, she doesn't remember to do Duolingo until it's too late. Duolingo ends on Sunday, pending when you started on Monday. We didn't do it last night and usually we do it Sunday morning to make sure we're in good standing when the Diamond League draws to an end that evening. But Beth has totally dropped the ball and now we've been demoted to Obsidian League. It hurts my pride. We're a team and she let us down.

The sun is setting and Beth pours herself a glass of wine. She's forgotten her temporary feeling of gratitude and appears malcontent again, on edge. She checks our eggs several times, turning them gently in their cups. I want to take her hand and say, "You're not alone. I'm here beside you. We'll get back in Diamond League, we'll hatch Little Leftie and Rightie, we'll harvest the fruit from the fruit trees and then move to Paris. I wanted to take Trixie but I can learn to live with Saucisson, we'll be a happy family."

I'm rehearsing these words, repeating them to myself, thinking how I'll whisper them over and over again in her ear tonight, when the chime sounds at the back door. We all jump. Thank god, it's just Miguel, back with Fernanda.

I feel bad for my amigo, he looks embarrassed and uncomfortable. Beth shepherds them in. Miguel tells Beth that too many people saw Fernanda this morning at their Sunday gathering spot. Word got out to Fernanda's *novio,* Dmitri, that Fernanda was back in the neighborhood. He came around and started making trouble.

Beth doesn't wait for Miguel to ask. She says how Fernanda is welcome to stay as long as she wants. She tells Miguel how empty the house felt after only having Fernanda one night. Miguel nods in agreement and looks sad, knowing now *his* house will feel empty.

Fernanda laughs. "Oh, *papá*, the boys are home, you're hardly alone!"

"Sí," he says softly, "But they are not you." He strokes her hair like she is still his little girl.

It's all so tender that I'm embarrassed to witness it. I see Beth watching closely too, I'm not sure if we're thinking the same thing. I'm trying to imagine under what circumstances I would be so tender with Evie.

None.

When I would complain that Evie was in conflict with the world, Beth would correct me. She'd say, "No. Evie is in *love* with the world. You're the adult, encourage her, don't hold her back." There seemed to be a grain of truth in those words but in the blink of an eye she away at college and then living across the country. When I dropped dead, I was just starting to learn there were other things in life, like fruit trees that blossom and apartments in Paris, things that we could have shared.

What is it about my amigo that allows him to bend and soften? Fernanda looks like an angel but the fact is, she's young, unmarried and has gotten herself pregnant. Evie would never be so stupid. In the wildest scenario, I try to imagine Evie pregnant, with a small growing belly. Then I try to imagine myself, strapping an egg to my body to gain understanding and empathy with the mother-to-be.

It just wouldn't happen, not in a million years.

My amigo Miguel inhibits a whole other frame of mind. A frame that can compromise and capture moments of humor under rigorous physical and mental conditions. The ideas of "flexibility" and continual "good humor" are foreign to me. As a physician, I wonder if maybe we're born with a "good nature" or a "bad nature".

I was born into a family whose father didn't take care of his dependents. He humiliated and abused both my mother and me. If I'd been flexible and good humored, how would I've survived? Probably, I'd taken the path of the least resistance and worked a dead-end job or put my mental acuity to criminal activities. Who knows? Who can say?

Miguel says, "*Buenas noches*," and Fernanda, Beth, Saucisson and I watch him leave through the back door. We're back to being a happy little family.

CHAPTER 22

Beth, Saucisson and I are having coffee outside in the morning when Beth gets a text. She puts her coffee cup down and stares at it. There's something wrong.

I jump up and look over her shoulder. It's from Jessica. It says, "I hate to ask but it's Carmen's day off, she's at her sisters and I can't seem to reach her. Can you come and stay with Sophia and Char? I have no one else. It's urgent."

Beth doesn't hesitate, and texts, "Yes, will be there soon."

Jessica shoots back, "Thank you. Please hurry!"

Beth looks at her watch, marches into the kitchen, closes the veranda door, plugs her phone into the charger, dumps her coffee and heads upstairs to dress. Saucisson and I stay downstairs, not sure of our course of action. Beth comes down moments later wearing leggings and a denim shirt that easily covers our hatching belts. She writes Fernanda a note, "7:20 Good Morning! I need to help a friend. Not sure when I'll be back. Help yourself to anything. Please take care of Achilles. Beth."

She bends down, picks Saucisson up and shoves him back in the crate. He's not happy, it's morning and this is not the routine. I have decided that I should go with Beth because I might be needed in some sort of medical capacity. I'm definitely alarmed by Jessica's text.

I'm leaning on the counter, where Beth's phone is charging, ready to fly out the door with her, when Beth walks into the mudroom, takes her purse off a hook and walks out the door. Slam. In her haste, she's forgotten her phone and subsequently forgotten me. I've missed my chance to slip out the door and rush to Jessica's aid!

I sit in my favorite chair, no better off than Saucisson locked in his crate, waiting for Fernanda to wake up. It's beyond frustrating to be held captive to a young adult's sleep schedule. I imagine if Evie was up there sleeping, it could be afternoon before she wandered down.

I wait and wait, formulating a clear but complex plan, which involves Spatula. It goes like this: when Fernanda wakes up and opens the door to take Saucisson out, I'll slip out with Spatula under my arm. I'll walk to 530 Round House Road to see if I can be of assistance, either to Beth or to Jessica. I'll bring Spatula to activate the gate and gain entrance. Having a tool like Spatula will allow me to be more independent and perhaps more helpful. I know it will take a few hours to walk up the road, but that's okay, I've done it once and it's good exercise. Paris is a walking city, I need to stay in shape anyway.

So I sit and wait.

It's 9:35 before Fernanda wanders down in an oversized tee shirt. She immediately reads Beth's note and goes over to the crate and lets Saucisson out. Instead of carrying him, like Beth does, she lets him out and calls him over to the open veranda door, halfway there, he stops and pees. Fernanda looks exasperated and gives him a smack on the butt, picks him up and carries him out the rest of the way. I grab Spatula from under the chair cushion, tuck her under my arm, so the rubber end sits comfortably in my armpit, and head out the door.

Bye. Sayonara. Have a good day! Good luck keeping Saucisson from peeing on the floor!

I march down the driveway and start my walk, it's five miles tops, probably closer to 4.5 or 4.8. I decide to count my steps to make the time pass quicker and calculate the distance accurately.

As I walk by Ray-the-Jerk's house, I have to veer off the sidewalk because of his overgrown bushes. It probably adds three to four steps to my journey and reaffirms why I hate him.

113

I'm busy calculating that each of my steps covers about 2.5 feet which equals about 30 inches. There's 5280 feet per mile and I'll need to multiple my number of steps times 2.5 and then divide by 5280. These might be messy calculations but overall the mental exercise paired with the physical exercise is very enjoyable.

I'm not thinking about Margaret and her possible struggles and I'm not thinking about Beth trying to entertain or maintain some sense of order with Sophia and Charlotte. I'm just lost in the flow of counting. At one point, I see a car slow down and I realize I'm holding Spatula like a baton and swinging her in my hand. I tuck her back under my arm.

Everything is going well, very well and then I come to 221 Round House Road, Gunther-Schlitz-Who-Shits-Money's house. I stop dead and look at the mailbox, losing count completely. I can still see the light pencil writing, "Schlitz 221 Round House Rd" on the post. Just to confirm what I already know, I take Spatula and flick open the mailbox door. There's some mail inside and it all says, "Mr. Gunther Schlitz Jr., Gunther Schlitz" or "The Schlitz Residence."

There's no doubt this is where our noble patron of the hospital lives. I take Spatula and spitefully sweep the mail out, so it flutters onto the ground. It's not raining and it's not windy and I know it's petty but it gives me great satisfaction and pleasure. Then I think about how I'm so much more empowered than the last time I was standing here: I have Spatula. I go over to the electronic sensor of the gate and wave Spatula in front of the eye.

The stupid, indiscriminate gate opens.

For a moment, just a moment, I am tempted to march up Gunther Schlitz's driveway but then I realize it's Monday, late morning, and no self-respecting man will be home. He'll be at work, but that's okay. I've proven beyond a shadow of a doubt that he lives here and Spatula has proven she can outwit the gate. How does the proverb go? "Revenge is a dish best served cold."

My expertise is needed more at the Kline's today. I continue my walk but now I'm not in such a good mood. The mere hint of Gunther Schlitz's toxic presence can still mess with my psyche. I've completely lost track of my steps and the rest of the walk is a trudge.

When I get to 530 Round House Road, I use Spatula on the sensor and the gate opens nicely. I walk up the loopy driveway like a man exploring the curves of a woman's body. I know when I get to the top, the beautiful house will greet me but in the meantime, I enjoy the meandering. I ask myself, in the future, if I attempt to count the steps, should I count the loopy driveway? Or is the true distance from the end of our driveway to the end of Jessica's gate? I'm contemplating the pros and cons and which calculation would be considered more accurate, when I hear the chatter of little voices as I approach the house.

Beth is sitting on the front stone step with her elbows on her knees, watching Sophia and Charlotte draw on the driveway with sidewalk chalk. The boxes are gone, leaving their shadows of yellow grass and the little pink roller blades, scooters, and bikes are lined up neatly on either side of the front door under the colonnaded portico. The lawn crew must have come and arranged them so they could do their work. I can't imagine Jessica or Carmen coming out and organizing the toys.

I wave as I approach. I can't help it. I've walked the entire way to join this little group and seeing them assembled brings me great joy. I sit down next to Beth and, together, we watch these two little girls draw, squabble, agree and hug. I can't figure out what they're working on but Beth says, "Your mom and Margaret will be so happy to come home and see this art!"

Charlotte is busy drawing bouquets of flowers and Sophia is carefully writing, "Welcome Home!" The drawing begins on the driveway with a rainbow (which seems to be their favorite thing to draw) and then continues on the slates leading to the front door. I get the impression they've done this before and they each have their assigned roles. When they squat, the hatching belts seem to get in their way. At one point, Charlotte gives up and kneels on all fours on the slate which hurts my knees to even look at.

When the mural looks done, Beth asks them if they're ready for lunch. Charlotte shouts "Yes!" and jumps up, leaving a pile of chalk. Beth calmly tells each of the girls to put the chalk back in the bucket, and then with no prompting, Sophia carries the bucket and puts it with the lined up skates, scooters and bikes. Thanks to Beth and the lawn crew, there's a sense of order.

We all go in and I sit at the kitchen island in the empty stool which is probably Margaret's. The kitchen is, for lack of a better word, a mess. There are dishes piled up and half empty containers sitting on the counter.

"When lunch is done, maybe the two of you can help me do some cleaning?" Beth says. "It doesn't look like anyone likes cleaning but we can make it fun."

"Carmen likes cleaning!" Charlotte says and she pokes her thumb into her mouth.

Sophia nods.

After lots of questioning and negotiation, Beth makes macaroni and cheese. The pantry is stocked with boxes and boxes of the ready to make orange pasta, so it must be a staple. After about two bites, Charlotte insists on a bowl of Cheerios.

Sophia shrugs and laughs, "Cha-Cha always changes her mind, it's fine."

Beth compliments Charlotte's posture, "You sit so straight, Charlotte, like a young lady."

Charlotte frowns. "It's the eggs, it's my turn to wear Mimi's." She lifts her shirt and there are two belts, one just below her belly button and one just above.

116

Beth frowns. "Maybe we could find somewhere warm to put the extra belt."

"No!" Charlotte says, "I promised Mimi."

There's a side to these children that I didn't understand before. I see their determination to support and show love to their sick sister. They look so young and innocent but there's a ferocity of feeling that I didn't expect. I know Beth sees it and is deeply touched.

"Now we usually watch TV and rest," Sophia announces. She and Charlotte get off their stools, go to the overstuffed sofa, climb into the corner, cover themselves with a blanket, snuggle and watch some kid show.

Beth foregoes her cleaning lesson. She starts to clean the kitchen, filling the dishwasher, finding the soap, and starting the machine. She manages to get the kitchen island cleared and wiped but then she literally *throws in the towel*, tossing the dish towel on the counter and joins the girls on the sofa, snuggled under the same blanket. Soon they're all leaning a little right, sound asleep.

I sit in a chair with a big ottoman that faces the sofa. I put my feet up and rest, too. It's only early afternoon but I've accomplished so much already, none of it typical or predictable for a Monday.

After they wake up, Sophia insists that she and Charlotte do some of their school work. "Mr. Smith will be coming tomorrow." It sounds like a threat. Beth wants to be helpful but there's a pile of work books and no lesson plan. Sophia announces that if they both do some reading and answer some questions, "that should be fine". She explains how Mr. Smith tells them they're all advanced and ahead of their grade level. She says it with great confidence and pride and I enjoy watching them concentrate on and off for the next couple of hours.

When dinner time comes around, the menu is discussed and macaroni and cheese is the winner. Charlotte gets whiney. She asks when her mom and Margaret will be home. Beth explains she has no idea, she forgot her phone. If Jessica is texting, she can't see it. I can tell she's very uncomfortable not being able to communicate with Jessica or knowing if Jessica is communicating with her. She offers to drive the girls to our house, show them Achilles and get her phone. Charlotte is excited but Sophia says, "We absolutely can't ride in any car without car seats. I still use a booster, it's the law."

Beth has to agree.

They spend the evening reading. Beth reads to them and they read to her. They really are advanced little girls. They insist Beth tuck them into their mother's bed. They want to know when she and Margaret come home. There's no mention of daddy.

The drapes are open with their vista onto the backyard and the pool. I can see the horizon turning pink. The girls ask Beth to leave the big door open and the hallway light on. There's still plenty of light and Beth can easily see their faces as she kisses their foreheads and pats their eggs. She goes downstairs, leaving the door open and the hallway light on as they requested.

I enjoy watching every minute of this routine between Beth and the girls. There's a tenderness that comes so naturally. Anthropologically, I believe I'm watching the elder of the species caring for the younger of a species. It doesn't matter who their rightful parent is, what matters is that the tribe provides safety and survival to its youngest members.

I go downstairs and try to be a help and comfort to My Darling. She picks up the landline and I watch her fingers dial our house, but Fernanda doesn't pick up. It doesn't surprise me, we don't pick up our landline either. It's mainly there for emergencies and for the alarm system. All of her numbers are stored in her phone. She can't contact Jessica or Fernanda, she just has to wait for Jessica to show up.

She starts cleaning, I think it's out of frustration rather than a sense of duty. I know My Darling is on edge and malcontent that she doesn't know the "plan" and that she can't check in with Jessica or

Fernanda, but I don't share her feelings. The sun has just dipped below the horizon and the light is soft in the kitchen. It's peaceful to just sit at the counter and watch Beth do domestic chores. It feels like we're a young family again and that we *did* make the move to Round House Road. I feel like a new husband and father and that I have not been at the hospital all day being asked to do the impossible. I'm mellow (I don't think I've ever used that word!) and appreciate my life.

Beth stops for a moment, cocks her head. She walks to the foyer, opens the front door and looks outside. The sidewalk chalk art looks festive and welcoming in the pool of light. She closes the door and locks it. Then she walks straight through the kitchen to the back of the house where there's a another entry, that's been made into a mudroom of sorts with little cubbies but it's really an old utility area where servants used to do the laundry in big basins. Beth locks this door too. *Smart girl,* I think. There's an alarm system but she doesn't know how to set it.

There is a bang! bang! at the front door.

Beth is already hurrying to the front. She glances out one of the little side windows on either side of the heavy front door and unlocks and opens it.

It's Jessica, straining under the sleeping weight of Margaret in her arms.

"What can I do?" whispers Beth.

"Just run ahead and pull the covers back on my bed," says Jessica, who does not stop but keeps her momentum going forward. Beth hustles and runs up the steps in front of her. I bring up the rear, wishing I could take the sleeping child from her. Jessica is either unusually strong for her size or Margaret is unusually light for her length. I have a feeling it's a combo.

Jessica gets to the top step and practically runs to the master bedroom where Beth has pulled back the covers on the side of the bed that looks out the window. She lays Margaret down and tucks the blankets around her.

"Thanks, Mommy," Margaret murmurs and falls back into a deep sleep.

Jessica looks at her eldest child, strokes her head, kisses her forehead. She walks around the bed and kisses Sophia and Charlotte. Their heads are together on a pillow with their bodies coming out making an inverted V. Both are on their backs with no chance of squishing the eggs. When Jessica kisses Charlotte, Charlotte's arm shoots up and she pops her thumb in her mouth. Jessica looks over her shoulder and smiles at Beth and Beth smiles back.

When I was alive, in the conventional sense, if you had asked me what being a mom was like, I would have thought of all the nagging, mess and demands, and concluded *thankless*. How could a woman feel anything else? But here, now, I am witnessing a side of motherhood I never thought about or imagined and I'm enchanted. The role is not packed with adrenaline bursts, like being a cardiothoracic surgeon, but it definitely washes the brain with a steady supply of oxytocin rewards.

Both women head downstairs and I follow, feeling pure bliss.

"What a mother-fucker of a day," Jessica says as she washes her hands. Then she opens the fridge, pulls out a wine bottle and yanks the cork out with her teeth. "I need this," she says as she pours herself a glass. She pours a second glass and slides it to Beth.

"I really should get home," Beth says, "I have a puppy." It sounds rather ridiculous after watching Jessica carry her sick, sleeping child up the stairs.

"Please stay, I can't bear to be alone with my thoughts."

Beth nods and sits down on one of the stools. Jessica remains standing, too wound up to sit. Beth apologizes for not being able to communicate, she forgot her phone.

"I figured."

Jessica thanks Beth and goes on to explain how the other mothers she knows have their own kids and she didn't want to uproot Sophia and Charlotte and dump them at a strange house. "This is home base. They need to stay here. They're traumatized enough."

Both women take sips and let it lie between them, a sad truth revealed – "traumatized."

"Well, I'm happy to come anytime you need me. Sophia and Charlotte are very well behaved and very smart. You're doing a great job." Jessica doesn't say anything so Beth continues, "Maybe next time I can bring my puppy. The girls could play with him."

"Sure. Absolutely. "

The women finish their wine and Beth stands up. "I should go." Jessica walks her to the door and hugs her. They both laugh as they pull apart, "The eggs," Beth says. "Let me know how Margaret is in the morning. I can always come back."

Jessica nods. "Thanks, but Carmen will be back." The adrenaline that allowed her Herculean strength is wearing off and she looks thin, tired and alone.

Beth is tired too and opens the car door slowly. It's easy for me to glide into the passenger seat. When we get home, a lot of lights are on and Achilles starts yelping in his crate. Beth immediately bends down and carries him through the kitchen area out the French doors and puts him down in the grass. Saucisson takes a long pee. She praises him up and down.

I notice two chairs are pulled out from the patio table. I can't be sure, but usually Beth neatly pushes in the chairs when she goes inside. I suspect someone was here with Fernanda while we were gone. It's no big deal, it could've just been Miguel, but then again, I think of the two dishes left in the sink and how Fernanda put them in the dishwasher.

It's probably nothing but I'm going to keep my eyes open. This is *my* house and my number one priority as The Greatest Husband is to protect and care for Beth.

Beth pushes the chairs in absentmindedly and heads in. While she stuffs Saucisson back in his crate and locks the back door, I check the sink for dishes – one plate, two forks, two glasses. She turns off all the lights, goes up stairs, cracks Evie's door and glances in. We can both see the mound of Fernanda's sleeping body.

When she goes into our room, she closes the door, which isn't her routine, usually she keeps it wide open. When Trixie was younger and could climb the steps, she'd wander in and out, in and out. Now I'm trapped in here for the night and I'm not happy about it. I'm even more unhappy because I don't have Spatula. The fact is, I don't remember putting Spatula under the chair cushion when we came home. This is very unlike me, I'm not a careless person, I'm purposeful and process oriented, but this was not a typical Monday and I could've been absent minded for just a moment and laid her down somewhere.

I can't remember the last place I had Spatula.

CHAPTER 23

I spend a restless night with absolutely nothing to do. I lie next to Beth and pretend to sleep but I can't. I check her position but she's gotten so used to the hatching belts, she lies like she's entombed, with her hands over her chest. Overall, the night is terrible. For a brief moment I commiserate with Saucisson, trapped in his crate, but I know he's probably dreaming puppy dreams of rivers of milk.

Beth is usually a very early riser but this morning she sleeps past 6:30. I hear Fernanda's alarm go off and I listen to Fernanda move around down the hall. Finally, about 7:00, Beth gets up. She looks confused because we can both smell the coffee aroma coming up the stairs and, for once, she hasn't made it. She leaves the bedroom door ajar as she turns back to wash her face and brush her teeth, I'm able to slip out.

I descend down the stairs just in time – "Nooooooo," to see Fernanda pick up Spatula, put her in the dishwasher and close the dishwasher door. I must have left her on the counter when I looked in the sink at the one plate, two forks and two glasses. The situation is not ideal but at least I know where she is.

When Beth comes down, she says good morning and walks immediately to Saucisson, hefts him out of the crate and carries him out the French doors. She praises him as the urine streams out on my lawn.

"So that's how you do it," says Fernanda standing at the door, "I didn't have much luck yesterday. He'd get about halfway to the door."

Beth gets a cup of coffee and thanks Fernanda for taking care of Achilles all day, she knows it's a big job. I know a bit of irony when I hear it. She's feeling out Fernanda's preparedness for motherhood. She believes Fernanda has no idea what she is getting into and I agree. However, right now, Fernanda, our *Pequeña Fleur* daughter, looks pretty perfect. She's well-rested, has her hair in a slick ponytail and her books are neatly stacked in a tote bag on the counter.

Fernanda tells Beth that Miguel will be here soon, to drive her to the train station and she'll go into the city for her final. After the test, she'll probably spend the afternoon in the library, studying before catching a train home. Miguel will pick her up and bring her back here, if that's okay. Beth assures her she's welcome for as long as she wants or needs.

"It won't be long, I have two more finals on Thursday and then I'm done!"

She says it like she's a kid getting out for summer vacation with thoughts of bonfires and camp songs on the near horizon. Instead, she is about five months pregnant, hiding out from some bad *novio*. To my understanding, she has at least another year of college and *then* she'll be "done." She will graduate and be qualified to do what exactly? From her stacks of books, she looks like she's a biology major or maybe organic chemistry, both fine majors but there's the business of internships and making contacts in the field and then you end up in a research lab or at a big pharma company working your way up the ranks. It's a long road. And all this with a baby? I'm not sure even if I could have done it.

"Oh, before I forget, a guy came by yesterday looking for you." Fernanda says casually, like it happens all the time. Both Beth and I perk up but probably for different reasons.

"What *kind* of guy?" Beth asks and they both laugh.

"I don't know... a guy about your age. I think he might have walked, I didn't see a car. He asked if you were home."

"He didn't have a black sedan?"

"Well, actually, while the guy and I were talking, a black car pulled into the driveway, that's what made me notice there wasn't a car here already. When the guy in the car saw both of us standing there, he turned around. It was kind of weird. The first guy thought so, too."

Beth doesn't look alarmed, she looks disappointed.

"The first guy said he'll come back today." Fernanda says this with a chipper voice, like this will cheer Beth up, but Beth says nothing.

We all hear a little "Beep, Beep" in the driveway. Fernanda grabs the tote bag and her purse and runs out the door to her dad's truck. Miguel smiles and waves to us as Fernanda climbs in.

Beth busies herself around the house. I wander outside to look at my fruit trees, curious if there's any progress since yesterday. When I wander back in, My Darling is looking at her phone. She has a new message. Friedrich smiley-faced the message, "I have a new puppy! Stop by if you're on my street, 22 Woodhill Road." She texted this on Sunday, which seems a lifetime ago after the long day at Jessica's. He must have responded, stopped by, saw Lovely Fernanda and Ray-the-Jerk and thought he either had the wrong house or just felt too awkward to come to the door... as he should. He does not belong here.

Beth stares at that little smiley face like it's going to reveal something more but it doesn't. The Lug is not effusive. He's barely responsive and yet she's driving to Bon Vivant more often than she needs. Even with Fernanda in the house, we have about 10 deli containers of the finest food that money can buy just sitting in the fridge. It's obscene.

Beth types: "I'm sorry I missed you yesterday. I was helping a friend (a fellow egg hatcher). Achilles the pup is growing by the day, come by anytime." She examines the message, deletes "anytime" and types "soon!" then she deletes "soon!" and just adds a "!"

It's not a long message but it's packed with information. The Lug now knows that Beth *knows* he came by and turned around. He understands that as an active member in the egg hatching community, he should have a vested interest in the other members (mainly her!). Also, the fact that Achilles is growing, gives the invite a sense of urgency because every man strives to see a puppy at its youngest. Haha! False.

If The Lug comes by, it will be to see my wife, with Achilles, a fat little excuse, unspoken between them.

I chuckle, imagining Saucisson growing, growing, growing until he's the size of a mythic one-eyed cyclops, chained, and secured by an iron bolt at the back door. The Lug "stops by" and Saucisson bites his head off. Chomp. It's just some silly cartoon image that scrolls through my brain, probably triggered by the cartoons at Jessica's house. The caption would be: "Beware cyclops!"

Beth then texts Jessica: "How's Margaret today? Is everything okay?"

Jessica responds, "Margaret feels much better, we're having a quiet day. I can't thank you enough for all your help yesterday."

Beth responds, "Anytime. Happy to help."

Jessica puts a heart emoji next to Beth's message.

I'm really getting the hang of texting. It wasn't my preferred mode of communication when I was alive, but I am warming up to the modern convenience of sending a person a short message when it's convenient for you and they can respond when it's convenient for them. Ironically, the inconvenience of the tiny keyboard keeps the messages short and cuts out all the fat and fluff of conversation that I despise, rendering it inconvenient (to type), convenient (to respond), perfect (number of words).

Beth then types "Sandy" in. The text thread is old and stale. It was very lively when Beth was working on the house and Stick-Your-Nose-In-Everyone's-Business-Sandy thought she was getting the listing. *Then* she was Beth's bestie and seemed to be thrilled by every paint swatch and upholstery sample. Since Beth stopped being a potential source of revenue, Sandy's interest has waned. Maybe it's mutual, I don't know, but with Sandy's recent puppy contact, it seems to be picking up again. Beth texts Sandy: "Do you want to come by today for lunch? You haven't seen my new baby!"

She puts the phone down and we both walk around the edge of the pond, observing its depth and water quality. By the time she returns, Sandy has texted: "What???"

Beth smiles and puts a little "HaHa" emoji. "The puppy, remember?"

It's just like Stick-Your-Nose-In-Everyone's-Business-Sandy to forget that she gave Beth the contact for the puppy. She has her nose in so many people's business, their plots and subplots, that she gets confused where she left off in her meddling.

There's actually a pause in texting. I'm picturing Sandy with her dyed hair and over plucked eyebrows which she needs to plump up with a little pencil now that thicker brows are in. (This is a detail that I would never have noticed but Beth pointed it out to me while I was still living.) It was fascinating to look for the little hairs drawn in when we were together. Honestly, I think she thought I was staring into her eyes, trying to mesmerize her with my classic boyish good looks. Meanwhile, Larry, her husband, who can be a nice guy but also a dope, orders everyone dessert because *he* wants it and doesn't want to eat alone.

"He just orders dessert to delay going home and being with Sandy," I would tell Beth and then kiss her, proving I was a different kind of husband, the greatest kind.

"Yes, lunch, your house, love it!" Sandy texts back after she's managed to trace Beth's narrative back in time to dead Trixie and the replacement pup. I recall that she never even offered Beth a condolence in her Facebook post, she simply commented: "I have a friend with puppies! Call me!!!"

Out with the old, in with the new. If you're feeling down, sell your house, forget your past! I can't believe Beth invited her over; it will ruin a perfectly good day. Beth goes into the kitchen and opens the fridge, with its 10 deli containers from Bon Vivant. She picks a few up, looks at the labels on the top, shoves Saucisson in the crate, looks in the mirror, grabs her keys and heads out the door. I have a hard time keeping up, I almost get left behind.

I'm not positive where we're going, but I *suspect* I know where and there's no way I'm letting Beth go alone.

We drive directly to Bon Vivant. Instead of parking close (after all, it's Tuesday morning, the place isn't packed) Beth parks in the far corner under the tree where I've seen The Lug parked with his black sedan. Thankfully, he's not there now. Beth and I walk in, she picks up some crackers and she lets Ben talk her into some shrimp with dill sauce.

At checkout, Sydney asks Beth, if she has everything she needs? Beth leaves with two items and ambles across the parking lot. There's no black sedan under the oak tree. Maybe luck is with me and there'll never be a black sedan parked under this tree? Maybe The Lug has lumbered into greener pastures?

Beth and I get in the car and she sort of waits, checking her phone for new texts but there are none. She sighs, it's not audible, it's more the way her shoulders drop that I know the warm, moist air left her lungs.

We drive home.

CHAPTER 24

Beth makes two plates with scoops of various prepared foods: greens with walnuts and Danish blue cheese, lemon rosemary potatoes, shrimp with dill sauce. It all looks mouth-wateringly delicious and I wish I could have a taste. Even a nibble. She pours two glasses of seltzer and puts it all on the patio table. It's slightly cool and she's changed into the turquoise sweater that's always been my favorite.

Sandy arrives punctually and walks around back. She knows our house and property inside and out; she sized it up for putting on the market. When she sees Saucisson, she chuckles, "He's as fat as Larry!"

Both Beth and I laugh. Sandy *can* be funny when she's not being annoying.

She sits down and starts talking. That's how Sandy works. Whatever she has to say, she's sure it's more interesting than what you have to say. "You know your neighbor Ray? I think he's getting a divorce. Do you know if he's going to list his house?"

Beth shrugs.

"I know I met him at Tom's funeral but could you introduce us? Maybe recommend me? I'd love the listing."

"Sure," Beth says. "If he's selling."

"That would be great. I'd really appreciate it." Sandy takes a few bites and adds, "If I recall, he's not a bad looking guy. Maybe you should think about inviting him over for dinner?"

Beth snorts. "He's already brought me a plant."

"A *plant*?"

Beth explains how he brought her a hydrangea to plant in the yard and how he fussed over Achilles.

"He sounds like a nice guy," Sandy says.

"He *is* a nice guy. I'm thinking he might be nice for Emily."

"Does your cup runneth over? Can you afford to pass him off so fast?" Sandy raises her brows, even I can see she's drawn one a little heavier than the other. "Beth, he's eligible *and* local."

"You make him sound like produce," Beth jokes.

They eat and occasionally Beth reaches down and scratches Saucisson.

When Beth gets up to clear plates, Sandy comments that she looks good. "Have you put on some weight? I don't mean that in a bad way. I just think you look like you're glowing."

"It must be the eggs," Beth says and lifts her sweater.

Stick-Your-Nose-In-Everyone's-Business-Sandy is completely dumbstruck. You can see she's following Beth's narrative back again, back, back, back. Then she remembers Beth's post on the happiness experiment of hatching eggs. She probably doesn't remember her rude comment: "Good Luck with *that!*" But I do.

"Oh my god, you did it! You got eggs and are hatching them!" Beth nods. "And it's working? You're happier?"

"Yes. Decidedly happier." She gently pats each of the belts. "It's kind of changed my life in a weird way." She smiles and I swear to all that is sacred, she looks like an angel. She looks young, beautiful and slightly mysterious, just like the night I met her.

Sandy sees it too. The fact that Beth looks so good and acts so happy is suddenly number one on Sandy's Stick-Your-Nose-In-Everyone's-Business proprietary information. Sandy will make it her business to dig, get details and dole out these details to whomever she wishes for their entertainment but ultimately to make *her* feel *more* important. If there's something you need to know, you go to Sandy or Page 6 of the *New York Post*.

Beth starts by telling Sandy how getting used to wearing the eggs was a little difficult, "You know, I have to lie flat at night and it definitely limits my clothing choices but, by day three, you see veins forming, if the egg is viable, and by day seven, you see movement. It's incredible, you really feel responsible for another life. Now I'm on day eleven, I have approximately eighteen or nineteen days left."

"Do you think you'll make it?" Sandy asks, taking a sip of her seltzer.

Beth cocks her head and looks hard at Sandy. "Sandy, I am fully committed to this. It's no different than a real pregnancy in a way. There's no going back. I'm committed to these two eggs but I'm also committed to the other people who've joined me in the pod. We're all doing our best to make this happen."

"Who exactly is in this pod, may I ask," Sandy says, raising the brow more heavily drawn on.

"Well, a woman I didn't know, who lives on Round House Road, joined me."

The detail of "lives on Round House Road" is the only detail Beth needs to fully describe Jessica, or any woman, who lives there to realtor Sandy. Sandy is completely comfortable lumping all them together as "high maintenance and self-involved". At face value, Jessica appears to fit the mold but the more I get to know her, I'm not so sure.

"Why did she agree to wear an egg?"

"Well, actually, she took three eggs for her adorable little girls." Beth describes how lively and smart Margaret, Sophia and Charlotte are.

"How does wearing the belts work with school?"

"Oh, they were tutored at home during the pandemic and their mom kept it going."

"Whhhhyyyyyy?" Sandy draws it out. She's digging deep now, looking for the juicy gossip.

"Well, at the moment, their lives are... complicated, let's say. I think the mom wants to keep them safe." My Darling wants to make everything sound normal and get Sandy off the scent, "They're all perfectly lovely."

"Who else is in your pod?"

"Well, Miguel, you know, my helper, the one who painted this winter and does all my lawn work, he took an egg."

"Why in god's name would *he* take an egg?" She leans forward. "What would be his incentive?"

"Well, his daughter is pregnant. He chose to wear a hatching belt to show Fernanda that they're a team. He didn't use these exact words but I'd say, 'To keep the dialogue open and to heal the rift the pregnancy caused.'"

Sandy narrows her eyes. "And where's the father in all this?"

Beth hesitates, choosing her words carefully.

"He's not in the picture. He's not a good guy. In fact, Fernanda is staying here to hide from him."

Sandy says absolutely nothing. She leans back. Something in Beth makes her feel compelled to keep talking.

"She's staying in Evie's room. It's nice, it's like Evie's back. I keep imagining if Evie was back and pregnant and Tom was alive..." She lifts her sweater. "This is Tom's egg." She points to Little Leftie. "I imagine Tom wearing the egg, like Miguel, to find common ground with Evie."

Sandy shakes her head, glancing at her watch. "Beth, it would take a lot more than a duck egg to make Tom find common ground with Evie, especially a *pregnant* Evie."

Both women laugh. It's harmless but I am slightly offended. I feel I've been misjudged. Sandy no longer knows me, I have changed over the last six months. Is it too much to ask to be understood?

Sandy looks at her watch and frowns. "I've got a house showing at one-thirty." Her voice changes. She uses the voice of a successful realtor, the one she uses when she's sitting with lawyers and bankers and is closing a deal. She uses the voice that makes her good at what she does. It's authoritative. I know the voice well. I used mine almost all the time.

"Beth, you are a big girl and I'm not telling you how to live your life but I'm going to give you some strong friend advice and you should think long and hard before you ignore it. Number one, don't serve your eligible neighbor Ray up to Emily on a silver platter. I think she's drinking again, but that's a topic for another day. Decent eligible guys are unicorns, believe me, I deal with divorced women trying to sell their houses all day long. Number two, don't get involved with a woman living on Round House Road in a complicated situation. That will be more drama than you bargained for. Lastly, don't make Miguel's problems yours. Fernanda is *not* Evie. Tom is *not* alive. You're alone and vulnerable. You're the perfect target."

Sandy stands up. "I'm sorry, I have to run. I'm sorry to be a bummer. It's just that you've been incredibly sheltered and I don't think you know how the real world works: eggs crack, people act shitty, and every day that goes by is time that we can't get back."

Beth walks Sandy to her car. They do an awkward hug due to the hatching belts and blunt advice. Sandy gets in her car, flips down her sun visor, uses the mirror to apply lipstick and then backs out of the driveway like a seasoned racecar driver.

Beth leans down and pats Saucisson until he's spinning in an adoring frenzy. She laughs, "And I didn't even tell her about Friedrich!"

CHAPTER 25

Watching Beth playing with Saucisson, I mull over Sandy's words.

Stick-Your-Nose-In-Everyone's-Business-Sandy is no ingénue. She's a realist who works her ass off hustling houses. Sandy and Larry would have slipped down the economic ladder long ago without Sandy's elbow grease propelling them up. I was always derisive toward Sandy when talking to Beth, but a tiny part of me gave her her due respect. She reminds me of a muscle fiber that started out average, but repeated exercise made it strong and efficient.

During the first year of retirement, I had the pandemic as an excuse not to go out to dinner with Larry and Sandy. But then, between vaccines and being retired, I had none. During the second year, I realized Sandy is actually voracious for information. It happens to be information about other people's lives but, in a sense, it's still information. She enjoys hearing how other people live, what their kids are doing, their pet names, their professional trajectory, the state of their marriage. She listens to it all, files it away and is sometimes able to monetize it at a later date.

I once told Beth, "If Sandy had been a researcher and focused her desire to know everything, she'd have been very successful."

Beth had laughed. "Sandy *is* very successful, she and William Crest vie to be the number one realtor every year."

This is all to say, Sandy's words of caution carried some weight with me; Sandy *does* know something about something. Naturally, the idea of Beth "serving up Ray to Emily" doesn't bother me in the least. Beth has me. Sandy doesn't know I'm still in the picture, so therefore her emphasis on "eligible *and* local" are irrelevant. Number two, her warning about getting involved with a woman with a "complicated" life on Round House Road is overly cautious. If Sandy knew there was a sick child involved she'd be more supportive; she has four kids herself. Number three, her attack on Fernanda has me slightly concerned. It's true, Fernanda is *not* Evie, but in some ways she's better. She's hardworking, tidy, and ambitious. True, she's pregnant but that's just an age-old morality tale. Aren't we all beyond that? It's too bad that *novio* Dmitri isn't a good guy, even though I've no idea what that entails exactly. If Fernanda holds the course, has the baby and stays in school, there will be plenty of nice men who will want to marry the jewel of *Pequeña Fleur*, should she want one.

The real problem is The Lug. Beth never even mentioned him. Sandy would have pursued him, even the *idea* of him, with bloodlust. I've plenty of my own concerns, mainly that Beth seems to be the driving force. But maybe that's how The Lug plays the game? He sits back, arms crossed, leaning against his black Town Car and lets women come to him. Maybe there's more to be worried about than the typical jealousy which occurs between a man of vapor and a man of flesh?

The rest of the day is rather dull. Beth carries in the dishes and puts them in the dishwasher. I catch a glance of my trusty Spatula but can do nothing about it. The house seems empty and quiet without our adoptive daughter, lovely Fernanda.

At 6:30, Miguel delivers Fernanda back to us. He talks to Beth about slate shingles for the roof, rocks for a wall, and slate tiles for the veranda. These all need a little repair and he thinks Beth should go to a couple salvage yards and try to match what we have, that way the repairs won't stand out like a sore thumb. She just needs to choose them, pay and then he'll pick them up with his truck.

Beth asks Fernanda if she can watch Achilles tomorrow afternoon. Fernanda says, "No problem."

When Miguel leaves, Beth invites Fernanda to eat with her. There are still plenty of containers in the fridge from Bon Vivant. Fernanda says, *"No, gracias."* She and Miguel stopped for enchiladas when he picked her up at the train station. Beth looks disappointed. Fernanda says she's tired and goes upstairs. It feels like the sun went behind the clouds. I follow her, trying to stay in her radiance but she firmly closes the bedroom door, I go back down to keep My Darling company while she eats a tiny plate of food.

When she's almost done, Saucisson starts to bark and the chimes sound at the back door. Beth brightens, like a little jolt of happiness raced through her body and she jumps up. Is she anticipating The Lug? I'm anticipating The Lug.

It's just Ray.

Ray-the-Jerk is standing at the back door. He's holding a bottle of wine but he doesn't look like the "eligible and local" paramour that Sandy imagines. For lack of a better word, I'll say he looks schlumpy. He's wearing a baggy shirt, baggy khakis and is standing with poor posture. Looking through the window at this man I've seen for years, I can objectively say he looks old. I'm not sure where the time went or how this happened but suddenly I feel like Ray-the-Jerk is a lonely old man standing at my backdoor.

I think Beth senses it, too. It's definitely a different Ray than the one who squeezed himself in between Beth and Emily with a martini. Maybe it's work-week Ray? Maybe tired Ray? Beth is solicitous and kind and welcomes him. He says he should've called but he's practically across the street, it seemed silly not to just walk over.

"Do you want to eat together?" he says. "This eating alone is getting to me."

Beth laughs, not in a mocking way, but in a kind way. "Sure," she says. "Eating alone gets old fast. I was just eating leftovers when you came."

She gets a plate and fork and brings out the containers from Bon Vivant while he opens the wine.

"Wow, what a selection. Much nicer than a frozen dinner in front of the TV."

They proceed to talk, really talk. I never thought of Beth and Ray as close. We were all just neighbors for years and years. Ray's wife and Bongo joined Beth and Trixie for a walk occasionally. If Ray and I found ourselves thrown together, Ray would try to find common ground with me through sports but that's a dead end. I'd just grit my teeth and not voice my irritation with his overgrown bushes which bloomed bigger and brighter each season. So listening to this neighbor and my wife find mutual understanding in their loneliness seems obscenely intimate.

"I really miss Linda," he says. "People ask, 'Didn't you see it coming?' As if that would make it less painful, but honestly, I didn't. I work every day and everything seems normal. Meanwhile, she met a guy walking Bongo during the pandemic. Then one Saturday morning, she sits me down and says, 'Ray, I'm in love with someone else. I'm sorry, but I need to take responsibility for my own happiness.'"

Beth nods, even though she's at a loss for the appropriate words of wisdom.

"Before I'm even fully awake and a chance to discuss things with her, she hauls out three big suitcases, calls Bongo, gets in the car and drives off, all before one lousy cup of coffee." He takes a big gulp of wine. "That's what I call a *bad* start to the weekend."

"You know, if it makes you feel better, I felt abandoned, too," My Darling says. "I know Tom didn't *want* to leave me, I know he didn't *plan* it out and pack his bags but nonetheless, the result is the same. I'm left alone. After he had finally stopped working, had time, we had a plan."

"And how are you now?

"I think I'm doing better. It's been six months, which I know is nothing but if the pandemic taught us anything, the time to find happiness is *now*." She bends down and strokes Achilles, he wiggles with pleasure. "I thought about selling the house, to move on, but I think that won't solve my problem." Beth pulls Saucisson up on her lap, "Emily, you know the woman I was with at Eggplant? She suggested therapy. It didn't take. Maybe it was the therapist, I'm not sure. She made me feel... combative."

Ray lifts a brow. "I can't even *imagine* you combative."

"Take my word for it, I was!"

"So what's better? What's the secret? Time?"

"Well," Beth says and I lean forward... I am learning a lot at this spontaneous dinner between neighbors. "I think time definitely is a factor but it's not everything. There are plenty of people who remain stuck in time. Take it from me, I've had nothing but *time* to think about it."

Ray nods.

Beth pets fat Saucisson. "This little guy is definitely helping me, he's greedy for life."

"And dinner!" Ray laughs.

"And the eggs, they're a little uncomfortable but they make me happy."

Ray looks confused. "Oh! The eggs! I was a little loaded that night. I completely forgot about the eggs. Do you have them on now?"

"Of course," Beth says. "I really only take them off to shower." She lifts the hem of her blouse just enough so that Ray can see the hatching belts.

"You have two? Would you like me to take one off your hands? I wouldn't mind wearing one. I've never dreamed of being a mother duck but it's better than being a failed husband."

"No," Beth says, "Thanks anyway, but this egg is for Tom," and she touches Little Leftie. "I think he would've enjoyed this home experiment. He was developing hobbies when he died. He was the one you'd see out in the yard with Miguel. It took him almost a year, and of course the pandemic came, but he was becoming unstuck after that disaster at the hospital. It was a terrible way to end his career."

Ray nods. "Yeah, that was a tough break."

I don't like how this impromptu therapy session is now focusing on my failures and shortcomings. I'd like to be left completely out of this conversation. Thankfully, it shifts away from me to puppies. Ray asks Beth if she would like to go with him to look at puppies, he might get another lab, it's time for yellow again. He's talked to his boss about permanently working from home two days a week. Bottom line, he's burned out.

"Oh! You know who'd really like to help you look at puppies? My friend Emily, the pretty one at Eggplant."

It's a smooth move on Beth's part. She's placed Drunk Emily on Ray's radar in the most innocent of contexts. "I'll have you both over. Emily is a lot of fun."

It's been an *enlightening* evening, there's no other word for it. Hearing Beth talk has been reassuring in some ways and unsettling in others. She doesn't seem to have taken Sandy's advice to keep the "eligible and *local*" bachelor Ray for herself. That's good but seeing him such a lackluster paramour at the door, I'm not surprised Beth would pass. However, I am unsettled by the vague talk about becoming "unstuck". I want to interrupt, "We will become *unstuck* when we move to Paris. That's *the whole point* of Paris!"

And then I think, "*Merde*! With all these moving parts, I just realized we've skipped Duolingo for three days. This is terrible."

CHAPTER 26

I know I don't have to worry about Little Leftie or Rightie, Beth sleeps flat as a board,-cognizant of her egg responsibilities even in her sleep. I spend the night, sitting on my favorite chair, missing Spatula. It's comforting to know she's in the dishwasher, clean. But inaccessible. I look at Saucisson a few times in his crate, behind bars, so to speak. He snores loudly and I wonder if it's possible for dogs to have sleep apnea. Overall, it's a very unsatisfying night.

My Darling and lovely Fernanda come downstairs almost simultaneously. Their presence is a relief from the idleness of the night. Suddenly, the kitchen is buzzing with female voices, percolating coffee and Saucisson's immediate needs of outdoors-pee, indoors-food, outdoors-poo. I love it, I just love it. It's not exactly the OR, where life and death hang in balance, but I'll take it.

Beth opens the dishwasher and I can see beloved Spatula's handle. But then Fernanda says she'll empty the dishwasher later, "Please, it's the least I can do," and Beth closes the door.

Fernanda is such a good girl. Beth and I enjoy having her in the house. It feels like she's always lived here. The three of us, (four if you count Saucisson) already have a domestic routine. I'm beginning to wonder if Fernanda should live with us after the baby comes, but that overlaps when we should be moving to Paris. Maybe Fernanda and the infant could live here in comfort and safety *while* Beth and I go to France. Why not?

Fernanda says she plans to study all day and Beth says she'll go pick out stones, tiles and slates if Fernanda can let Achilles in-out, in-out. The plan is formed and now I have to decide. Do I go with Beth?

Or stay with Fernanda? I decide to stay, not because I don't want to be helpful to Beth in her search for stones, tiles and slates, but because I feel insecure going somewhere new without Spatula.

Lovely Fernanda has on a sundress and her books under her arm when we wave goodbye to Beth. With the sun shining, Fernanda, Saucisson, and the entire yard bursting with life, and I feel I've made the right decision to stay, rather than be stuck in the car. Fernanda keeps the French doors wide open. She turns on some lively music and puts her books on the patio table. The veranda is nothing like a library cubicle and her dark hair sparkles in the sun. For maximum concentration, she should probably be indoors but she's youthful and it's spring and the outdoors suits all of us just fine.

I notice that as she studies, she looks at her phone and texts. I don't approve of this distraction. We didn't have phones and texting when I was young but I don't think I would have fallen prey to the temptation even if we did. Occasionally I try to look over her shoulder and see who she's texting but she's quick with the tiny keyboard and the glare of the sun on her screen makes it virtually impossible.

At one point, Fernanda goes into the house but I don't notice because I'm examining an aphid infestation. When I notice Fernanda is not at the table, I rush indoors. The kitchen is dim compared to outside and I realize my eyes need a moment to adjust, my pupils to dilate, just like if I was living.

Fernanda is standing near the dishwasher and it's door is hanging open. She's holding the silverware basket in her hand. She places it on the counter, right in front of the utensil drawer and starts putting the silverware away. There's never a moment where I can grab my beloved Spatula, whose handle stands out like the long straw in a schoolyard pick. I watch her put a butter knife with butter knives, salad forks with salad forks, teaspoons with teaspoons, until only Spatula is left. She holds Spatula and looks into the drawer.

It was the only non-silverware utensil in the dishwasher and it clearly doesn't belong in the neat and orderly silverware drawer. She holds it in front of her with two hands, like a pioneer woman holding a sputtering candle in the dark. The brittle, irregular rubber end nearly touches her pursed lips. She's thinking, "If this was my kitchen, where would I put this?"

The correct answer would be, "Next to the stove," but instead Fernanda opens the warming drawer.

I've pretty much forgotten about the warming drawer and it's leftover egg and I'm quite sure Beth *has* forgotten. The egg has been lying for 12 days, nestled in its pink dish towel, waiting to be found. Fernanda discovers it and says, "Oh." It's very soft, maybe it's just a sigh, I'm not sure. She puts down Spatula, picks up the egg cloaked in the towel, touches it to her cheek and holds it there. Spatula is right on the edge of the counter and the towel obstructs her downward peripheral vision. With the smooth, warm egg laying against her cheek, she closes her eyes for just a moment and I snatch Spatula.

In a blink of an eye, I put its yellowed, brittle end in my armpit.

Fernanda gently puts the egg back in the warming drawer and closes it. As I walk over to my favorite chair, I watch her look around the counter and floor, confused. She opens the warming drawer again to make sure the spatula didn't fall inside. Then she gets down on her knees to look under the overhang of the kitchen cupboards. At that moment, I easily pull Spatula out from under my arm and put her under the cushion of the chair where she belongs.

My staying home has just proven to be the right decision. I feel a deep sense of satisfaction that the one object I'm capable of owning and possessing is back safe, sound *and clean* in my hiding spot. The rest of the day could go to hell but I've got this win under my belt. I feel a little sorry for Fernanda because, being a conscientious girl, she keeps looking for the lost spatula. I can't imagine Evie being so diligent. Evie's thought process would go something like, "It was a crappy old spatula, who cares?"

Late in the afternoon, Beth comes home. She's carrying a bag from Bon Vivant. It's true, she and Ray managed to polish off about five of the to-go containers last night but we still have about five in the fridge. Bon Vivant used to be *our* Saturday lunch treat. Occasionally, we'd pick up Sunday night dinner, too, but it was never an everyday occurrence like it's become. I don't begrudge Beth spending the money, I'd never deny My Darling a single dollar. It's the location she chooses to spend it at that bothers me. It's inappropriate.

She puts the bag in the fridge, pats Saucisson and tells Fernanda that she's going to lie down. Traffic was a mess and she got stuck close to an hour in a queue of cars and trucks filing down to a single lane. I know the exact spot. They've been doing construction at that junction for years, even before I died.

I feel badly that I had such a wonderful day while Beth's was so grueling. To show solidarity, I go upstairs with her, even though I'm not the least bit tired. I'm never really tired, I just go through the motions. Saucisson follows us upstairs. Maybe he feels a sense of solidarity too, but it's humorous to watch him drag his sausage body up the steps on his short legs. The three of us go into our bedroom and, much to my surprise, Beth closes the door. Click.

And locks it. Click.

I've never really known Beth to lock the bedroom door. Even Saucisson turns his head when he hears the second click of the internal bolt sliding into place. Beth opens one of the closet doors and pulls out Trixie's old bed that used to be on the floor beside our bed. Beth had just bought this new one when Trixie became incapable of climbing the steps. She puts it beside the bed and pats it. Saucisson waddles over, sniffs it, climbs in, turns three circles and closes his eyes.

Beth props her feet up, lies in bed and holds her phone. I think we're going to watch an old movie, which is absolutely one of my

143

favorite things to do. Instead, Beth googles: *Dating middle age*. The first article in the search is New York Times: *Stop Languishing, Start Dating – At Any Age!*

The article is dated July 17, 2021. I was still alive. Beth would have had no reason to read this article when it was published. I start reading the opening paragraph but don't get very far. Essentially, it's starts: make the most of your time, don't put off your happiness, seize the day – clichés of that sort. I don't get very far because the phone falls forward as Beth falls asleep. It lies face down at an angle between Little Leftie and Little Rightie. My Darling is tuckered out. I bend down and whisper to Little Leftie, "Don't worry, papa's here."

CHAPTER 27

It's a warm evening and Beth sets the table outside. She carries out all the Bon Vivant containers and some spoons and calls Fernanda. They're about to start eating when Miguel walks around the corner of the house.

"*Hola!*" he calls out.

Miguel says he was driving by, which is probably close to the truth. He's taken off whatever shirt he must have worn that day and put on a clean tee that still has fold lines in it. The tee is fitted and shows off his strong physique with the only flaw being the unnatural bulge of the hatching belt. I'm sure he wants to stop by and see Fernanda. I'm sure he misses her and does not want to end this beautiful day without laying eyes on his lovely daughter. I don't blame him, these two women would buoy the most tired man's heart.

Beth invites him to stay. At first he objects but it's all just for show. I can see he wants to stay and is probably much hungrier after his physical labor than either of the women. He and Beth ask Fernanda about her exams tomorrow and Beth tells Miguel about her success at picking out stones, tiles and slates. They make a sweet scene of domestic bliss with pregnant Fernanda sitting between them.

Miguel tells Fernanda that he'll be by in the morning and bring her her favorite Mexican coffee for good luck. He'll drive her to the train station then pick up the stones, tiles and slates and bring them back here. There's no discussion about what Fernanda is going to do after tomorrow, after her exams, after she finishes her third year of college but *before* she has her baby.

I'm beginning to worry about the unborn child and what kind of life he or she will have. I truly think Beth and I offer the best solution to this human conundrum. If Fernanda lives here, Beth would be able to help her, guide her. Beth could hire some child care, if need be, while we're in Paris. Fernanda could finish her last year of college, allowing her to go out in the world with a college degree. It's not like a degree alone is the golden ticket, but at least it's a good start.

At dusk, mosquitoes come out. The three of them carry their plates indoors and Beth closes the French doors. Miguel says he has to go. He thanks Beth profusely for dinner, *"Gracias, gracias, gracias!"* He says he needs to work on billing tonight. There aren't enough hours in the day; in the spring, the work is double. He needs to stay up late doing billing to keep money coming in. I remember his account notebook on the seat with its straightforward simplicity and hierarchy of customers. There was no negotiated rate, no arcane codes, no inflated pricing. It was honest work for honest pay.

I imagine Miguel in his simple kitchen with the family's shoes lined up at the door, his head bent under the kitchen light, adding columns of numbers and doing simple multiplication. Maybe he sips a beer. It's a humble, straight-forward task that might take him late into the night. It appeals to the egalitarian in me. Besides, I don't want to be stuck in our master bedroom all night, or locked out, either. Nights with closed bedroom doors and the dog in the crate have become interminably long. I liked it much better when I could float between our bedroom and comfort Trixie with Spatula.

Knowing that Miguel will be back bright and early, knowing that I might gain some insight into running a small business, knowing that it might be a late night with male camaraderie, I pull clean Spatula out from under the cushion and follow Miguel out the door to his truck.

"Adios, ladies! I'm going to have a guy's night out at Miguel's!"

It seems like a sound decision as we drive the four miles to *Pequeña Fleur* with the windows open and country music playing. I'm already pleased that I made the decision to go. A little male bonding is important and I've had a lot of female companionship over these last few days. Don't get me wrong, I enjoy female energy, and in fact, I am enjoying it more and more.

Towards the end of my career, a lot of the specialists were women, which was fine with me. Often they were more competent than the men and easier to work with. That being said, I look forward to a night with "the guys" even if it's only one guy and we're doing simple math.

When we pull up to Miguel's house, he gets out, opens the chain link gate and drives in to park on the concrete slab front yard. On his side of the house, the lights are off. Miguel reaches for his accounts notebook at my feet, he gets the dirty tee and empty thermos on the passenger seat. He puts the windows up and we get out of the pickup. Miguel carries the items to the front door. Once again, his neighbor sticks her head out of the second floor window and yells the exact same question, "*Cómo está el huevo?*"

Miguel puts the items down, lifts his tee up, higher than he needs to. "*Muy bien!*"

She yells back, "*Muy, muy bien!*"

I think of schlumpy Ray coming to my back door with a potted plant, what would Beth say or do? The mere thought of this interaction makes me chuckle. Already the evening is so much more lively than back at 22 Woodhill, where I'm sure it's lights out.

There's a thick chain secured around one of the front door railings next door. It wasn't there before or I didn't notice it. It warns of a dog, definitely not a small dog, but a large dog, which puts me a bit on edge. In the waning light, I see a few dark mounds on the neighbor's side of the concrete slab. It might be dog shit, large dog shit. My only comfort is that I don't hear a dog barking.

With no warning, Miguel leaves the notebook, dirty tee and thermos on his top step and turns back to the truck. I'm confused, I thought we were home for the evening. He goes back to the truck, unlocks it and gets in. He actually climbs in, so naturally, I scramble in too, climbing into the passenger seat. My amigo Miguel reaches across my body and flips open the glove compartment. It hits my knees but makes no sound. No little light comes on and I can't see what he's reaching for. I sit very still and straight with Spatula hidden under my right arm. He's practically leaning on my left thigh.

My amigo Miguel pulls out a gun!

I only see it for a split second because it's dark and fits snugly in his hand, just like Spatula fits snugly under my arm. I've never even touched a gun. Guns did not factor into my life. Occasionally, I fixed the violence done by a gun but that's as close as I came.

I sit very still and wait for him to reach back over and slam the glove compartment closed again. But Miguel doesn't reach across, he does what I'd never do; he just leaves the door hanging open, slides out of the driver's seat and slams the truck door shut in one smooth motion, like an octopus slipping into a crack. Click. He locks the doors and I'm left inside. Trapped.

My sleepover at Miguel's just got a whole lot less fun.

Miguel walks to his front door, picks up the items that he left on the steps and goes inside. I see his kitchen light flick on and a warm yellow glow over the kitchen table. I imagine him getting a beer from the fridge and sitting at the table with his greasy notebook and a 4x5 formatted billing pad. He'll run his finger across the top line that says "Señora Paradise", add up the hours, multiply by $20 and write the total twice, once in the greasy notebook and once on the clean billing pad. Looking at the glowing light, I'm sure it's just like I imagine… except now there's a gun in the picture.

I never imagined the gun. How could I? I never knew the gun existed. What does my amigo Miguel do with the gun once he brings it in the house? Is it sitting on the kitchen table next to his beer? Does he holster it in one of the shoes lined up inside of the door?

My amigo Miguel has a gun and I have Spatula. I could use her handle to depress the unlock button of the car door, but Spatula isn't agile enough to pull *up* on the door handle and successfully open the door. I am consigned to sit tight, pass a long and boring night in Miguel's truck with my only comfort being that Miguel has promised to bring Fernanda her favorite cup of Mexican coffee in the morning and drive her to the train.

I put my head on the seat rest and tell myself I wouldn't be doing anything more interesting back at home. I close my eyes. "Feel gratitude, Tom," I tell myself over and over.

Around midnight, the kitchen light blinks off and the neighbor's lights turn off, too, except for a dim, flickering light on the second floor, where the neighbor yelled out the window. I try to imagine what she's doing. Is she reading a romance late into the night? Is she watching a game show? Did she fall asleep and accidentally leave the TV on? I start to let my imagination run wild and envision her as a sorceress and the heavy chain is for her dragon that lies beside her…

Some shadow of a movement catches my eye.

I look in the rearview mirror and I see a red car idling on the street. The windows are tinted and I can't see a driver or any passengers. There is movement inside the fenced front yard, I know it, I *feel* it. The hair on my arms stands on end, which I didn't even know was possible. I clutch Spatula in both hands on my lap.

A shadowy figure goes up to Miguel's door. It's the figure of a tall, thin man holding a long, tubular object. I see him reach for the door knob and I hold my breath. He nudges his shoulder against the door but it doesn't budge. I'm squinting, trying to see everything but there's no light outside the front door. Most of my attention is riveted by the figure on the front stoop but I think I might have just seen a movement at the second floor window. I feel utterly helpless that I can't warn my amigo.

The neighbor's door opens a crack. No wedge of light comes out. I can barely make out the door on the right moving and opening. But there's no missing the white object that comes hurtling out. The moment the object shoots out, the door slams shut. It's all quick and seamless. The object is a dog, a white dog, a big dog, a fierce dog.

The truck windows are closed, making it hard to hear, but I don't think the dog makes a sound, no growl, no bark. The dog's intent is set and he needs no reason to announce it. He charges for the figure at Miguel's door.

The figure turns, I can't see his face but I would relish his look of surprise. Instead of running, however, he stands his ground, plants his feet and takes both his arms back. Now I see the long object is a baseball bat and he's taken the batter stance. He swings the bat and catches the white ball of fury on the side of his head. The white dog that was all movement and momentum, staggers and drops. Like any decent batter, the figure starts to run after his successful hit but unlike a batter, he doesn't drop his bat. The white dog lies on its side, there's nothing to hinder the runner's progress.

Much to my surprise, this runner slows to a casual lope, he already knows he hit it out of the park. He stops at Miguel's pickup truck and gazes directly into the passenger window like he's looking in a mirror, staring directly at me as I sit perfectly still and stare back. He's an unusually handsome young man with high, Slavic cheekbones and full lips, in the bloom of youth, the apex of his strength, a fine physical specimen. With no warning, not even a clench of his jaw, he takes his arms back and swings the bat. My window explodes! The glass shatters into a thousand tiny prisms and then folds into itself and falls onto my lap.

The young man jauntily walks to the chain link fence, like a homerun hitter returning to the dugout, all of his attention is focused on the celebration ahead. He doesn't see the white dog rise like a ghost, only stunned, but he hears him roar. The white dog charges!

I'm watching this unfold from the passenger seat, through an open square where the window used to be. The young man fluidly vaults the fence and jumps into the passenger seat of the red car as it peels out.

My amigo Miguel runs out of his front door in time to see the car peel away. He's in his boxer shorts and I can see the hatching belt around his middle. He's holding a dark object in his right hand. The sorceress pokes her head out of her window. Miguel looks up and says, "*Gracias.*" She replies "*De nada.*" What more is there to say?

The white dog trots up to Miguel. Miguel strokes his tremendous skull, scratches under his ears and then turns and goes back inside. The big white beast surveys his chain link domain, lifts his leg and pees on the bottom rail of the front stoop. Then he trots over to Miguel's truck, stands on his hind legs and sticks his massive head into the broken passenger window.

He's some sort of pit bull-mastiff mix. I can see why the bat didn't kill him, just stunned him. I have no idea if he can smell me or how he perceives me: a man? A ghost? A former heart surgeon? Or a *jefé* stowaway? Thankfully, Miguel comes back out his front door. He calls, "Diablo!" and Diablo pulls his head out of the truck and trots to Miguel.

Miguel hands him something. It looks like a chicken drumstick but it's gone in a second, bone and all. He pats Diablo again and goes into the house. I move over to the driver's seat, away from the glass fragments. Diablo trots around the truck but seems disinterested in my presence inside. He squats down by his stoop and pushes out a tremendous turd.

Momentarily, another truck pulls up. One of Miguel's sons jumps out and opens the gate while the other brother drives through. They survey the damage, pat Diablo and hurry inside. Diablo does one more inspection of the area, satisfied, he lies down on his own's stoop, and rests his massive jaws across his front paws.

I sit very quietly in the driver's seat with Spatula. I think of the loyal neighbor in the second floor bedroom, I think of Miguel and his sons now asleep in their beds and I think about fearless Diablo guarding the side-by-side stoops. I try to have an open mind. I know my children have lived in a rarified, sheltered world and that others aren't as fortunate. It seems that my amigo Miguel can take care of himself. It seems the friendly sorceress isn't easily frightened by a night intruder. But what about Fernanda? Lovely Fernanda, the jewel of *Pequeña Fleur*, moving back here with her tiny, helpless infant and living one flimsy wall away from Diablo and one vaultable fence from danger.

I can't reconcile that.

CHAPTER 28

My amigo Miguel is up bright and early this morning. He looks no worse after the excitement of last night. His hair still stands up, his teeth gleam and there's a bounce to his step.

I, however, feel old, tired and misplaced. I've been forced to sit in the driver's seat all night with thousands of cubed glass crumbs beside me. Diablo didn't prove an imminent threat but I kept quiet and sat still, as far away from the broken window as possible. When I retired, I became a dog lover, a dog aficionado, but I'm not 100% comfortable with this beast and I don't think I ever could be. There are few similarities between Trixie or Saucisson and Diablo. Objectively, one could wonder if they were the same species.

Miguel has a garbage bag, dust pan and hand brush. He pats Diablo, who wags his tail and possibly smiles with his massive lower jaw hanging open. Miguel opens the passenger door. The glove compartment is still hanging open. He reaches behind him and pulls the small hand gun from the waistband of his jeans, places it in the glove box and pops the door closed. He does it so casually and quickly that I almost miss the action entirely.

He sets to work sweeping the glass, first off the seat and then off the floor. He hums while he does it. Lastly, he gets the glass scattered on the concrete slab. Just when I think he's done, he walks around to the three mounds of dog shit, scoops them up with the dustpan and dumps them into the bag with the broken glass.

The second floor window opens and his neighbor yells out, "*Gracias!*"

It's Miguel's turn to say, "*De nada!*"

A few seconds later, the neighbor's front door opens a crack and Diablo goes running inside. It's almost like the night's events never happened, except the passenger window is gone.

Miguel goes inside the house for a few minutes. I move over to the clean passenger seat and enjoy knowing that Diablo is inside, probably wolfing down a bear-sized breakfast. Miguel comes out, carrying his notebook and thermos. He tosses them both into the open passenger side onto my lap like this new arrangement, no window, is the most convenient thing ever. He opens the chain link gate, backs out, closes it, turns on loud music and off we go to the Mexican coffee bodega.

Coffee in hand, we drive the four miles to my house. I'm having a good time, between the music and my open window, but I'm relieved when we turn onto Woodhill and I know there are no surprises ahead of me. Miguel pulls into our driveway, jumps out and taps lightly on the back door.

I hear Saucisson barking and Fernanda comes out. She's wearing a white ruffled dress with a sweater around her shoulders and Beth's Palm's Resort tote bag over her shoulder. She looks like a woman of leisure. Miguel smiles and opens the passenger door for her. I slip out, she slips in. She will have to ride with the broken window playing havoc with her hair.

I'd love to drive to the train station with them but I know Miguel will be on the road today, picking up the stones, tiles and slates. I need to spend quality time with Beth and frankly, I've had enough excitement. I walk around to the back, where Beth is sitting at the table having a cup of coffee. The French doors are open and Saucisson is sniffing around in the grass. He looks in my direction and gives his short tail a mild wag. I feel the same way. I don't love him like I loved Trixie but right now he looks pretty good beside Diablo who, although useful in *Pequeña Fleur,* would be stressful at 22 Woodhill.

Everything is just as it always is and I feel gratitude without even having to remind myself.

The day goes smoothly and Miguel shows up with his heavy load and his passenger window already fixed. He backs the truck up the driveway, closes both the driver and passenger windows, takes off his hatching belt and lays it carefully on the seat while he tosses the heavy rocks out of the bed of the pickup. He stacks the materials until he's ready to tackle each project at a later date. I admire the forethought of the warm pickup cab and how this arrangement allows Miguel to work without fear of bumping the belt or the egg cooling.

At one point, Beth walks out and asks Miguel what Fernanda's favorite cake is. She's going to make a cake to celebrate the end of Fernanda's exams. Miguel says, "Chocolate." She's holding her car keys and purse and has pulled her hair into a ponytail. I suspect she's going to Bon Vivant and decide my time is better spent watching Beth than watching Miguel.

I'm right. We drive straight to Bon Vivant and Beth parks in the corner of the lot under the oak tree. She leaves the spot open where The Lug likes to park in the shade. I'd like to go in but I decide it's best to wait in the car. I'm curious – if the black sedan drives into the lot, will he do anything differently when he sees Beth's car? Is he expecting *her* to be here? Is she expecting *him* to be here? I'm not sure how far this flirtation has gone.

I wait.

No black sedan comes. Beth comes out with her shopping bag, glances right and left and looks disappointed. The skip in her step is gone. She gets in the car, puts the bag on my lap and checks her phone. No texts. When we get home, Miguel has unloaded all the stones, tiles and slates and piled them neatly on the side of the driveway where there is no lawn, only mulch. He looks sweaty and actually tired.

Beth asks if he wants to join them for dinner again. "No," he says, "Fernanda just texted. She's taking a later train and doesn't need

155

a ride." Now all three of us look a little disappointed. Beth carries the bag in and puts the beautiful little chocolate cake in the fridge. As if reflecting our darkened mood, the sky gets dimmer and a couple rain drops plop down.

The only good thing that comes from the suddenly deflated evening is that we devote ourselves to Duolingo. Last week, Beth allowed us to slip down to Obsidian League but this week she seems determined to be one of the top three students and get promoted back to Diamond League. This buoys my spirit slightly. While we're working assiduously on our French, Beth's phone makes a ding. It's from Jessica, "How about coming for that tea party on Saturday? The girls would love it." Beth texts, "That would be lovely." Jessica gives her a thumbs up.

Although Jessica's text did not demand further action, Beth looks long and hard at the screen. Then she hits the back button and goes to the queue of conversations. She runs her finger down and finds The Lug, aka Friedrich.

Beth isn't as quick of a texter as Fernanda, thank god. I have a fighting chance to see what she taps out and sometimes I can even go back and read one or two texts before. The last text from The Lug says, "I'll be there in 5 min."

I can't see the tiny date stamp above it, but regardless, I don't like it.

Beth taps out, "I was at Bon Vivant today. I looked for you. How's the egg?"

She gets an automated message back: "I'm driving with Do Not Disturb While Driving turned on. I'll see your message when I get where I'm going."

I panic. What if he's driving to our house right now? But Beth doesn't look like she's anticipating The Lug's arrival and she sighs, putting her phone down. Then I remember his job *is* driving. He drives all day, presumably when he's not sitting in the parking lot of Bon

Vivant waiting to stare at my wife and, hopefully, other women. And then I start to do something that I would never have done as a living, breathing person, working or not working: I start to wonder who The Lug is as a *person*.

People have never deeply interested me. Their hearts have but not their whole self, their hopes, their dreams, what path brought them to where they are, what they do day to day. The *context* of their biases, fears and passions didn't interest me or I didn't care; I'm not sure there's a difference.

So that brings me back to The Lug, who I have so aptly named. He's a two dimensional presence to me (be it large), just like my amigo Miguel *was*, but now Miguel is so much more. Through observation, I now know details about my amigo's life. Whether this is a good thing or a bad thing, I am not sure.

I worked beside Miguel in my yard year after year, well, stood beside him, and I never knew he had a concrete slab for a front lawn, Diablo as a protector, a gun in his glove compartment and a daughter who is the jewel of *Pequeña Fleur*. In some ways things have changed but in others they haven't. He's still my amigo Miguel, showing up with his gleaming smile and porcupine hair.

Because I have time and I'm never tired and am incapable of falling into an exhausted sleep, I find myself thinking more and more about humans, specifically people I interact with in my ghost life. *Their* lives haven't really changed, they just keep living them. It's *my* life that's changed. Perhaps, since I don't have a life, in the conventional sense, I'm more curious about *their* lives.

I wonder about The Lug. Where does this man who wears cheap suits live? He has a French accent but I'm quite sure he's not from France proper. Assuming I'm correct, then where's he from? And why would he accept the obligation of an egg and hatching belt from my wife, a perfect stranger, in the Bon Vivant parking lot? I could say I'm "curious" but that would be a lie. I feel it's grown critical, perhaps life or death, *my* life or death, that I find out The Lug's story.

Late in the night, I hear a key in the back door and listen to the door open and close. Beth must have shown Fernanda where she hides a spare key. Beth didn't close our bedroom door tonight, a mother's instinct to leave her door open to listen for her child to come home. I stand at the top of the steps and watch lovely Fernanda quietly walk down the hall and go into Evie's old room.

It's 2:00 a.m. As a doctor, I feel it's far too late for a pregnant woman to be out. As a father, I feel nothing good happens this late at night. As a ghost, there's absolutely nothing I can do about it.

CHAPTER 29

Friday morning starts out promising but takes an unpleasant turn that I never saw coming. Beth gets up as usual, makes her coffee and leaves a cup out on the counter for Fernanda. Saucisson goes in and out of the French doors and we all sit outside together, me in my preferred chair. Without even reminding myself, I feel extreme gratitude for the beauty and serenity of my environment. The night at Miguel's is still fresh and has left a definite impression on me. Even though I'm a ghost, I lead a pretty cushy life and appreciate all I have.

My amigo Miguel arrives. He's his usual energetic, cheery self. He looks like he had the best night's sleep of his life and that he doesn't have a care in the world. I know otherwise. I now know about the gun in the glove compartment and the watchful neighbor with fierce Diablo. It makes me admire Miguel and his sunny, breezy manner even more.

He says, "*Huevo*," and pats his hatching belt. Beth replies, "*Huevos*," and pats hers. It's like a code, no more words need to be said

Miguel asks about Fernanda. Beth says, "She got in late." I can tell he doesn't like this news and Beth can see his displeasure so she tries to soften it with "not too late", but all three of us know it's not true.

It's almost 11:00 before Fernanda wanders down for a cup of coffee. Beth asks her how her exams went and tells her it's healthy to sleep in while she's pregnant. "Enjoy," she says.

But all is not peace.

Fernanda goes outside to the driveway with her cup of coffee and stands by Miguel's truck, I'm watching from the back door window. Miguel stops edging a bed and walks over. I can see he's not smiling. He starts moving his hands and possibly yelling. I run back through the house and out the open French doors. I'm so curious what can arouse my amigo Miguel, he's usually so unflappable. When I get there, I'm disappointed to hear he's yelling at Fernanda in Spanish. I only catch words like *"malo, bébé, novio."* I'm much more fluent in French than Spanish. But there's one word that catches my attention. It's how Miguel says it, he draws it out phonetically compared to the other staccato words, "droe-guz."

It could be "drugs" but I'm not sure.

Lovely Fernanda stands straight and defiant. At no point does she bow her head or look apologetic for provoking this displeasure in her father. I can't help but think of Evie and me. She slings a whole slew of words back at Miguel, all in Spanish and rapid fire. The only word I really catch is the last word. It's *amor*.

She turns, takes her coffee cup and goes back in the house. She leaves Miguel standing with his porcupine hair but no white smile. I feel badly for my amigo. I run in the house and get Spatula from under the chair cushion. Beth must be upstairs, I don't think she caught any of this *Pequeña Fleur* drama played out in our driveway.

I decide to stay out in the yard and work beside Miguel, like old times. There's not a lot I can do with Spatula, but when Miguel's back is turned, I pull her out from under my arm and flick any stray pieces of mulch back into the bed with surgical precision. It's the least I can do, we are *compadres*, Miguel and me.

We're working for about 20 minutes or so when Fernanda comes back out of the house. She's wearing the white ruffle dress that I like and she strides down the driveway. Miguel stops what he's doing and watches her. My first thought is that Beth asked her to get the mail but then I notice her purse is slung over her shoulder. She never looks over at Miguel and me and Miguel doesn't shout out. As she hits the bottom of the driveway, a red car pulls up. I'm certain it's the same red car from the other night with the same smoked glass windows. I can't see the driver but obviously Fernanda is expecting him. She opens the passenger door, slips in and the car roars away.

My amigo Miguel is left leaning on his shovel and I am left sitting cross legged on the lawn with Spatula under my arm. Here we are, two strong men. One is strong, with gleaming teeth and a gun in his glove compartment and the other is... well... I have Spatula and many other useful qualities. Between the two of us, we're impotent to save lovely Fernanda, against this threat in a red car. If I had a heart, a functioning heart, I'd say it's "disheartening".

Beth comes out of the house an hour later. She's smiling and has Saucisson on Trixie's old leash. Seeing how light-hearted she is, I'm sure she doesn't know Fernanda left and I'm sure she doesn't know that Miguel is so unhappy. She yells over, "First real walk, wish us luck!"

Miguel rouses himself. He smiles and yells, "Achilles needs no luck!"

Beth laughs and keeps walking. I know I could go with her but I decide to stay.

I watch Beth as she passes Ray's house. Saucisson keeps stopping and smelling and getting distracted, like a toddler, and Beth is being patient, letting him explore this new world. It's slow going and I'm glad I didn't go, I'd just be irritated.

Miguel and I are hard at work when a black sedan glides into the driveway. It's so quiet and elegant after the sound of the souped-up red car that we hardly notice it. Miguel pauses for a moment but then keeps working. Beth's visitor is none of his concern. His world has already been rocked and he's not looking for extra entanglements.

Even from across the lawn, I can see the big, black head of The Lug. I thought the red car was an intrusion but the gall of the black

Town Car to actually pull into my driveway is infuriating. I stride across the lawn. Spatula is not Diablo, nor is she a gun but she will have to do.

The Lug is standing at the back door that goes into the mudroom. He must have finished knocking or ringing the doorbell or whatever he did and now understands that Beth isn't home. He's pulled out one of his humble business cards that simply states: "Friedrich Ngoy, Driver," with a phone number and he's writing on the back with a pen that he's pulled from his suit pocket. I can't see what he's writing because he has it cupped in his massive hand. When he's done, he puts the pen back in his pocket, touches the bump of the hatching belt and tucks the card so it's sticking out of the closed door like a little white surrender flag.

I can't help but loathe this man from his big, shaggy head to his signature pointy shoes. Seeing him at my backdoor is a cruel insult. I follow him back to his car. He glances at Miguel but my amigo doesn't give him the time of day. As he folds his bulk into the Town Car, I hit him on the rear with Spatula. It makes no sound through the thick layers of the suit pants and suit jacket. He turns, looks confused, and gets into the car. He glides out of the driveway as silently as he came in.

I think, "Not on *my* watch." I take Spatula and flick the card out of the crack. It falls onto the slates. Then, flick by flick, I move it off the stoop and down the stairs. My ultimate goal is to get it to a bed and cover it with mulch. I am squatting, hard at work flicking it across the driveway to the nearest mulch bed when I hear Saucisson growl. He is standing a few feet away and has seen Spatula, mysteriously floating in the air. Beth is standing there, too.

I was so intent on my task that I didn't see or hear them walk back up the driveway. Beth, thank god, seems to be looking out at Miguel. It gives me a moment to tuck Spatula under my arm. Beth turns, pauses, bends and picks up The Lug's card. She reads it, smiles, tucks it in her pocket and walks across the lawn to talk to Miguel.

I'm left squatting, with Saucisson staring me in the face. I dare not move, even though I'm dying to run over and hear what Beth is saying or asking Miguel. About 30 seconds into the dead surgeon vs. fat pup stare-down, Saucisson wags his tail, trots over and pees on my trouser leg, marking me as his.

CHAPTER 30

Miguel leaves and Fernanda doesn't come home. It looks like it's going to be a dull Friday night, which would have been perfect when I was working, but it's a letdown, now that I have all this time and consciousness. Beth is sitting quietly at the counter, shopping for sneakers on the Internet, when there's a knock at the back door. She jumps up, like she's been shot through the heart by Cupid himself, and hurries to the mudroom door with Saucisson at her heels.

I follow, gnashing my teeth. The Lug's card, in the worst handwriting possible, doctor scrawl, had said, "See you soon. F." This is far sooner than even I expected.

But surprise of surprises, it's Evie!

She is standing with a small duffle slung over her shoulder, smiling broadly through the window. Beth screams with delight and opens the door. "Evie!"

"Mom!"

They hug and I enjoy watching their pure happiness. Evie pulls back and frowns. She touches Beth's middle and says, "What's that?"

Beth laughs and gives her the short version of the hatching experiment and how it's a "dynamic force of change". Naturally, Evie thinks this is "fantastic", "brilliant" and "should do it with my friends." I snort at the thought of Evie being saddled with this responsibility for a day, much less a month. I'd place my bet on Charlotte before I'd place it on Evie.

Evie bends down and struggles to lift a squirming Saucisson up. He's getting bigger by the day and this is probably the last time he'll be picked up in this house. She kisses him on the nose. "So nice to meet you, Achilles!"

Beth asks Evie why she's here and how she got here.

Evie laughs, "Flew, Mom." She tells Beth that there was a conference in the city and her co-worker was supposed to go but he broke his leg rock climbing. Evie went in his place. but she wasn't sure she could change her ticket to leave Sunday instead of Friday after the conference. Obviously, she was able to change her flight.

"Voila! I'm here 'til Sunday noon!"

Evie says she'll take her bag up to her room. Beth frowns for a moment and tells Evie how Fernanda is staying in it. Evie is slightly surprised but doesn't seem the least upset. Beth suggests the second floor guest room, Tyler's room, or the first floor guest room, which is away from everything, back by the bar and study.

Evie just shrugs and asks if she can just stay in our room since she's only home two nights. "It will be cozy, like when I was little."

Beth is delighted with this arrangement. She asks Evie if she wants to go out to dinner or stay home. She'd rather just stay home tonight. Evie runs her bag upstairs and wants to clean up from her day at the conference. Saucisson follows *her*.

I watch My Darling move around the kitchen. She's so visibly happy and I can confidently say that I'm happy for her. It's a lovely evening and she sets the patio table with some candles and linen napkins.

Then the back door chimes.

Is it The Lug? I hope it is. I'm sure Beth will send him away now that Evie's here.

It's schlumpy Ray, peering in. He looks pathetic as usual. He's wearing a loose, floppy Hawaiian shirt and holding a bottle of white wine. He looks like he's about 40 years late getting to Margaritaville. Beth opens the door and is polite. Beth is always polite.

Ray asks if she wants to have dinner again as "lonely neighbors". Beth says that Evie surprised her and is home for the weekend and I think that will be the end of it, but then Evie comes around the corner wearing my stethoscope around her neck and actually *hugs* Ray, like we've always been so close, and asks about his daughter Mia.

Much to my annoyance, Ray is invited to stay for dinner. The wine is opened, the Bon Vivant containers are taken out and Beth puts portions on the plates. Evie proclaims, "It's a party!" It's all so Evie, spontaneous and random and Beth is laughing and Ray is obviously thrilled to be in the company of these two vivacious women. *My* two vivacious women.

Very quickly, a second bottle of wine is opened because, to quote Evie, "It *is* a party." Evie asks Ray some polite questions and understands that his wife left him, took Bongo and that Mia doesn't really talk to him. They change topics.

Beth asks Evie why she's wearing my stethoscope, which is something I would've liked to ask myself. Evie laughs. She says how she saw my old leather medical bag still sitting on the counter in my dressing room and put it on so she'd remember to tell a story about Dad, *me*. She starts the story, "Well, you know how Dad and I always fought…"

Beth grimaces and Ray nods his head, which is so much bullshit. Ray-the-Jerk did not know the tone and tenor of my relationship with my daughter. I'm sure he's thinking of his own sorry-ass relationship with *his* daughter.

"Well, we'd have a particularly bad fight, I'm talking, I'm a little kid and I'm defying this man like nobody has had the nerve to do all day, he says, 'Go to your room, young lady!'" And Evie makes a grumpy face that's supposed to be me. "But in the night, he'd come check on me. I'd be asleep and I'd feel this cold stethoscope touch my chest." She puts the stethoscope to her chest. "And I'd lie still and pretend I was asleep and he'd listen for about three seconds. Then he'd gently cover me and leave. We never mentioned it between us. I never let him know that I was awake but I understood that his checking my heart was his way of saying he loved me."

Beth wipes her eyes and Ray has no comment. I'm not sure how I feel about the story being told out loud. I think I liked it better uncommunicated, a quiet secret to take to the grave. Which, for my part, I did.

Beth brings out Fernanda's chocolate cake that was bought to celebrate the end of her exams. It has thick ganache and light mousse like only Bon Vivant can do. I wish I could taste it with all my heart but obviously I can't.

After two bottles of wine and dinner, Ray stands up to leave. Beth is a little tipsy, I can tell. She announces to Evie, "Ray wanted one of my eggs but one is for your father," She lifts her blouse and touches the left side, Little Leftie. It's nothing she would say or do if she was 100% sober.

Evie frowns. "You should give the egg to Ray, Dad would've never worn one."

She says it with a derisive tone of voice, like she really wants to say, "Ray is a kind, thoughtful, warm human being, Dad never was." It's Evie chasing a sweet story with a low blow. I'm not sure Beth hears her, she's carrying some plates to the kitchen.

"You know where to find me if you change your mind!" Ray adds breezily as he walks out the door.

When Ray leaves, Beth checks under the doormat for a key. It's right where we always keep it. Then she steps inside and locks the door. Evie laughs and says, "Still the same spot? Might be time for a new one."

"Maybe when Fernanda leaves. I'm not sure where she went but I'm sure she'll be back soon."

Before she and Evie go upstairs, Beth leaves the last slice of cake on a plate with a note, "Celebrate your accomplishments! Evie surprised me and came home. She's sleeping in my room. Beth."

Saucisson gets put in his crate. Beth assures him, "Not much longer. You're such a good boy." Beth, Evie, and I trudge upstairs. The two of them appear very tired and tipsy and I feel drained, too. I think this fatigue is more emotional than physical. Witnessing the fight between Miguel and Fernanda wasn't a good start, followed by the outrage of The Lug's visit, and the shock of Evie's arrival, which stirred up twenty-five years of old emotions, many of which I regret now.

Beth reminds Evie to put my stethoscope back where it belongs. It's still a beautiful bag and perhaps the only item my mother truly splurged on in her life. It has a small gold plate, Dr. Thomas Paradise. I carried it for many years, even when I didn't need to because all files were electronic and all equipment was at the hospital. At this point, it's an anachronistic accessory but I still enjoy looking at it.

Beth, thankfully, leaves the door ajar. Evie gets in bed with Beth and they chat with the lights out. Apropos of nothing, Beth says, "Would you like to meet the man I mentioned to you on the phone?" There's a quick intake of breath from Evie's side of the bed. "Yes!"

Beth laughs. "Okay, tomorrow I'll introduce you but I have to warn you, he's nothing like your father."

"That's okay. Maybe better, in fact."

Beth doesn't dispute it or argue it, which is annoying. She says quietly, "It still might be nothing. I don't know. He's just a man I'm drawn to."

"Okay, now I don't know if I can sleep!" says Evie.

"Me, either!" laughs Beth.

"Me, three," but I don't laugh, I pace back and forth, back and forth. Dark hours pass quickly when hatching an evil plot.

CHAPTER 31

Fernanda uses the key under the mat and comes in at about 1:00 a.m. She reads Beth's note and eats the slice of cake. In her white ruffled dress, she looks like a tired child eating at a confectionary counter.

I don't follow her upstairs. I sit in my favorite chair, contemplating all the things I *can* do to The Lug versus all the things I *can't*. As the sun comes up, I think I've devised a plan. It's risky and I have limited tools but battles often come down to the wit of the commanders, not the brute strength of the combatants. In short, Spatula and I will outwit The Lug, buy ourselves time and get to Paris.

When Beth and Evie come downstairs they're still chattering. It's like they never stopped and slept. Beth texts Jessica that Evie surprised her, came home for the weekend from San Francisco and she can't do the tea party today. Maybe Monday? Jessica texts back a sad face. "The girls will be so disappointed."

Beth, who's usually so accommodating, doesn't budge. She texts back, "Sorry! I never see her." She puts her arm around Evie and takes a selfie to prove to Jessica she has her own living, breathing daughter and sends it. I wonder if Jessica will see herself in that picture? There's Beth, aging but beautiful, there's Evie, a young version of Beth but more sporty and robust and there's Jessica, who would fit perfectly in between the two, the missing link, the younger sister, the aunt.

Fernanda comes down dressed in shorts and a tee shirt. Her hair is in a high ponytail and she looks well rested and radiant even though she slept less than Beth and Evie.

Evie squeals and hugs her, which mystifies me. She acts like Fernanda is a long lost sister when, in actuality, they occasionally played as children. It's a typical, over-the-top Evie display. Fernanda smiles and is warm but much more reserved. Evie touches Fernanda's baby bump and tells her what a beautiful mom she'll be. It's just like Evie not to think of the sleepless nights, the dirty diapers and Fernanda's inevitable financial strife. With Evie, it's always the here and now.

Beth invites Fernanda to go to dinner with them that night but Fernanda declines. She says she's hanging out with friends on her last free weekend. Monday she needs to look for a job. "And on that note," she looks at her phone, "my ride's here." I follow her to the back door but once she closes it, I can only see about half way down the driveway. I can't see if there's a red car with smoked windows waiting at the end to take her away from us.

The day and evening are planned and I decide to join them on their walk, even though Saucisson's constant stopping will aggravate me. As we walk down the sidewalk, Saucisson is more distracted by me than by random scents. He keeps turning his head and wagging his tail to see me behind him. Instead of being annoying, it's kind of cute.

There's a disappointing amount of talk about straight leg versus bell-bottom pants. It's so boring I actually feel relieved that I'll be missing tomorrow's drive to the airport. But then Evie says something that catches my attention. Her tone of voice changes from light and airy to cautionary. "Mom, I think you need to be careful when it comes to Fernanda."

Beth says nothing but looks confused and listens.

"Remember when we were young and you took Tyler to play in that baseball tournament and you spent the weekend away? You went with Tyler and Dad stayed with me, I was probably about nine years old."

"Yes," Beth says with some hesitation.

"Well, Dad went into the hospital in the morning and said he'd be home soon."

"Anyway, in the late afternoon, he calls and says there was a big car accident and he has to do emergency surgery. I went and sat on the front stoop with Trixie and started crying. Miguel was working in the yard. He came over and asked me what was wrong."

"Miguel *is* so sweet."

"He is. So we wrote Dad a note and Miguel took me, to his house." They stop and let Saucisson sniff my leg. "Fernanda and I played until Dad called and Miguel brought me home."

"Why didn't you ever tell me this? Your father shouldn't have left you."

"The point isn't Dad! The point is that going to Miguel's house freaked me out." She picks up a piece of litter and tucks it in her pocket. "Miguel's yard had a fence that he closes and locks so no one *steals* his truck. They *locked* their front door when we were eating dinner. I was a kid but I *still remember.* The point is, you live alone; you're the perfect target, Mom. I had to learn these lessons the hard way when I moved to San Francisco. I've gotten ripped off at least three times. Everywhere isn't like here. You need to be more careful. For starters, you can't just keep a key under the mat."

I'm very surprised by Evie – I'm not the only one changing. She's actually giving Beth prudent advice. And Evie doesn't even know about the gun in the glove compartment, fierce Diablo, or the red car with the smoked windows.

I always knew it was my job to protect and provide for Beth, she wasn't meant to make her own way. The night we met, she arrived with the dessert course. She was all sweetness and froth and I ate her up.

When we get back from our walk, I get an unpleasant surprise. Beth looks at her phone and says, "Yep, you'll get to meet him, he has his regular Saturday schedule."

"Do I look okay?" Evie says playfully.

"Do *I* look okay?" Beth asks back.

They look like the perfect mother-daughter team, both wearing blue, toned, trim and brimming with health. It's a look that education, skill and massive workload bought for them. Don't get me wrong, I don't begrudge them in the least. I'm proud of them, I revel in the abundance of health and beauty and I don't plan to share my bounty with anyone, especially not The Lug. I grab Spatula and tuck her under my arm, *locked and loaded.*

We all climb in the car and head to Bon Vivant. In actuality, I don't have a well formulated plan, but I have some *ideas.* All I really know is that The Lug is a physically powerful adversary but I have my superior intelligence. And Spatula.

CHAPTER 32

Beth pulls into the Bon Vivant parking lot and parks in the corner under the oak tree. The Lug isn't there yet. "This is where he parks," she says to Evie, like it's some kind of sacred site.

We all go into Bon Vivant and Evie hangs a basket on her arm. She puts some crackers in and then we make a beeline to prepared foods. Gentle Ben is working the counter as usual. When he sees Beth and Evie he says, "Ah, I see Paradise!" He holds up a big serving spoon like an explorer's staff. "What do you lovely ladies desire today?"

"Give us what's the best," Evie says.

Of course, Gentle Ben reaches for the lobster salad at $45.99/lb., followed by the baby roasted carrots with dill at a more reasonable $9.99/lb. I begrudge My Darling nothing, but it irks me that Evie grew up so oblivious about money and resources, but then I remember her cogent advice to Beth and I am mollified.

Sly Sydney robs us, oh, excuse me, rings us up and in a blink of an eye we're back out to the parking lot. The Lug doesn't disappoint, he's parked in his spot, under the oak, arms crossed, leaning on the hood of his black Town Car.

Evie turns towards Beth and softly says, "Is that him? He's so handsome!"

It's just like Evie to talk in such hyperboles. It's such an utterly ridiculous comment that it pains me to overhear it. His face is so dark in the shade of the oak tree that you can't even see his features, much less his cheap suit and outdated, pointy shoes. He's merely an lug of a man leaning on a black car, no big deal.

He straightens up and takes a few steps toward us.

Beth says, "Friedrich, this is my daughter Evie. She surprised me from San Francisco."

"Enchanté," The Lug says and gives Evie a big smile.

"Ooooh, what a beautiful French accent!"

It's just like Evie to get sucked into this pseudo French accent. If I had anything in my stomach, I'd promptly heave it up, right here, right now, in this parking lot. On his shoes.

"It's French via the Congo," The Lug says and then laughs deeply, like a man playing a king in a Shakespearian play.

There's a lot of talk, all spearheaded by Evie, about "beautiful spring weather," "possibilities," "eggs" and "coincidences".

"The coincidence" of The Lug helping Beth when she fell. "The coincidence" of The Lug taking an egg. "The coincidence" of them always running into each other in the parking lot.

It's all such bullshit. "Coincidence" is no part of this equation. This has all been carefully choreographed. It seems that Beth is the aggressor in this slo-mo chase, but I am not ready to admit that. If I can get rid of The Lug, I'm sure things between Beth and me will fall back into place.

While he lifts his shirt and shows Evie his thick waist with a preposterously tiny hatching belt strapped around it, I check out his Town Car. The backseat is wide open and the passenger seat only has his phone and sunglasses on it. When he opens his door, I should have no problem jumping in. It's sad to think I won't be able to spend any more time with Evie, but she leaves tomorrow and, quite frankly, she's managed to aggravate me even as a ghost.

I have no idea where The Lug is going and how my imminent attack on him could pose a terminal threat to me and my existence. There are so many scenarios running through my head that I can't even begin to plot solutions. For instance, if Spatula manages to pull the steering wheel while he's driving and we kill him, will I be trapped forever in the car, like a genie in a bottle? That's just one horror I've been running through my head. I have a lot of improvising ahead of me but it's not so different from opening a body cavity. You never really know what you'll find and you must make life or death decisions as they come.

So when The Lug looks at his watch and says he has to go, I whisper in Beth's ear, "I love you, My Darling, I always have and always will. I will try to make it back to your side, at all cost. Please wait for me. I promise I can do better."

I'm quite sure Beth hears me on some level, because she takes her hand and waves it by her ear like she heard a buzzing insect. I wave goodbye to Evie and with trusty Spatula under my arm, I jump into the passenger seat when The Lug opens his door.

His window is open and he calls, "*Au revoir!*"

I look directly at him, from the passenger seat and mimic back, "*Au revoir!*" Only I say it with a Parisian accent and my tone is dripping with sarcasm. I say, "*Au contraire*, you won't be back."

I am trying to get Spatula near the steering wheel but we barely get going, maybe ¼ of a mile, when we pull up in front of Mademoiselle Mimi's Ballet School. This ballet school is a town institution. When Evie went through the little girl ballet stage, she took lessons here. Mademoiselle Mimi looked about 80 years old back then, I can't imagine how she's still around running *her* ballet institution and yet *my* surgical legend has faded away. I also can't imagine what circumstance brings The Lug to be parked out front of a Mademoiselle Mimi's.

We sit and wait, him patiently, me impatiently.

At 12:05, the door opens and a herd of charming, wispy girls and one boy emerge, making a wave of pink chiffon. One reed detaches herself from the group and runs to our car. She's maybe ten or eleven years old. She's that age when girls are all vertical, with long coltish legs. The thought of burdening them with hips and breasts seems cruel.

I'm about to scramble into the back seat when The Lug opens his door, jumps out. He looks like a bear but moves like a gazelle. He opens the back door with a flourish and says, "*Ma petite chou.*"

"*Merci*," The Reed says and jumps into the back seat.

If we were kidnappers, we couldn't ask for a more cooperative or polite victim. The Lug closes the back door, gets back behind the wheel, and looks in the rear view mirror. I begrudgingly admit he is checking that The Reed has her seatbelt secured before moving the car.

The Lug drives with meticulous precision through town, no rolling stops, no lane changes without signaling, hands positioned at 10 and 2 o'clock. I try to find fault in his technique but I'm at a loss. We drive only about a mile or so when we turn off the main road and wind down a drive called Breezy Point. On one side, you can see water, an inlet, and on the other side are old gracious homes up on the hill. We make a right and drive up the hill to a big white clapboard house. It's a little bit like my house except it's tall, with five chimneys. My house hugs the ground, has a front porch and only three chimneys.

He pulls up, stops, gets out, opens the door for The Reed and she jumps out, waves and runs into the house. The Lug glances at his phone and leans on the hood of the car with its back door still open. I'm not sure if I should join him or stay put. I stay put.

After about 10 minutes, the front door opens, a woman waves and a young boy lopes toward us. He is about the same size as the girl, also like a reed, with none of the bulk or coarseness of a man. He's in full baseball gear: red jersey, hat on, baseball glove on left hand, cleats clicking on the driveway. He reminds me a bit of Tyler when he thought he wanted to be a baseball player. He has a goofy smile.

The Lug high-fives The Boy. The Boy jumps into the back seat. We meticulously drive The Boy to the town baseball fields behind town hall. When we get there, The Boy opens his own door and starts jogging to join his team, a cluster of red.

The Lug opens his door, planning to join the other parents on the bleachers although, clearly, he's not The Boy's parent. Admittedly, I'm not a baseball fan and never will be, but I'd rather sit on the bleachers than be resigned to sit in the car like some misbehaved lap dog. I get ready to get out but The Lug is quick and he slams his door closed, almost catching the back of his suit jacket. The window, or shall I say the door of opportunity, has closed and I'm stuck, the misbehaved lap dog.

From inside the car, I watch The Lug on the bleachers. He cheers and claps like the other parents and occasionally checks his phone, just like the other parents. At one point, he peers at his phone, jogs over to the car, leaving The Boy with his team, gets in the car and off we go. Once again, we don't drive far, to a beautiful little street called Old Creek. We pull up in front of a two-story stone colonial as a teenage girl runs out. She passed the fleeting stage of The Reed's perfectionism. Her adolescent features might come together with maturity but right now, she is self-consciously awkward.

"Madame," The Lug says with a flourish, holding open the back door.

"Thanks," says The Teen, not deigning to play the French game.

I applaud her ability to deflect The Lug's airs of exaggerated French manners. Good for her, she could teach Beth and Evie a thing or two about being gullible.

We drive The Teen back to main street. She's texting the entire time. Without looking up, she says one word, "Joey's".

We drive down main street and The Lug stops in front of Joey's, a store I've never heard of it or knew it existed. A whole gaggle of teen girls is outside and our teen jumps out to join them. Before she slams her door, she says, "Thanks, Friedrich. I don't need a ride home."

He and I drive back to the baseball fields and this time I am ready for The Lug's quick exit. We sit side-by-side on the bleachers and cheer for The Boy when he hits a double. When the game is over, I have to admit it wasn't as dull as I thought it would be. Walking back to the car, The Lug lays his arm across The Boy's shoulder and says, "You did well." It's a simple statement but The Boy looks up at The Lug and smiles. It's a smile to melt any father's heart.

We carefully drive The Boy back to his house on Breezy Point. His mother and sister come out and greet him and all three wave good-bye to The Lug and me. We wave back as The Lug carefully backs down the driveway and heads to the main road. I have no idea where we're going, or how I'll vanquish The Lug or when I'll get back home again to My Darling. I just know this afternoon did not go the way I anticipated and the evil task still lies before me. It doesn't matter that I'm emotionally drained and already feel I've put in a full day.

Off we go, north, well within the speed limit of 35 mph.

CHAPTER 33

We are heading north for only a few minutes when The Lug's phone dings. Being a rule follower, he pulls over, reads the text and we turn around, back to town. We drive directly to Bon Vivant. Is he meeting Beth for a second rendez-vous? The adrenaline jolt helps awaken my sense of purpose.

But Beth's car isn't under the oak tree, we're alone. I'm torn; if he goes into Bon Vivant, should I go with him and see what he buys? Or should I give up my plan for the day and just get out and walk home? Quite frankly, my resolve is flagging and I feel a little carsick. I'm contemplating the pros and cons of each option when my decision is made for me. The Lug jumps out of the car with unusual agility and slams the door. Now I'm stuck. I can't go *in* and spy and can't get *out* and walk home.

Ten minutes pass and The Lug comes out holding a large Bon Vivant bag. I have only needed a large bag twice and it was when Beth sent me to pick up food for Tyler's graduation party and then again three years later for Evie's graduation party. A large Bon Vivant bag is equivalent in status to a women's luxury purse. I know these delicacies can't be for The Lug himself. He's clearly driving this Town Car for a service catering to the tippy-top of the elite.

He puts the Bon Vivant bag on my lap, the bottom is a little warm and a delicious smell wafts through the top. I sigh. Off we go. Again we head north but this time we drive up Woodhill, right by my house. I yearn to tap him on the shoulder with Spatula and ask to get out at my driveway, *"S'il vous plaît."* He drives well within the speed limit and does a quick glance at my gentleman's farm as we pass. I'm

179

wishing I were home and, much to my delight, we make two turns and head up Round House Road. I'm excited. Not only do I love the road and the real estate but I'm hoping we drive by Jessica's house and I can catch a glimpse of her and the children. I picture them standing at the bottom of their driveway, waving to me as I pass by, like I'm some sort of important personage. Not realistic, I know, but I am expectant, nonetheless.

We're still at least a mile away from Jessica's when The Lug starts to slow down and turn on his left signal. The Lug could be a driver's ed teacher, there's no one coming toward us, there's no one behind us. I am so preoccupied with my scorn for his unflagging, law-abiding driving that I don't initially recognize the gate we pull up to.

We've arrived at Gunther Schlitz Jr.'s house, *The* Gunther-Schlitz-Who-Shits-Money.

The gate opens, revealing a massive piece of heartless architecture. It is three stories, with large columns that make it resemble a moderate sized museum. The driveway is not like the Klines', which needlessly curves and detours the driver for the tasteful surprise at the end. This driveway is a bee line, a plumb line, a straight incision. The whole set up screams, "I'm Gunther Schlitz, I shit money!"

The Lug drives straight up the driveway (where else could he go) and pulls in front of a four car garage. He hits a button, the first door rises and The Lug pulls in. Inside the garage, the concrete floor looks as clean as an OR floor. A few tools are hung on the wall like surgical instruments on a tray, there's nothing superfluous.

Once again, The Lug moves quickly. He gets out and slams the door and for a moment I think I'm trapped but then he walks around to the passenger side and opens my door. He lifts the heavy Bon Vivant bag off my lap, supports its bottom with his left hand and I am able to get out. It's kind of nice, almost like he's opening the door for me.

He closes the door and I follow him very closely, with Spatula tucked under my arm. I now know how The Lug moves and I'll have to stay on my toes. We walk briskly to a door that goes into the house, he opens it (no key needed) and we move in tandem through a very large mudroom, past a laundry room with two washers and two dryers and a small woman ironing.

"*Hola*," The Lug says.

"*Hola*," she says but doesn't look up.

We arrive in a white marble kitchen. The kitchen is cavernous, there's no better word. It has a huge island in the center with no less than eight stools, chrome, black leather, pure Italian. The counter is immaculate except for a beautiful espresso maker, which I'm sure is also Italian. There's a 9-burner stove, three ovens and a Sub-Zero that looks like a chrome wall. You could easily cook and plate for 50 people in this space. It's a chef's dream but it's under-utilized, unemployed, unloved.

The Lug puts the bag on the counter, turns on his heel and we travel back the way we came. It's a sudden reversal and I have to remind myself not to get distracted. He hangs the car keys on a little panel by the door that goes into the garage. Each hook on the panel has a little label with its own set of keys.

We walk back through the garage, past the four parked cars: the black Town Car, a Silver Cadillac Escalade, a white Corvette, and the last bay has an old, beat up Fiat. In the far corner, there's a set of wooden steps. The Lug bounds up these steps and I hurry after him. At the top, he opens the door (no key) to an apartment above the garage.

The apartment is simple and very neat. We walk directly into the kitchen, just like at Miguel's. Just like in Gunther Schlitz's kitchen, there doesn't appear to be one extra item anywhere, except an old Mr. Coffee maker on the counter.

The Lug sighs and suddenly looks weary, just like I used to after a long day in the OR. He hangs his suit jacket on the back of a wooden kitchen chair, untucks his collared shirt and checks his hatching belt. He opens a small white fridge, takes out a can of seltzer. The pull tab makes a satisfying hiss and he takes a long swallow.

I haven't formulated a plan and I'm staying very close. I was hoping to do my mischief while in the car but I imagine if I had tried to obscure his vision, he would have had the presence of mind to turn on his hazard lights before easing to the shoulder and coming to a complete stop. I'm thinking I'll need to do whatever I do while he's sleeping.

We walk into the living room and I'm deep in thought when, suddenly, I notice two figures sitting on the sofa. Children. A boy and a girl. They are small and spindly, maybe they are eight years old or nine. The boy is in a collared shirt and shorts, the girl wears a jumper. School uniforms. They both wear flip-flops.

They look up, startled. Their eyes widen and they press against each other, actually frightened. I feel so sorry for them and want to comfort them by saying, "It's okay, you can't see me but I'm here. I won't hurt you, I'm here for The Lug. Whatever trouble you're in, why ever you're here, I'm here to help you."

The Lug sits down in a well-worn armchair. He never even glances at the huddled children. He's as oblivious to their fright and misery as any cold-hearted stranger could be. But then I realize their eyes are on *me*, not him. They're frightened of *me*? Dr. Tom Paradise, Surgeon Extraordinaire, Saver of Lives.

They see me and I see them but The Lug sees nothing. The Lug has proven an even more wily opponent than I expected. The Lug has his own secret: ghost children.

CHAPTER 34

The Lug turns on soccer. I stand behind him and the children watch me; their fear is palatable, which I find absurd. I don't know how to reassure them, so I don't.

The Lug is an enigma, there are no two ways about it. He came into my life completely uninvited and I don't understand what brought him here, to Gunther Schlitz's house or why our lives should bisect. He looks like he's going to stay in his chair for a while with his eyes glued to the TV. He's obviously tired and content with the drone of the soccer game.

So I begin poking around. I start with the bathroom. There's nothing to see, a cup with a toothbrush and a tube of toothpaste. There's no women's cosmetics, no telling pill bottles.

I move to the bedroom. It's like I imagine a Franciscan monk's room: a twin bed with a wooden frame and a faded plaid comforter, one wooden chair and a dresser. It's all cheap pine, like you'd buy at some furniture warehouse. There's a pair of folded pajamas on the chair. Three framed images, sitting on the dresser, are the only items of interest.

The smallest frame holds a faded photograph of a tall couple with a boy standing between them. They each have a hand on the boy's shoulder and he is holding up a certificate of some sort. The couple and the boy are beaming proudly.

The second photo is clearly the two ghost children, huddled on the sofa, with The Lug standing beside a tall woman in an elegant orange headwrap. The children wear their school uniforms, the same ones they still have on.

My eyes travel to the third frame. It's the most informative and I wish I could pick it up and really examine it. It's a certificate: *Université de Kinshasa* in an arc across the top. Below it says: *Friedrich Ngoy*. There's some small type I can't read and the next line says: *Obstetrics & Gynecology*. The year is 1996. There's a gold seal and some signatures. I realize it's a standard medical diploma!

This explains a lot. First of all, I calculate The Lug's age – he's about 50, so ten years younger than Beth. Second, surprisingly, I know exactly where Kinshasa is, it's the capital of the Democratic Republic of the Congo. I know this obscure fact because my hospital sent a team to Kinshasa as part of Doctors' Without Borders. I had a colleague, Dr. Patricia Musa, who was a pain in the ass do-gooder. I don't recall which African country she was from but she went to Pierce, president of the hospital, and insisted we assemble a team of professionals to help in the aftermath of the Congolese War. She, herself, planned on going, I believe she was in pediatrics. She fundraised to help pay for the mission.

When I explained to Beth that I needed to find a volunteer from the cardiology department to go to Kinshasa for three months, Beth became deeply interested in this brutal war that was hardly acknowledged by the Western press. I remember she told me there were six million fatalities, which is shocking, considering I never heard of it. Beth thought *I* should be the one to go, chief of thoracic surgery, but I sent a new doctor, Charlie Thayer, who actually runs the department now.

When our hospital team came back, they were lauded as saviors. They showed horrific pictures of the war's toll, life-altering wounds and botched repairs. It only confirmed my decision *not* to go. I told Beth, "I'm glad I didn't go. I would've been forced to do a subpar job under primitive conditions." Then I added one of my favorite adages: "If you can't do a job well, you shouldn't do it at all."

Beth disagreed.

These images and their clues lead me to conclude that the children sitting in the family room could be victims of this war declared over about 17 years ago. They're trapped in time, like a beetle in amber, forever on their way to school. Death is the true cleaver, when a child is ripped from a parent, a husband from a wife. Yet, somehow, it seems My Darling has managed to blur that divide and I live on. It seems The Lug has also blurred the divide, but is not even aware of it.

Where is his wife, their mother? How did he dodge the fate of his family? And lastly, why is a Congolese OBGYN living in Gunther-Schlitz-Who-Shits-Money garage and driving his cars?

Life is strange, no doubt about it but, perhaps death is stranger. I say this because here I am, a ghost, above Gunther-Schlitz-Who-Shits-Money garage with Congolese ghost children and The Lug – my sworn enemy – whom I plan to kill. We *all* find ourselves together under one roof, the roof of the man who killed me, be it indirectly.

I go back to the family room. The children are good children and sitting right where I left them. The Lug has one hand on his hatching belt and is snoring. The two sets of frightened eyes watch me as I walk up to The Lug in his chair. I turn my head and watch their reaction as I gently place my ear against The Lug's chest. I listen and hear such a loud, clear heartbeat that I almost jerk back. The Lug, as I was beginning to suspect, has a tremendous heart.

This begins a long night. As I've mentioned, ghosts don't sleep but we pass the time. Every once in a while, the boy and the girl whisper but otherwise they don't move. They're the definition of "sit tight". I perch on the corner of The Lug's footstool, fidget and occasionally pace around through the apartment. But the space is small and bare, without even steps to climb up and down. There's nothing to *do*. The two children never take their eyes off me.

As the morning light starts to come in, I realize they no longer look frightened. Time has proven me to be a harmless curiosity. When it dawns on me that their fear has passed and my boredom has become unbearable, I do something that I've never done in my life, not even with my own children...

I act silly.

I take out versatile Spatula (good for almost all occasions!) who has grown hot and moist tucked under my armpit. I pantomime stirring cake batter and then I lick her moist rubber end and rub my stomach. They smile. Success! I decide to try flipping her in the air and catch her again by the wooden handle. They look at each other and giggle. I balance her on the tip of my finger while looking really worried. The boy and girl are laughing and swinging their legs. I'm amazed at how many clever and funny things I can do with Spatula. It's like we're Siegfried and Roy, a well-oiled performing team. For my grand finale, I'm embarrassed to report, I stick my rear out and pretend to wipe it with Spatula. It's such a roaring success that I bring Spatula to my nose and pretend to smell her. (Forgive me, Spatula.) The little boy tips over on the sofa; he's laughing so hard. They appear so much happier than when I found them and so am I. I'm actually enjoying myself.

The Lug grunts and wakes up, startling the three of us. Spatula goes under my arm and fun and games are over. It's Sunday morning and I have no idea where or when The Lug will drive but I need to be ready to leave. He brushes his teeth, showers and eats some cereal. Instead of putting on a collared shirt, he puts on a worn tee that has a UPenn logo on it. I think Gunther Schlitz went to UPenn.

I almost get left behind when he doesn't stop to put on shoes but walks out of the apartment with bare feet. I look behind me when I realize we're actually leaving. The boy and the girl have followed The Lug and me to the door. While The Lug's back is turned, Spatula and I wave goodbye.

Very quietly, the little girl says, "*Au revoir*" and the little boy sadly says, "Goodbye, mister."

CHAPTER 35

I follow The Lug past the three shiny cars and old Fiat, to the unlocked door to Gunther Schlitz's mudroom. I'm right behind him when he snags a set of keys off the panel of hooks and spins back around. We almost collide. We go back out to the garage and he hits a button to open the first garage bay. When he gets into the Town Car, he does it so quickly, I'm left standing flat footed in the garage. But The Lug only backs the car out a short distance, then he gets out again and begins filling a bucket from a tap. Sunday morning, or at least this Sunday morning, is car-wash morning.

I think about Beth and Evie at home. I'm sure at some point this morning they'll call and FaceTime with Tyler. They'll laugh and put their faces together so he can see the perfect mother-daughter mirror images. There will be talk of all of them getting together, an idea I'm warming up to. Post living in Paris, who's to say Thailand shouldn't be next?

I thought I was irritated by the endless mother/daughter chatter and resigned to not spending more time with Evie on this visit, but now I long to be included in the drive to the airport. I want to cherish those last minutes, like any good parent. So, while The Lug is sudsing the car, I decide it's a good time to walk down the straight, charmless driveway to the gate. I wave Spatula in front of the electronic eye, not knowing what will happen and if the gate gets locked each night or if it's ever locked on this side. Spatula doesn't disappoint, the gate rolls opens.

The Lug stops his washing and looks down the driveway, expecting someone to drive in. No one drives in, only a ghost walks out.

I know this walk, I know I can do it, I know it will take 60 to 80 minutes. It's a warm late spring, almost summer morning and my heart should be light but it isn't. I am filled with a sense of failure. I completely flopped at what I set out to do: destroy The Lug. Furthermore, I'm not sure if it's possible, or if my heart is in it. After listening to The Lug's heart, I know he's incredibly strong and the thought of ghost children with no parents is... unsettling. Moreover, I had the perfect opportunity to put my Duolingo skills to use.

I should have tried communicating with the children during the night. I should have known that French is one of the languages they speak in the Congo, a remnant of colonization. It could have been so pleasant and productive to practice. I'm annoyed at myself. I could have done so much more to communicate and I didn't.

However, these two failures hatched a larger possibility. I now have the means and knowledge to right the greater wrongs done to me. When I look past my immediate failure and shortcomings, I see that I have gained access to my true archenemy. If I just step back, cool down, and examine the situation objectively, I know that The Lug is not directly trying to harm me. His actions might very well harm me but his intent is not malicious.

On the other hand, my actions to save Schlitz Sr. were never meant to be harmful, they were just a series of unfortunate events, but Gunther Schlitz Jr. came after me professionally *and* personally with malicious vengeance. He embodied spite and vicious intent, which one could say killed me. That December, if I'd been working as a surgeon, which was the intention (I had no plans of retiring), I would never have been shoveling snow... not in a million years. I would have been at the hospital, or sleeping, or getting ready to go into the hospital. I wouldn't have had a catastrophic heart attack.

Perhaps this venture was not a waste of time. Perhaps it was part of a necessary odyssey and the best thing that could have happened to me. All our paths are not as straight and vulgar as Schlitz's driveway. I now know where Gunther-Schlitz-Who-Shits-Money lives, how to broach his gate and the unlocked access point into his house. I've only seen Gunther Schlitz once or twice but I've seen many pictures of him. He's not a virile type like The Lug. If I recall he's short with a gray complexion. He's most likely more killable than The Lug and he's definitely less likeable.

These are my thoughts as I walk home on this late spring morning.

I haven't even crossed the street to walk up our driveway when I notice the red car with smoked windows parked near our garage. The brilliant red is like an open, bloody wound against the white clapboard of our house. I panic and I start to jog up the driveway. I'm alarmed at the thought of Beth, Evie and Fernanda in the house with The Slugger, who vaulted Miguel's fence, knocked Diablo in the head and then smashed the truck window, almost hitting me in the face.

The front door is closed, the garage door is closed, the side door is closed, I can't turn the knobs to see if they're locked. (Spatula can only do so much.) I jog to the back of the house and, thankfully, the French doors are open. Saucisson is sniffing around when I round the corner. He looks at me and wags his tail.

I go in the French doors, preparing myself for the worst case scenario but am met by lovely Fernanda humming happily at the counter, making two plates of food. I don't see Beth or Evie and don't know if they're home. I also don't see the handsome guy, The Slugger, the driver of the red car. I run upstairs to the master bedroom and go into my dressing room. Evie's bag and small pile of clothes are gone so I can assume that she and Beth are on the way to the airport. Knowing they're not in the house is an instant relief but also disappointing. Despite my best efforts and hurried walking, I missed my chance to go with them. I start to relax, coming off my cortisol high, when I hear drawers closing from across the narrow hall in Beth's dressing room. I walk over to investigate.

There, standing at Beth's built-in drawers, is the young man from Miguel's, The Slugger. He's wearing jeans and a tee shirt with a Pacifico Beer logo. He's going down the line, systematically opening and closing Beth's drawers. I can see he's five drawers away from Beth's jewelry drawer. I've begged Beth to hide her jewelry but she always said it was meant to be worn and enjoyed. If she tucked it away, she'd never find a reason to pull it out. I really shouldn't care that much, it's all insured, but for lack of a better word, I believe we're about to be *robbed.*

The Slugger is in the process of *robbing* us. There's really no other explanation and there's nothing I can do but *witness a robbery in progress.*

I watch as he opens and looks in the next row of drawers. The first drawer has Beth's velvet jewelry tray with little indents to hold rings, earrings and necklaces. I watch him open it and start picking up one piece of jewelry at a time. He picks up her delicate evening watch, which has diamonds around the face. He looks closely and slips it into his front jean's pocket. Then he picks up a ring, it's a band of sapphires. I'm particularly fond of this ring because it matches Beth's eyes and I bought it for her after the birth of Tyler. It's a memento and I'm helpless as The Slugger assesses it and adds it to his pocket.

Suddenly, I have a moment of pure inspiration. I remember that we have an alarm. We never use it but it's installed and monitored as a prerequisite of our homeowner's insurance. There are three key pads, one by the front door, one by the door in the mudroom and one in our bedroom. I know if I hit * and # simultaneously a panic alarm signal will be transmitted directly to the police station. We've never used it but occasionally I'd remind Beth of the feature.

I hurry to the bedroom and look at the alarm keypad. In order to hit both the buttons at once, I need two objects but all I have is one Spatula. Once again, in a moment of genius (and regret), I break Spatula's handle in two. It breaks where Trixie or one of the children chewed, about a third of the way down. With the two wood pieces in hand, I'm able to hit the two buttons simultaneously.

Nothing happens.

But nothing *should* happen. I remember it's a silent panic alarm and yet I have my doubts. I walk back to Beth's dressing room to keep witnessing the robbery. I see another piece of jewelry added to the jean pocket. Suddenly The Slugger stops. He cocks his head, hearing the siren before I do. He stands completely still. As it gets louder and louder, he pulls the four pieces of jewelry out of his pocket.

When it's clear that the police car with the siren howling is pulling into our driveway, he tosses the jewelry back in the drawer and slams it shut. As he rushes past me, he's so close that I smell his spearmint gum. I fumble Spatula and the new broken piece falls onto the floor. There's no time to pick it up as I hurry downstairs after him. He positions himself innocently beside Fernanda when the police pound on the door.

Fernanda answers. She's obviously flustered and has no idea why these policemen have come to the door with their sirens blaring. They ask her if she's okay. They look her directly in the eyes. Her tee shirt is pulled tightly over her small pregnant belly, The Slugger is standing behind her at her right shoulder. Fernanda would be the perfect victim in a Mexican telenovela for these men in blue to save.

She swears to them that she's fine, that she's staying at the Paradise House, and that she has no idea why or how the alarm went off. One of the policemen walks back to the car and makes a call. The other policeman talks affably with Fernanda while keeping an eye on the handsome young man. His partner comes back and says, "It checks out. She's a guest." They give her one long look (blink twice if he's threatening you) but she just smiles.

As she closes the door, her cell phone rings. It is Evie, calling on Beth's phone, because Beth is driving in heavy traffic, asking if Fernanda is all right. She assures Evie everything is fine, say thanks for calling, good-bye, and turns to The Slugger. "Dmitri, what did you do?"

"Nothing, I didn't do anything!"

"What were you doing upstairs?"

"I was looking for a bathroom."

"There are two down here. You don't need to go upstairs."

"I'll remember that next time." He gives her a brilliant smile and kisses her.

Fernanda, her curiosity and suspicions satisfied, says, "Okay, let's eat." After they eat two plates of expensive Bon Vivant food, she looks at the clock and says he better leave.

He gives her a casual kiss and tells her he'll pick her up tomorrow. He even bends down and kisses her cute pregnant belly.

My Darling comes home a full hour later. The drive was brutal, even on a Sunday. She looks weary and sad, most likely because Evie's gone and suddenly the house lacks vitality. She says she's glad Fernanda is okay, she was worried when the police called. Fernanda says she didn't even realize there was an alarm and that she wouldn't know how to sound the panic function even if she needed to. Beth says it's an old system and that we probably need a new one.

But I don't think Beth is completely dismissing the alarm and letting it slip from her consciousness. I see her glance in the sink but Fernanda has tucked the two dishes in the dishwasher. I see her open the fridge and ask if Fernanda has eaten. It's total speculation on my part but I am hoping that Beth is doing a little recognizance. I'm thinking she listened to Evie's sage advice just like on some level she listens to me whisper in her ear.

Fernanda tells Beth that tomorrow she's beginning job hunting, she's looking for a summer job before school starts and the baby comes. Then she plops down on the sofa and starts texting, like any lazy teenager.

Beth goes upstairs and Saucisson and I faithfully follow her. When she walks into our bedroom, she spies the bit of wooden spatula handle on the floor below the alarm pad on the wall. I completely forgot to go back upstairs and pick it up. She bends down and looks closely at it. She also looks at the alarm pad but there's nothing to see.

She holds the piece in her hand and walks into my dressing room. My medical bag sits like a lovely relic on the counter. Beth has given away probably three-fourths of my clothing but my favorites hang neatly waiting for my return. Stick-Your-Nose-In-Everyone's-Business-Sandy said it was better to leave some articles "for staging" and Beth thoughtfully left all my favorites. She scans the room and sees nothing out of place. Then she walks into her dressing room, looks around, doesn't notice anything out of place and puts the piece of Spatula down on her dresser.

I'm wondering if I should come and claim it during the night. Is it too strange if it just disappears? It's proven useful and might in the future. I'm contemplating my choices when Beth turns, opens her top drawer, her jewelry drawer, and slides the wooden remnant in. Now the decision is made for me. The 1/3 of Spatula's wooden handle, so crudely amputated, might as well be buried six feet underground.

CHAPTER 36

What used to be my favorite day, Monday, is dreary. There's nothing to get my adrenaline flowing, nothing to make me feel alive. I feel like the weather or the weather feels like me, I'm not sure which. Misty and noncommittal.

"Today is not a good day for the tea party," Jessica texts early.

"I agree, the weather :(" Beth texts.

"Margaret doesn't feel well either."

"Can I help?"

But there's no answer. Whatever is happening at 530 Round House is either private, too mundane, or too painful to share. Part of me feels like I should walk up there and see if I can help, an extra set of hands. It looks like nothing is happening here today. If I leave now, I can be up at Jessica's by 10:30. As long as the gate is not locked, the ¾ spatula will most likely work. The problem is entering the house. With no puppy constantly going in and out, there's no guarantee when or which door or even *if* Jessica will open a door. I could make the walk and end up locked outside all day and all night. That's not very appealing, not to mention demeaning.

Then I imagine, if I got stuck outside Jessica's, with no door opening or closing, I could turn around and walk to Gunther-Schlitz-Who-Shits-Money house. I know I could get in the gate but I need Friedrich to drive in or out of the garage.

I'd also love to "pop in" and see his ghost children again. I have a couple simple things I'm ready to say, "*Je m'apelle* Tom. *Je suis un docteur.*" I feel like we were just getting comfortable with each other when I had to go. I'd also love to get into Gunther Schlitz's house, this time getting past his kitchen, polished and soulless. I'd like to visit his inner sanctum, where he shits his money. A man like Gunther Schlitz has secrets, no doubt about it. I need to find those secrets to destroy him.

But today may not be the day. Today feels like a stay-at-home day.

Fernanda comes down. She's wearing an untucked yellow blouse with jeans and looks fresh and at odds with the monotone day. The blouse hides her pregnancy so she just looks glowing and well-fed. Beth asks her if she needs a ride anywhere but she says she's going job hunting with "a friend". I'm suspicious but Beth doesn't show any reaction. If this was Evie or Tyler, she'd definitely advise against showing up with a friend to fill out job applications. I think Fernanda is going to look for a waitress or hostess job to get her through the summer.

She glances at her phone and jumps up. "My friend is here." I follow her to the door and see the red car. The Slugger is waiting; just as I had figured.

So it's just Beth, Saucisson and me on this overcast, hazy, drizzly Monday. I can't drink coffee to spike my emotions, I can't save anyone's life and I can't even do Duolingo without Beth's help. *Frustrated* is the word that comes to mind.

But then Beth jumps up and pulls out an old beloved cookbook, *The Joy of Cooking*. She turns to a dirty, dog-eared page that has the recipe for Four Layer Coconut Cake. Beth would always make this cake for family birthdays and special occasions; it was my absolute favorite. She's had no occasion to make it since I died.

Like a scientist, she checks her supplies. We have unsweetened and sweetened coconut, coconut milk, and plenty of eggs. She takes out measuring cups and measuring spoons. I absolutely delight in the precision of the portioning and the fact such simple ingredients can be orchestrated into such an impressive dessert. I wonder if she's thinking of me while she makes it; I don't see how she couldn't. I certainly think of me, all my birthdays and the accomplishments that called for the cake.

The cake is time consuming. She has to use our layer cake pans through two bake cycles, let all four layers cool, shape them and whip egg whites into a glossy meringue before she can construct the cake on its pedestal. When it's done, the cake stands tall, like a fancy woman in high heels. It's a work of art but I can't figure out who will be the recipient of this extravaganza.

Later in the day, Beth texts Fernanda, "How's the job hunt?" She texts back, "Good." I'm skeptical. Beth eats dinner alone and we do our Duolingo, which is nice. I learn the verb "to like" – *aimer* – which might come in handy when I communicate with The Lug's ghost children.

When we go up to bed, the cake is still standing tall on the counter and Beth lets Saucisson follow us up the stairs. He's proven very dependable and can now easily make it through the night without any accidents. He's not Trixie, but he's turning out to be a decent dog. After Beth changes into her pajamas, she opens her jewelry drawer, pauses and slips her wedding ring off, dropping it into an indent. Instead of closing the drawer, she stares, surveying its little compartments. She carefully picks up each piece of jewelry, examining it. She starts with the sapphire ring.

I'm deeply satisfied that she's discovering first hand there's something amiss, but deeply disturbed that her wedding ring is being put to rest, so to speak. No doubt, she needs to understand her vulnerabilities but that starts with wearing her wedding ring. People should know there is a man of the house. She carefully arranges each piece in its proper indent, leaving Spatula's 1/3 handle to nestle with her marital band.

I hear the door open and close downstairs. Beth gets a text, "Home!" She gently closes the jewelry drawer and I think she's going to go downstairs and confront Fernanda about the jewelry being moved. It's important that she understands the subplot going on under her own roof. Maybe, if she confronts Fernanda, Fernanda will realize just how bad her *novio* really is. Fernanda doesn't know her *novio* was pilfering Beth's jewelry when the alarm so mysteriously went off. I'm not even sure she knows about the assault of Diablo and the smashed pickup window.

I rush out of the bedroom and wait on the stairs, but Beth and Saucisson don't follow. Beth very quietly closes our bedroom door and I hear the lock click into place. Locked out, I go downstairs to check on Fernanda. She's staring at the cake, it looks so beautiful and perfect. She opens the silverware drawer and takes out a teaspoon. She gently runs the curved side against the waves of frosting and licks the spoon. Her lips are full and sensual, her tongue is pink and when the tip hits the meringue, she closes her eyes in pleasure.

Then she goes upstairs.

I'm left downstairs with no one, nothing, just my own devices. I can't help myself, this is my favorite cake and it's completely accessible. I get my ⅔ Spatula from under the chair cushion and gently touch the brittle, rubber end across the top of the cake. I don't think I'll be able to taste it, but I just want to try. I'm about to touch the end to my tongue when Fernanda rushes down the stairs to the back door. I leave Spatula on the counter and go to see what's happening. She's anxiously or eagerly looking out the back door window while texting. She's a very fast texter but I see her text, "NO! Not now!" We both stand and peer into the darkness for a few minutes.

When it seems as though no one's coming, Fernanda walks back to the kitchen. Her spoon and Spatula with a bit of frosting on the tip are lying, side by side, on the counter. Fernanda takes the back of the spoon and smooths the frosting wave where Spatula and I touched and she licks it. Then she promptly takes both utensils, runs them under hot water and dries them. She opens the silverware drawer and puts the teaspoon back. Then she turns and surveys the options of which drawer the spatula should live in. She opens the warming drawer *again* by mistake.

I haven't thought of the warming drawer for over two weeks and I'm sure Beth hasn't since she put the leftover egg in it, that had no hatching belt and no one to wear it. The egg is nestled in the pink dish towel, right where Fernanda left it. Fernanda looks at the egg and then again lays it against her cheek. I'm sure it's warm, it's got to be, it's in the warming drawer.

I'm trying to imagine its weight and heft in her hand. Has the embryo grown to comfortably fill the egg with its head positioned at the larger end? Or is inside the egg a slimy putrid slur? Fernanda seems to enjoy its smooth warmth and to be deep in thought. She then lays it back in its pink towel and carefully closes the drawer. Instead of continuing her search for the utensil drawer, she calls it quits and simply puts beloved Spatula in the silverware drawer where she doesn't even belong.

Monday is becoming my least favorite day.

CHAPTER 37

I pass the night completely and utterly alone. I can't lie on the bed next to My Darling, I can't listen to Saucisson snore (which can be amusing) and I can't sit in my favorite chair with the satisfaction of knowing that Spatula is directly under me, ready for action. I sit, wander, and stare at the silverware drawer. For the first time I think about all those cliché ghosts depicted wandering and moaning through the hallways dragging their chains. Even dragging a chain would be better than nothing right now.

When Beth comes down in the morning, she and Saucisson look happy and well rested. I try not to feel resentful but the fact is that I feel underappreciated in my own home. Beth makes coffee and we sit outside while Saucisson sniffs around, trying to decide where he's going to defecate. The resentment dissipates and I start to feel less angry and more in sync with the bright dewy morning and My Darling.

"Ding!" I stand behind her and read the message from Jessica, "Today works for us! Noon?" Beth gives her a thumbs-up emoji. (Ahhhh, the coconut cake was in anticipation of the tea party!) So we're set, noon, Jessica's, 530 Round House Road, Tea Party. I'm not sure I'm a tea party type of guy or that it's something I'm capable of enjoying but I definitely enjoy knowing the schedule for the day and what to expect. I'm tired of surprises.

Later in the morning Fernanda comes down. She isn't very talkative and takes a cup of coffee back up to Evie's room. Beth asks her how the job hunt went and she's vague, actually, the more accurate word is *evasive*. I know there's so much more going on than her fresh looks divulge, but I'm not sure Beth knows the extent.

199

As noon approaches, Beth looks long and hard at the cake. She must notice the tiny wave that wasn't the way she made it. She opens the silverware drawer and stares. There's Spatula, MIA and now reappearing with ⅔ a handle. She picks Spatula up and recreates the peak the way she intended it. Then she absent-mindedly licks Spatula and lays her on the counter. She covers the cake, using a special cake cover that fits securely onto the stand and carries it out to the car. She leaves the door from the house into the garage wide open.

I pick up Spatula. I hold her to my nose. I can smell My Darling's saliva on her, a cakey kiss. I kiss the yellowed rubber. Spatula is mine and from this point on, I'll be more careful not to let her leave my sight, I tuck her under my arm. Beth has conveniently left the back door of the car open. I climb in while she goes back in the house and then returns with Saucisson on a leash.

We drive north up Round House Road. I stare at Gunther Schlitz's gate, 221, as we pass by. Beth doesn't slow down or even glance to her left. I'm sure she has no idea that Gunther Schlitz Jr. lives here and so does The Lug. She sits very straight because of the hatching belts, keeps her eyes on the road and drives a good 10 to 15 mph over the speed limit.

When we get to Jessica's, all the usual pink outdoor toys – bikes, scooters, roller skates plus a wagon – are scattered around the front door area. Sophia and Charlotte are hard at work doing a sidewalk chalk mural and scream when they see Achilles. They each wear a hatching belt and don't seem the slightest encumbered by its presence. It goes to show how incredibly adaptable children are.

Sophia opens the big front door and yells, "Mom!" leaving the door open and she and Charlotte keep playing with Saucisson. Beth and I walk through the foyer to the kitchen. Beth carries the cake and I carry Spatula under my arm.

Jessica is in the kitchen, unpacking a large box with gold lettering – "Nibbles – on it. She decided to order their tea party. I've seen Nibbles' front window a hundred times but I had no idea what was inside. Our allegiance was and *is* to Bon Vivant but it seems Jessica has found an even pricier, more exquisite place to spend her money. She uses words like, "makes it easy," and "delivers," with Nibbles taking "tea party" to a whole new level. She pulls out a tray of petit fours that make Beth's homemade cake look positively primitive.

Margaret sits very quietly on a stool at the counter. I can see her skin is ashy and she desperately wants to smile and be cheery but she's just too tired. Jessica chatters with Beth and keeps trying to loop Margaret in but Margaret only nods. When Jessica has unloaded the box and put all the finger sandwiches, vegetables cut into special shapes and tiny cakes on a large tray, she calls Sophia and Charlotte inside. Saucisson comes galloping in with them.

I would think a tea party would be on a blanket on the lawn, but maybe that's the definition of a picnic? The concept of this frivolous activity is completely foreign to me, but I am finding it fascinating that there's a whole business built on making 2x2 inch cakes, each individually iced and decorated. I think about Mr. Kline and wonder what he does that allows the females in his life to inhabit such Marie Antoinette-like luxury.

I carefully watch Margaret and monitor what she eats. And although Jessica is talking breezily to Beth, I can see she's also carefully watching Margaret. We've both made a mental note that she's had two bites of a cucumber sandwich and one bite of a *petit fours*. She yawns, murmurs, "May I be excused," and lies down on the sofa. Jessica gets up, covers her with a blanket and kisses her on the forehead, holding her lips there one second longer to check for a temperature.

Charlotte is chewing and says, "Mimi, do you want me to wear your egg?"

"No thank you," Margaret says.

I had no idea children this polite and sweet existed. I don't believe Evie has ever said the words "May I be excused" in her life. This sick child is an angel. She's Angel Margaret. When Jessica comes back to the counter to join Beth, Sophia and Charlotte, she pretends to be light-hearted and engaged but I know her thoughts are lying like heavy lumps next to Margaret on the sofa.

The tea party is over much sooner than I would have liked. Saucisson has found a toy stuffed cat and torn it apart on the floor. Beth is apologetic but Sophia and Charlotte think it's hilarious and Jessica doesn't care a lick. Beth insists on leaving the cake and drags Saucisson to the front door. Before leaving Jessica casually asks Beth if she'll be "around" later today and tonight. She's worried that she might have to take Margaret to the doctor and Carmen is at her sister's, who just had outpatient surgery this morning. Can she trouble Beth?

My Darling Beth assures her that she's "around" and will keep her phone by her. She can come any time and spend the night, especially if she can bring Achilles, aka Saucisson. Jessica "can count on her".

Standing by the front door, the two women look like a pair of matching earrings. They both have white tees, cropped jeans and ponytails. Jessica is maybe an inch taller and a bit more muscular. They both lilt their voices up and down like two birds in a tree.

When Beth walks out to the car with Saucisson, I linger in the doorway. I'm more needed here and I have a bad feeling that Jessica will have to call on Beth and Beth will be back soon enough. Besides, I know how to open the gate and walk home.

I also know Gunther Schlitz's house is between Jessica's and mine. I know this stretch of road well and it has everything I need.

CHAPTER 38

The front door closes and I become very alert. I say to myself, "I'm needed *here*, now." I hover over Jessica's shoulder and watch her constantly touch her lips to Angel Margaret's forehead. There's no stainless steel, scrubs, or monitors but I'd have to say the next few hours pass as tense as in any ICU. I feel my adrenaline pumping and my intellect laser focused on this small, corrupted body. I never dreamed a tea party could be an overture to an intense professional experience.

By about four, Jessica can't stand it any longer. She walks to the kitchen and gets the digital thermometer. She aims it at Margaret's forehead. It instantly beeps and we both see 103.2. Margaret immediately starts to say, "It's not so bad Mommy, please let me stay. I don't want to go to the hospital."

Jessica texts Beth: "Can you please come?" Beth, like a champ, immediately responds, "Be there in 15 min." For a moment, I allow myself a burst of pride, Beth knows the gravity of the situation and is on high alert. It must be all those years of living with me, a thoracic surgeon, that helped her understand that Jessica's house is a war zone between life and death.

Jessica calls the hospital. She tells whoever picks up, "Please tell Dr. Musa that Margaret Kline will be there in twenty minutes."

Margaret is whimpering, "Please, no, please, no." Her unflagging politeness tears my heart and I actually have to remind myself that I *don't* have a heart and to remain unemotional and professional.

Jessica lifts Margaret's striped tee and gently un-Velcros the hatching belt. She lays it carefully on the coffee table. "Do not fight, you can take turns wearing Mimi's egg until she gets back. Beth will be here and she's bringing Achilles to play." She switches 100% of her attention back to Margaret. She puts a pink blanket around Margaret's shoulders, picks her up and carries her to the door. Sophia runs to the front door and opens it. I can tell they've all done this drill.

Beth is standing at the door there like a warrior ready to fight for the innocents. As she helps Jessica bundle Margaret into the backseat, she says, "Don't worry about anything here, we'll be fine." It's good advice. Perhaps that's how our whole marriage worked. Perhaps, every day when I left for the hospital, Beth, on some level, transmitted to me, "Don't worry about anything, I'll be fine" and that allowed me to do my job faultlessly.

When Jessica opens the driver's door, I climb in and sit in the passenger seat. Sophia and Charlotte are standing in the open doorway, looking bereft. They both wave but Jessica's mind is elsewhere, probably where we'll park. I'm not as focused as I should be, I'm out of practice. I take 2/3 Spatula and wave goodbye.

Pulling up to the hospital is like coming home. If possible, my ghost brain is emitting dopamine and adrenaline at the same time. It's wonderful, I feel so alive and know my place in this mini-ecosystem.

Jessica pulls up to a covered entrance. It's adorned by a life-sized sculpture of a pink cow with daisies around its neck. We head in, pausing to let Margaret pet the cow's nose for good luck.

I knew they had valet service at the south wing but when I had my emergency ride to the hospital, I was in a screaming ambulance and pronounced DOA. There was no pink cow to pet, just rush, rush, rush. A few violent jolts to the heart and that was that – sudden and catastrophic – no luck to be had.

Margaret's illness is different, slow and insidious. I'm not an expert on cancer but I do know it's a war of attrition. The body has its

204

walls of defense and the doctor's job is to keep morale up within the walls while the foreign troops, outside the walls, maraud and feast and multiply.

Jessica rolls Margaret up to the front desk. One nurse hands Margaret a stuffed teddy bear, saying, "Let's see what's going on today, Maggie." It's all casual, non-urgent but efficient. We all go to an examining room and she starts taking Margaret's vitals: blood pressure, pulse, temperature. Moments later, Dr. Patricia Musa walks in. I don't really know her, the hospital is big and departments didn't inter-socialize much, compounded by the fact that I tried not to socialize at all.

I know *of* her from her work with Doctors' Without Borders and her efforts to send a team to Democratic Republic of the Congo. I know she was a pediatrician but I didn't know her specialty was childhood oncology. She, herself, exudes health and vitality. She wears her hair in a big afro which makes her look electrified and energetic. She looks exotic but is down to earth, warm, homegrown. Jessica and Margaret seem to genuinely adore her. If Dr. Patricia Musa hadn't been working, she should have been invited to the tea party.

In med school, the teaching doctors talked a lot about "bedside manner." Thankfully we weren't graded on the subject. It was just a concept that was floated out there. My feeling was, "I focused 100% of my being on saving your life, you were under anesthesia the whole time." Before I retired, websites were springing up with doctor reviews. Occasionally I'd look at them. Some patients had the audacity to write: "Lacks bedside manner." This only caused my blood pressure to rise. Excuse me. You're alive and your heart was a mess. I'm the maestro in the OR who just gave you a second lease on life. The end.

Dr. Musa looks at the chart and the recorded temperature of 103.4. She sees a pulse of 120 and a blood pressure of 90/60. She walks over and lays her cool hands (I imagine they're cool) on Angel Margaret's forehead. She gently lifts her shirt and runs it over the emaciated rib cage, "No egg today?" she says. It's a mother's touch, it tells her more than the numbers in the chart. I can honestly say, as a doctor, a professional, a great surgeon, I admire her. There's a humanity to her professionalism that I never thought about until now.

Dr. Musa, while maintaining eye contact with Margaret, calmly tells them they'll need to draw blood. She knows Margaret's white blood cell will be low from chemo but she's worried Margaret's hemoglobin and hematocrit are low, too, and if so, she will need a blood transfusion. She'll need to be running a normal temperature before she can go home. Jessica closes her eyes but Margaret doesn't react at all.

Thirty minutes later, Dr. Musa returns and says Margaret's white blood cell count is 2,000, (normal is around 7,000, but she doesn't say this) and her hemoglobin and hematocrit are low. Jessica looks out the window when a tech comes in with a bag of blood. When Margaret is hooked up and situated, Jessica texts Beth that they'll be spending the night and then gets into bed beside Margaret and begins reading a book called *Coraline* out loud.

I sit in the recliner, close my eyes and listen. It's the story of a courageous girl entering an alternative world. I may possibly enjoy it more than Margaret and am disappointed when Jessica stops reading and takes out her iPad for them to watch movies. Dinner comes but Jessica has brought protein bars and health shakes. They leave the hamburger and french fries untouched on the tray. As the sun goes down, Jessica brushes her teeth, takes my place in the recliner and settles in for the night.

I decide to wander over to the cardiac ICU to cheer myself up.

CHAPTER 39

When I pass through the double doors to the north wing, I'm not disappointed. There has been an accident and an ambulance gurney is being pushed down the hall with at least six EMS workers around it. The tallest EMS worker standing at the patient's head says, "Car accident. Had to cut him out. Jaws of Life. Pressure dropping, multiple internal injuries." Two nurses rush the young white male to imaging.

The patient is back and we all jump on the service elevator and go up a floor. We're immediately met by three doctors. I recognize Charlie Thayer, the surgeon who took my place as Chief of Cardiothoracic Surgery. I don't know the other two, one is a woman. Each doctor does one quick visual check and the three doctors turn and rush for the scrub area. I stay with the patient.

They roll him into the operating room. There is a swarm of nurses already scrubbed, masked and gloved. They shave him and start swabbing him down with surgical prep. Lines were run into his veins in the ambulance and the anesthesiologist is already sitting on a stool, watching his vitals as he puts him under. The three surgeons enter like three amigos ready for a gunfight. The only way to tell them apart is by their heights and voices. Everyone becomes a player with a very defined role, just like in a symphony. Charlie is the conductor (that would have been my role); he also assigns himself solos.

The patient codes and Charlie brings him back. It makes me sad that I was never brought back. They said I was DOA. I wish I'd had the chance to fight back, like this young man.

After the second coding, Charlie yells, "Come on!"

One of the nurses quietly says, "Jason."

So Charlie yells again, "Come on, Jason!"

It is jarring to hear a name given to the patient. I always just called the patient "The Patient". When Charlie yells, "Come on, Jason!" It reminds me of Tyler's baseball coach yelling as he rounded third base and it makes me imagine if Tyler were lying here instead of Jason-The-Patient.

There is something about this splayed open young man that reminds me of Tyler, besides being about the same age and Charlie yelling at him with the gusto of a baseball coach. There's something vaguely familiar about him, but with a breathing tube and surgical cap, it would be hard to recognize your own mother.

After the fifth code red, they're unable to bring him back. There's a decided down tick in the tempo of the symphony and the room loses energy. Charlie and I walk out to the waiting room. I know I should head back to watch over Angel Margaret and Jessica but as the once chief of thoracic surgery, I need to see this job to completion.

The waiting room has sofas, a flat screen TV and a saltwater aquarium. It could be a decent living room if it wasn't a waiting room. Much to my surprise, sitting slumped on the sofa is Stick-Your-Nose-In-Everyone's-Business-Sandy and her husband Larry. When Charlie walks in with his shoulders curled forward, Sandy starts to moan, "No, no, no." She clings to Larry, who tries to stand straight

I visualize the day Beth sat in this very room waiting for news of me. The day that began so magical but ended so tragically. She wouldn't have had long to wait, after all, I was DOA. Did she have time to appreciate the coral in the fish tank? Who came out and told her? Did one of my old colleagues trek over from cardiology? Did President Pierce push himself away from his desk and walk over? It took me a while to come back to join her, so I'll never know first-hand how it unfolded.

Unlike Jason, I wouldn't have needed cleaning up, I probably looked pretty good. My hair would have been messy from my cap, I know it was long and I was due for a haircut and I still am. I probably looked relaxed, like a man taking an indulgent nap on a snowy day.

Out of professional curiosity and because I have the time, I follow Sandy, Larry and Charlie into the room where they've wheeled Jason, cleaned up with a neatly tucked sheet around him. A grief counselor stands quietly by Jason's head and, much to my surprise, Charlie doesn't leave the room.

Sandy is whimpering like a beaten puppy and Larry is mute. They both touch Jason's hair and face. Charlie, in very simplified language, explains to them there was a puncture to the aorta, small but a puncture. Even if they had gotten him out sooner and even if he'd been able to address that first acute situation, there was extensive damage to other internal organs.

At first I think he's telling them this to clear any doubt of malpractice but then he lingers, hugs each of them, and repeats all the same information. I realize this is the important information he'd want to hear if his son was lying dead. It gives the bereaved no forks in the road, no "what ifs." It's a straight tunnel with no light, only a definitive dark end.

When Charlie and the counselor leave, I linger. Larry has never been anyone to me, just Stick-Your-Nose-In-Everyone's-Business-Sandy's husband. The few times I was forced to socialize with him, I just let him do all the talking. It's a great strategy unless you have two non-talkers, then it's a problem. Larry turns to Sandy and says, "Maybe if Tom was alive, he could have saved him."

The unexpected praise shocks me.

It's not true, I couldn't have saved him, I know that, but a great warmth spreads through my body. I have an unexpected urge to hug my grieving almost-friend Larry but, of course, I can't.

Back in the south wing, morning dawns and Margaret's fever is gone. She looks so much brighter after getting some fresh blood that hasn't been ravaged by chemo. Jessica is smiling and Dr. Patricia Musa says they can go home. It all sounds so good, so positive.

Before leaving, Dr. Patricia Musa calls, "Let me know when the eggs hatch!"

Back at Jessica's, all loose ends are soon tied up and I'm suddenly anxious to get home. I left the house on Wednesday for a tea party and now it's almost noon on Thursday. Fernanda has been left to her own devices for over 24 hours with The Slugger idling around in his red car. If there's one thing Grieving-Sandy and I can agree on, it's that the job of a parent is never done, you can never stop being vigilant, even when they've grown up.

CHAPTER 40

When the three of us get home, Beth, Saucisson and I, there isn't a dish in the sink, the mail is neatly laid on the counter and the sofa pillows are fluffed. There's a note from Fernanda by the coffeemaker in curly, girlish writing:

> Dear Beth, Thank you for your hospitality.
> Dmitri and I have worked out our problems
> and are going to raise the baby together.

Beth reads the note. I myself read it through twice trying to process what raising a baby with The Slugger – almost thief – looks like.

My sadness, disappointment, sense of betrayal makes it obvious that I got too attached to the vision of Lovely Fernanda living here and raising her child under our roof. Somehow, I got lost thinking we could seamlessly meld and become a happy family. Fernanda arrived, a fully formed human being, with her own behavior and personality. It was arrogant to imagine I could alter her course, it would be like changing the flow of a river.

I think about Evie and how, even as a child, her current ran contrary to mine. I wonder if Jason's was contrary to Sandy's or if they flowed side by side. I wonder if Jason, even as a child, was rash, a wild risk-taker, or if this was just one moment of carelessness. I feel I've experienced two losses, Fernanda and Jason, in one day.

Beth's phone starts dinging. Texts are rolling in, mainly from Drunk Emily. She is texting Beth that Sandy's son, Jason, died last night. Beth goes outside, sits curled in a chair and calls Emily. I don't need to hear the details, I *experienced* them and even though I never liked Sandy and only *now* like Larry, I don't want to relive them. The OR left me oddly unnerved... powerless might be a good word.

I'm poking around the front yard, avoiding listening to Beth's and Emily's conversation, when my amigo Miguel pulls into the driveway. His energy and beaming smile is sorely needed. But Miguel isn't his usual self. He gets out of his pickup and I swear, his porcupine hair is wilted and his lips remain firmly closed, no smile. He walks around back, where Beth, looking devastated, is off the phone and curled up in the chair.

Miguel sits down at the outdoor table. He looks Beth straight in the eye and says, "I'm sorry, Señora Beth, I don't want the egg anymore." He lifts his shirt, un-Velcros the belt and gently lays it on the table.

Miguel and Beth morosely stare at the egg in the hatching belt. "I just don't have the heart to keep carrying the egg." I gently rest my hand on his shoulder, I swear I know how he's feeling. "They're young and in love. The attraction is like fire. I can't keep Fernanda from the flame. It was the same thing between me and my wife, we were seventeen."

They both look again at the egg lying between them. Beth touches the smooth shell. It now seems silly to all three of us that we thought this little inanimate object could hold such power and change the outcome of young love and the pull of sexual attraction.

"It's okay, Miguel," Beth says softly, "I'll find someone who wants it."

Miguel doesn't stay, he gets back in his truck and leaves. I'm tempted to go with him but think better of it. Beth puts Saucisson on a leash and gently adds Miguel's hatching belt to her torso. I think she's going to take Saucisson on a walk and really don't feel up to the exercise. I walk them down the driveway to send them on their way but as I stand at our mailbox, I see Beth cross the street and walk only a few houses down, to Ray's. She stands at the front door, ringing the bell, and eventually he opens it; I guess it's a work-from-home day. They talk for a while and then she hands him the belt. He lifts his shirt, she helps him strap it on and he joins her for her walk.

I cross the street and run to catch up. He and Beth are talking in soft voices about Sandy's son.

Stick-Your-Nose-In-Everyone's-Business-Sandy had stopped by Ray's house a while ago to introduce herself and remind Ray that they met briefly at my Celebration of Life. She told Ray that she'd be happy to sell his house if he was interested.

"I told her, I really don't know what I want, at this point." Ray adds, "That's terrible about her son." Then Ray, who I dubbed Ray-The-Jerk, says, "I wonder if Tom could have saved the boy? He saved me."

Beth is caught as off guard as I am. She says, "What are you talking about?"

Ray explains how when they first moved onto our street, he had chest pains and was rushed to the hospital. I was the surgeon who did the emergency stent procedure on him. I never realized it was my new neighbor lying on the table. He had been scrubbed and capped and maybe someone said his name, "Raymond Little," but that wouldn't have meant anything to me. He was just a patient, no different than any other patient. I did so many of these procedures every week/month/year that I never put the pieces together. I find it very odd he never reminded me over the next 20 years that I put an emergency stent in him.

"Did you ever remind Tom that it was you he did a procedure on?"

"No," Ray says but doesn't elaborate.

The next day is Friday, there's lots of texting. Beth texts Tyler and Evie to tell them about Jason. Neither one was close to him but they both knew him. Beth texts Sandy but Sandy never replies. Beth texts The Lug; he doesn't reply either. Beth texts Jessica and checks in. Jessica texts, "All good." Throughout, Emily texts Beth frenetically. Finally Beth calls her and says, "Come over tonight and eat dinner with me. We can talk."

It's as though tragedy has set off a chain reaction of everyone checking in on everyone. A text and a response is the same as two fingers to the radial artery to check the pulse.

Beth gets her purse, a clear sign she's going somewhere and even though I don't know where, I decide to go. I jump in and we drive to Bon Vivant. She parks under the oak but doesn't look expectantly for The Lug, which is good; we've way too much on our minds. We go in and Beth buys a lot, way more than she needs. She has Sydney put it in two separate bags and says, "One is for a friend."

We drive to Sandy's and Beth writes on the bag, "Thinking of you. Let me know how I can help. Love, Beth." The driveway is full of cars. I'm sure Sandy's three other children have all come home and the family has closed ranks to grieve. I wait in the car while Beth puts the bag at the front door and we leave. I wonder if Jason is inside with them.

When we get home, Beth texts Jessica again, "Do you need me?" Jessica confirms, "No, we're good, Mimi is playing!"

Beth sets two places at the table and Emily shows up on time and drunk as a skunk.

CHAPTER 41

Emily is a mess. No one can doubt that I was dead-on with my original moniker: Drunk Emily. It seems sober Self-Aware-Emily was just a fleeting stage.

Emily, Sandy, Beth and I, even Ray, we all have kids about the same age, young adults. If something happens to one, it sends a thunderbolt of fear through all. My guess is that Sandy's son had dabbled in dangerous behavior before, but this time a slick road, a big tree, another car, made the danger decisive.

Emily sobs in Beth's arms, surveys the bottle of S. Pellegrino and says, "For Christ sake Beth, don't you have anything stronger?"

Beth opens an oaky chardonnay.

Beth and Emily talk about Jason in subdued tones and then touch on different topics, one being "that nice single neighbor". Beth tells Emily that Ray is wearing an egg now. She explains how Miguel lost heart and she gave it to Ray with only a week left before hatching, "It's a good deal for him."

Emily pouts and says she needs an egg and that Beth should have thought of her. Inwardly, I sigh with relief; the egg seems much safer with Ray.

Beth apologizes to Emily but I know she doesn't mean it. "Did you know, Tom operated on Ray when they first moved in. He saved Ray's life. But Ray told me himself that he never mentioned it to Tom."

"Strange."

"It's a shame, because maybe Ray and Tom could have been friends. Ray obviously admired Tom and they both seem like gentle, quiet souls, bookish. Tom could've used a friend."

Beth sounds like a mother trying to arrange a playdate between two awkward toddlers. I'm getting irritated. I'm about to go inside and sit in my favorite chair when Emily says apropos of nothing, "I have something I need to tell you, Beth. I need to come clean."

I freeze.

Is Drunk Emily, the drama queen, going to bring up our dalliance in the china closet *now*, one and a half years after the fact? If so, I wish I could stick Spatula down her throat right here and now. Undisputedly, a lifetime has passed (mine!) since that ridiculous slip of judgement during those dark days after my forced retirement. I hold my breath.

Beth sighs and puts down her wine glass. "Emily, I already know. Sandy told me the day after the party. I forgave you a long time ago."

Drunk Emily sits agape and then stands and awkwardly hugs Beth.

"In fact," Beth continues, "I've thought of thanking you a few times. That transgression, that misstep, that illogical action on Tom's part, changed him. It jarred him out of his self-pity and apathy. He woke up a different man. The very next morning, he started talking about moving to France and learning about fruit trees."

They both take a few bites and then Beth continues. "He wasn't the only one struggling. His constant, weighty presence around the house was too much. I was used to him being gone and I felt stifled. I didn't know how much longer I could live with his constantly moping and the bitterness. But after that party, after that terrible night, everything got better. He really was the greatest husband... for a year."

Whoa, *for a year*! This is a low blow. There's a lot to unpack. This dinner is over for me. I stumble inside to find Spatula. Beth, My Darling, thinks I was a great husband for *one* year, that's 35 million heartbeats, that's nothing, a blink of an eye.

CHAPTER 42

Saturday morning comes and my mood matches the weather, drippy and dim. I'm really not happy with what I heard last night. I didn't even go upstairs last night. I feel as though Beth has twisted almost 30 years of a perfect marriage into something like an endurance trial, followed by a year of *constant, weighty presence.* The one year I was dubbed "the greatest husband" is nothing. It's like an amateur-hour, like bad surgery closed up with some neat stitches. It's negligible and unacceptable.

Beth comes down looking rested and happy in her kimono we bought in Japan. I want to remind her of everything I've given her, everywhere we went. I'd like to defend my status as The Greatest Husband. In fact, I'm *still* The Greatest Husband... evidenced by the fact that I'm still here, beside her.

But rather than engaging me, righting her wrongs, she acts as though nothing happened. She has her coffee, gently rotates Little Leftie and Rightie and seems overall peaceful and satisfied. When she gets dressed and take Saucisson for a walk, I stalk after her. I think of all the ways I could approach this misinterpretation of history and how at one point, I even wonder if I could write my defense in dirt using Spatula. Saucisson keeps looking back at me and giving me a little tail wag. He's attempting to broker peace between us.

No deal.

On the way home, I'm still so offended and exasperated, I veer off at Ray's house. I need some good ol' male camaraderie. It's true, Ray doesn't trim his bushes but Ray at least understands that I was a great surgeon, a maestro who saved him. If I were still living, I'd actually walk over, maybe pop a beer (even though it's 9:30 in the morning) and shoot the shit with My Neighbor Ray.

He could complain about his wife leaving him and how she took Bongo. We could both gripe about our daughters, his daughter doesn't talk to him, mine doesn't listen to me. I could confide in him how Beth didn't think I was The Greatest Husband for all those years and then I could refute it and go into microscopic detail of all the ways that I *was*. I'm sure he'd agree. Then Ray and I would go fishing. I've never been fishing but it seems like a decent way for two guys to spend an afternoon and it suits me because it doesn't include a ball or running.

Just thinking of My Neighbor Ray and all we have in common makes me realize we're already buddies. He's My Buddy Ray.

My Buddy Ray's house is smaller and newer than ours. It's not the original farmhouse for this parcel of land. His front door is closed tightly but I know his back has sliding glass doors (instead of French) and a stone veranda, a bit like ours. Sometimes Trixie would wander back there looking for Bongo and I'd have to retrieve her.

I walk to the back of the house, hoping My Buddy's sliding glass doors are open. They aren't open but the drapes are. I put my face to the window and peer in. I think My Buddy Ray's wife must have come home. There's a woman sitting at the kitchen counter with a cup of coffee, a thick dictionary and a newspaper. She appears to be doing a crossword puzzle. Occasionally, she brings the pencil to her mouth or taps the eraser on the counter in frustration.

I realize it's *Ray* sitting at the kitchen counter; there's no mistake; it's my buddy, the man I imagined fishing with. I can see his profile, his facial stubble, even the black curly hairs sprinkled on his shoulders. My buddy is wearing a woman's flowered nightgown and has giant pink fuzzy slippers dangling off his feet. When he stands up, he touches the bulge around his middle, (which must be the hatching belt) and adjusts the spaghetti straps of his nightgown. He walks over to the coffee pot and tops off his cup. He shuffles back across the kitchen to resume the crossword puzzle and pauses, staring at the sliding glass doors. I know, *intellectually*, he can't see me staring in, jaw dropped, but it *feels* like he sees me. My buddy reaches out and yanks the drapes closed.

Show over.

This isn't what I expected. I'll be the first to admit, I am flabbergasted. But as I walk across his lawn to return home, the shock kind of rolls off me and it all starts to make sense. Years and years ago, I recall doing an emergency stent operation on a man. His name (if mentioned) meant nothing to me but it must have been My Buddy Ray. I had no way of knowing he was my new neighbor but he must have realized I was *his* neighbor.

A week after the procedure, Dr. Brett (a real ass) says to me, "You know that poor bastard you put a stent in last week? He changed doctors and is doing his follow up with me! He doesn't realize that the whole cardiology department already knows he was wearing a woman's bra and underwear when they cut his clothes off." Hahaha.

I actually feel sorry for My Buddy Ray. All those years he had a secret and he thought if he reminded me that I did his surgery, I'd know the secret and despise him. Little did he know that I already despised him for his overgrown bushes. I could have more readily forgiven him his propensity to wear women's clothes than not trimming his bushes. Afterall, sexual orientation is a mystery locked deep within the brain and not trimming your bushes is just inconsiderate. I wish he had a chance to confide in me – in or out of our hypothetical fishing boat. Suddenly, unexpectedly, I see the humor; I'm a ghost; my buddy's a cross-dresser; and I wish we could go fishing. I laugh. Life, Saturdays in particular, is full of surprises!

By the time I walk down the sidewalk, across the street and up my driveway, I decide I'm going to catch a ride north with The Lug today. It's Saturday, he should be hanging out under the oak at Bon Vivant. I feel Beth and I could use some space and time to work through our feelings. I could keep walking to Jessica's or I could stay with The Lug and maybe practice French with his kids. It's a good plan for a very unpredictable Saturday.

I go back to the veranda, but the French doors are closed. I need to get back into the house to get Spatula for my travel plan to work. Time passes. Saucisson grows by the day and his bladder and bowel movements get more and more dependable. But sure enough, just before 11:30, Beth comes and opens the door. She encourages Saucisson to "go pee". I hurry in and grab Spatula. Beth's purse is already on the counter so I wait by the mudroom door. She calls "Achilles," closes the door, looks in the mirror and off we go to Bon Vivant.

The Lug is already there, leaning on the Town Car under the oak, arms crossed. He gives Beth a big "*Bon jour!*" I still hate him but I also respect the dignity in which he does his job, even with his great losses. And I can't imagine what it must be like to have been a doctor and now… but this is the story of so many professionals who immigrate.

They laugh and talk about their eggs. Beth claims she forgets they're strapped to her body. She tells The Lug about her friend's son who died. He frowns and asks how old he was. Beth says twenty-two. The Lug shakes his head, "No good, no good." She does not tell him about Drunk Emily's confession and how she felt about our marriage. If she had confided these details, the betrayal would be too much for me and I would leave her. I'm not sure where I would go, maybe I'd just live outside, under one of my dwarf fruit trees, I don't know.

The Lug looks at his watch. "It's time for pickup."

Beth says, "Come by this week… for dinner."

The Lug nods and smiles. When he opens his door, I jump in; I know all too well how nimble he is. We both wave "Au revoir" to Beth as we drive off.

We drive to Madame Mimi's Ballet School, just as I predicted. A few minutes after noon, the same frothy group of girls pours out. The Lug holds the door and says, "Mademoiselle." We deliver this delightful child to her mother on Breezy Point. Then we drive to the house on Old Creek, this time a teenage girl *and* a boy come out. They look the same age and are definitely brother and sister. The Lug says, "The house of your cousins', yes?"

"Yes," they simultaneously confirm without looking up from their cell phones.

We actually get on the highway and drive 30 minutes and four towns over. It's probably the furthest I've been from my house since I died. It's definitely further mileage-wise than the therapist in the city. We exit off the highway and wind around, pulling up to a beautiful stone house with cars parked along the edge of the road and balloons tied to the mailbox. It's some sort of party. The siblings jump out and the teen boy says, "Thanks, Friedrich!"

We drive the 30 minutes back to our town.

This is all taking a long time. It would have been quicker to walk straight up Round House Road, but the driving hasn't been unpleasant and it definitely isn't physically taxing. When we take the exit ramp for our town, The Lug glides over, stops, and texts something. He waits. He almost immediately gets a response. He texts again and we're off. This time The Lug drives down main street and parks in front of Babe's BBQ. It's an upscale BBQ restaurant next to Eggplant. They have live music on the weekends and very expensive tequilas and whiskeys. Beth and I went once but it's not my type of place.

The Lug jumps out and is back in moments with two large brown bags. He puts them on my lap and I feel the warmth spread over me. The smells coming out of the top are heavenly, deep umami and burned molasses. He pulls a piece of candy from his pocket. It's a little red hard candy shaped like a pig. The waitress leaves them with the check. They're hot cinnamon and burn the smokey taste out of your mouth after eating barbeque. The Lug unwraps the candy, drops the wrapper in the cup holder and rolls the candy pig around his mouth with relish. Even with the urgency of hot food, The Lug drives the speed limit up Round House Road to the house of Gunther-Schlitz-Who-Shits-Money.

It all goes as planned. The gate opens, we pull into the first of four car bays, The Lug takes the bags off my lap and we both get out. He opens the door into the giant mudroom, and he strides into the cavernous kitchen. It's immaculate, like last time, but this time the small woman from the laundry room is standing at the kitchen sink. She is rinsing a spoon and bowl and filling a sippy cup. "Hola," The Lug says. "Hola," she says and turns to leave. She is wearing the same white, starched dress and the same spongy white shoes but in this context, I realize she's a nurse or nurse's aide, not a housekeeper.

Could Gunther Schlitz be sick?

Seeing the nurse or aide is like a Rorschach test for me; I immediately think of sick Margaret. I feel a pull, a sense of panic, to go straight to Jessica's. As The Lug hits the first button in a row of garage door buttons and the garage door starts to close, I decide to dodge out. I feel pretty confident that if I come back here tomorrow morning, Sunday, The Lug will be washing cars. He's quick but predictable.

When I duck under the closing door and hurry down the driveway, I feel I've made the right decision. It's warm and a soft golden light is illuminating the trees; the landscape is beautiful and it's a nice evening for walking. I'm very concerned about Margaret. I wonder if Mr. Kline is finally home.

CHAPTER 43

Have I told Spatula lately how great she is? How versatile in a multitude of situations? How I grow to appreciate and rely on her more and more each day as my world expands? I wish I knew the word for *spatula* in French. I get to Jessica's gate, wave her in front of the electronic eye and go in. No problem.

I hurry up the winding driveway to the front door. The usual mess of pink toys is scattered around, the Range Rover is parked in the circle, but when I peek in the front windows of the house, there's no sign of life, so I walk around back. As I venture around the corner, I hear lilting voices and splashing. Jessica and the girls are in the pool. There's a wrought iron fence enclosing the pool and patio area, so I have to stand, leaning on the fence and watch. Jessica is playing in the pool with Sophia and Charlotte. Margaret is lying on a lounge chair covered with a thick beach towel. Jessica is saying, "It's like bath water, sweetheart, I swear. I turned the heat way up this morning."

Margaret shakes her head. "I'm keeping the eggs warm," she says.

I wish I could vault the fence and check her pulse.

The girls' chatter reminds me of exotic birds nesting for the night. Jessica's brown hair is shining and I feel I'm part of some tableau of feminine charm. I could stand and watch the four of them interact for a lifetime. Peace.

Suddenly, the little-used back gate opens and Jessica's head swivels around, alert, like a lioness. A black Porsche purrs into the service drive and parks at the back door. Mr. Kline gets out, all smiles and tousled hair. He's dressed in Bermuda shorts, a golf shirt and flip-flops.

"No one told me we were swimming!" he yells, opening the gate, stripping his shirt off and kicking off his flip-flops. He dives into the deep end and swims underwater to the shallow end, popping up right by Sophia and Charlotte and spurting water like a whale. They laugh and squeal. There's no two ways about it, Playboy Perry is a fun guy, plus he's a decent swimmer.

Jessica stands as rigid and stern as a school marm. He pretends not to notice and kisses her on the cheek. "Your mommy looks as beautiful as always," he says to Sophia and Charlotte and they giggle with delight.

Then he does a few perfect strokes to the steps, climbs out and walks over to Margaret. He kisses her forehead and says something to her that I can't hear. She gives him a weak smile. His presence has completely changed the tenor of the evening.

"Well, I think it's time I get out," Jessica says.

As she walks up the steps of the pool and wraps herself in a towel. Kline watches her and I watch him. I can say with certainty that I hate this man who has so much and is so confident that he can be careless with it.

"Mommy, I'll go in, too," Margaret says and between them, they carefully carry the three hatching belts into the house. I go with them.

"Don't drop mine!" Charlotte yells.

Jessica, Margaret and I head upstairs. The kids' pajamas are lying on Jessica's big, unmade bed. She helps Margaret take her dry bathing suit off and step into her soft pajamas. Margaret looks exhausted, she has dark circles under each eye. Jessica pulls off her suit and drapes it over the side of the tub and puts on shorts and an oversized tee.

I hear Kline come in and a cacophony of kitchen noises.

"Can I just stay here, Mommy? I'm tired."

"Of course, my angel." Jessica kisses Margaret and she and I go downstairs. Kline is making the girls big bowls of ice cream.

"Really, Perry? Sugar right before bed?"

At some point, Kline takes Sophia and Charlotte upstairs. Jessica says their jammies are in her room. She says he can read to them there.

I follow and observe him. He's not a terrible father, he's very playful and Sophia and Charlotte seem to enjoy it. He gets them into their pajamas and then goes into his own dressing room, he comes out in dry shorts and a dry tee shirt. He looks like he's here to stay. He sits on the edge of the bed and reads animatedly from a stack of books. Charlotte picks one, then Sophia. Margaret just listens with her eyes closed. I don't remember reading to my children and being so playful. I'm quite sure I wasn't. I'm not sure why not.

After about 45 minutes, Margaret's breathing is regular, she's sound asleep. Charlotte is struggling to keep her eyes open, only Sophia is still wide awake. He kisses each one on their forehead and turns off the bedside lamp, leaving the drapes and door open, just how they like it. We both go downstairs, stepping softly.

Jessica is sitting at the kitchen island with a glass of wine. Kline walks over to a cupboard, takes a cut crystal tumbler, reaches into a high cupboard, pulls out a tear shaped bottle and pours himself a glass of scotch. He drops one ice cube into it and sits down next to Jessica.

"You look great, Jess."

"Oh, just shut up, will you? How many times do you think I'll fall for this? Did you get the papers? My lawyer said they were delivered Thursday."

"Yes, yes, I did. It all seems rather... impulsive."

Jessica narrows her eyes and slowly, slowly, as if rehearsed, says, "Perry, you're a scumbag. You've always been, you always *will* be. You're never going to change. I don't know why it took me so long to see it, that's on me." She takes a deep gulp of wine. "But my dad saw it from a mile away. Thank god he had the presence of mind to protect me from my own stupidity."

Perry stands up and starts pacing.

Jessica keeps talking. "You'll get $250,000 cash, no more. You can keep your stupid car, consider it a bonus. Bring boxes next time you come and get your shit out of my house. You can see the girls but you need to contact me ahead of time, no surprises like tonight. I should have locked the gates. That won't happen again. You'll get fair visitation rights."

"Jess, don't make this mistake. You know I love you. You know you've always been my girl."

She laughs, "What? Did your latest bimbo drop you?"

This makes Kline's head jerk around. He's tired of being conciliatory. His back is against the wall. "Look at this place," he sweeps his hand around, encompassing the dishes on the counter and the toys scattered around the family area. "This place is a shithole."

It's true, Jessica doesn't seem particularly concerned with cleaning but the location, the lot, the architecture, the furnishings, it's about as far from a "shithole" as you can get. I should know, I grew up in a shithole.

Jessica doesn't react. Kline finishes his scotch, puts down the glass and walks out the back door.

When the door shuts, Jessica and I walk over and watch his tail lights fade and the gate close. Then she looks at the alarm pad and hits a button. The gates are locked for the night. We're safe from Kline and his arsenal of boyish charms but I am trapped from going home.

This situation is new to me, like a hatching belt. I didn't know it existed... here's a woman, a good woman, a beautiful woman, a devoted mother and she doesn't need a man. All this wealth and status has been heaped on her, she was born the lucky daughter of some rich father who had the foresight to see Kline for what he is: a charming, manipulative playboy.

I find it refreshing that this particular woman, Jessica, whom I've grown so fond of, is safe and sound in her historic mansion with her old money. She doesn't have to worry that Sandy swoops in and sells the house from under her. Angel Margaret is safe in her silken cocoon bed, or as safe as Margaret can be, given her condition.

I spend the entire night thinking about Jessica as a powerful spirit and it pleases me. I walk upstairs and look at them lined up in the king bed, Sophie, Charlotte, Margaret and Jessica. Jessica sleeps on just a sliver, next to the window. She's ready to spring up and get ice or water or anything Margaret might need in the night. I keep watch out the back door. I now know Kline physically enters through the back gate and tries to work his charms to unlock Jessica's heart. It's better if he just stays away.

Unfortunately for me, Jessica wakes up and announces this is a "lazy day". I guess this means that none of them have to get dressed or do anything in any particular order. It doesn't seem so different from any of their other days. Sophia takes a book and climbs into a club chair, letting her legs dangle over. Margaret and Charlotte sit on the sofa and watch some animated show with a rat chef that cooks in Paris. Margaret keeps her arm draped around Charlotte. Jessica sits down with coffee and starts reading the paper on her iPad.

Carmen cleans the kitchen, loading two dishwashers and makes us all breakfast.

With no dog to let in and out, I am trapped inside, no different than the ducklings developing within their shells. Being a "lazy day" means I have to reign in my expectation of making it to Gunther Schlitz's house for car washing. I am trying to accept the things I cannot change, namely closed doors, but I'm getting impatient.

I suffer through a marshmallow roast over gas burners, pace through naps and finally, at about three, Charlotte announces she wants to go "Schwimming!" Margaret doesn't want to but Sophia says, "You can be the mother duck and sit on all the eggs!" Everyone seems happy with this arrangement. Sophia and Charlotte give Margaret their belts and run off to put their suits on. I feel like Saucisson, just waiting for the door to open to get outside.

Jessica runs down the back steps, pretending to chase Sophia and Charlotte. They grab towels hanging in the mudroom and then we all go out to the pool. I can see steam rising off the surface; Jessica has set the heat so high to accommodate Margaret. I've heard heating a pool is like burning dollar bills and I'm proud that my independent, Amazonian woman has money to burn.

The mood is so cheerful and I've already missed the car washing, and the call with Tyler, and I might even miss the call with Evie, but I don't really think about my actions and their repercussions when Jessica lifts the latch and holds the gate. We all just run in and the gate swings shut with a decisive clang because it has a strong safety spring. I settle myself on a lounge chair near mother duck Margaret and watch my girls play. I feel like a man of leisure enjoying the fruits of his hard labor.

Later, it's decided they're going in the house to get some lemonade. They leave all the towels and the eggs, so Spatula and I stay and float, enjoying the warm water.

Time passes, they don't come back but I remain a buoyant ghost, looking up at the sky. I wonder if this is how it feels to be dead or if this is how it feels to be alive. A little wren comes and perches on a lounge chair to sing an evening song. Hours have passed when I see some lights turn on in the house and the back door opens. Margaret walks across the lawn to the pool. She looks tired but calm. Sophia sticks her head out the door and yells, "Get mine, too!" Towels are draped on the lounge chairs and one has a mound under it with all the hatching belts. Margaret is finally coming to retrieve them, which is perfect; I'll be able to escape.

I reluctantly climb out of the pool and stand by the lounge chair. Margaret comes into the pool area and touches the eggs, I'm guessing they're still warm. She seems to look nervously in my direction as she gathers them up like a little farm girl. She walks to the gate, holding the eggs in the towel like it's a sack, opens the catch of the latch and pushes the gate with her boney hip. I'm standing right beside her, Spatula tucked under my arm, I know full well the gate will snap shut with its safety spring.

We move through the gate together, like two people with one token, coordinating their strides through a turnstile. Margaret seems to look directly at me and with a little shriek takes off running across the lawn to the back door. I had no idea she could run like that and am left flat- footed and agape. If we *had* been sneaking through a turnstile, the transit police would have easily grabbed me and not her. She yanks open the door and slams it shut.

I'm out of one enclosure, the wrought iron pool fence, and trapped in another, a walled and gated yard. I have a powerful desire to go home and check on Beth. I missed the weekly Sunday calls with Evie and now I'm missing Duolingo. Beth is probably sitting in bed, right now, doing our lessons.

I walk down the loopy driveway and wave Spatula in front of the gate sensor. Nothing. I walk to the back service entrance, and wave Spatula in front of that sensor. Nothing. Jessica has remembered to lock the gates for the night from the control panel. From my previous entrapment and recognizance, I know that the back gate offers more options for scaling the wall and escaping than the front. I can climb on the recycling bin or shimmy up the nicely placed branches of some scrub pines. The drop down on the other side of the wall doesn't excite me. Technically, I don't have bones, but I still carry the memory of them and, at the moment, they feel old and brittle. I'm not sure what the reality is.

I choose to scale the pines because just getting on top of the big blue recycling bin poses its own set of problems. Clenching Spatula between my teeth, like a pirate climbing the rigging with his cutlass, I climb a scrub pine, alternating right hand, left foot, left hand, right foot. When I get a little higher than the wall, I gently lower myself onto the top of the wall, so I'm kneeling on all fours, like a very uncoordinated cat. The top of the wall is about 10 inches wide and rounded and there's nowhere to cling, to lower my old bones down to the ground. I'm wondering where the best place is to jump and I'm considering crawling along the top to look for possible softer landings when... I just sort of tip over and fall, like an uncoordinated old cat that had a catastrophic heart attack.

I'm glad no one is here to see the indignity of the fall. I momentarily imagine how Kline would have expertly navigated the escape. All in all, it isn't my finest moment. I sort of roll when I land, not tuck and roll like a gymnast, I just roll like a can of soup falling off the counter. I roll down a slight incline and rock to a stop. I can feel my arms and legs and they seem intact and attached, and Spatula is still between my teeth. All good things. But when I rise to stand, I feel my back, my 73-year-old ghost back. It has been jarred and the pain is excruciating. I lie back down in the deep grass. It doesn't hurt if I lie still, so I just lie and do nothing.

The grass is thick and long. It tickles the back of my neck and my ankles where my khakis have hiked up. I ponder how this grass thrives so well outside the wall, away from people's incessant fussing and I watch the stars come out and wonder at their punctuality. I'm not in pain if I lie still and I have the same sensation as floating in the pool. I, Tom Paradise, am one with the universe. I'm not sure I've ever had this sensation while I was alive. But then I remember being a boy and lying in a hammock – *hammock*, such a funny word. I floated for a few stolen moments in empty peace back then, too.

The stars make their slow arc across the sky and as the sky lightens, I decide it's time to make my way home. I get up and sort of shake the dew off myself, like a bear waking from slumber, put Spatula under my arm and hobble out to the road. My back is slightly better, not in active spasms, but I still can't stand straight. I start walking down the road, bent like a candy cane.

CHAPTER 44

My plan was to go home. I really wanted to, it was definitely the plan, but when I got to the Gunther-Schlitz-Who-Shits-Money mailbox, I got the brilliant idea that, if I played my cards right, I could catch a ride back to town with The Lug. My back was killing me and walking was only aggravating it. Revenge, the dish best served cold, isn't even on my menu. I'm too consumed by my own discomfort.

It's Monday morning, everybody goes somewhere or does something on Monday morning (except maybe Jessica). I think the chances are very good that The Lug will drive toward town. Maybe he'll drive one or more of those kids to school, that would be ideal. We live almost in the dead center from the elementary, middle and high school, I would have a short walk from any of the schools. I wave Spatula in front of the gate's electronic eye and think *open sesame* and it opens.

As I shuffle up the driveway, I see the first garage bay door is already open. The Lug is staring at the bottom of the driveway, frowning at the gate that just opened and closed for no apparent reason. I'm almost glad to see him in his worn suit and pointy shoes. The Town Car is shiny black, not a speck of dust on it, apparently it got its Sunday wash. Its back door is wide open waiting for a passenger. At the moment, I'm that passenger. I climb in and sigh. Sleeping under the stars had its charms but, right now, the deep leather upholstery is what the doctor ordered for my aching back.

The Lug frowns, looks at his watch and then hurries up the plywood steps to his apartment. He leaves the door to his apartment wide open. The two ghost children poke their heads out and look around the garage. The boy's eyes lock on mine in the back seat and he gives me a big smile. I smile back but can't think of anything silly to do with Spatula, I'm just too tired. The Lug hurries out with what looks like a folded towel, tee shirt and book.

Gunther-Schlitz-Who-Shits-Money comes out of the house. He's a frog of a man, short, plump, with jowls that are smaller versions of his hips. His frog figure is clothed in a very expensive suit. I can see from the fabric, stitching and the fact that it actually fits his not ideal body, that it must be custom made. No designer would ever sew such an atrocity of dimensions without being ordered and paid in advance. He has a camel-colored briefcase that looks like the younger, thinner version of my beautiful doctor's bag.

I've only met Gunther Schlitz Jr. a few times, twice to be exact: once to explain how I turned his father into a vegetable and once with his lawyer and my malpractice lawyer. Now I'm sharing the backseat with him. I'm more than happy to move as far away as possible and position myself in the furthest corner.

Even me, a candy cane propped in the corner of the backseat, has a natural line of vision that grazes the top of Schlitz's head. There is no amount of money that can change the fact that Gunther Schlitz Jr. is short, very short.

The Lug hurries over and gets in the driver's seat. "Good morning, sir," he says.

"Morning, Friedrich."

"Where are we going this morning?"

"Downtown, lower east side. I'll confirm the address when we get closer."

As we exit the gate, The Lug says, "Sir, I think the gate might not be working properly..."

He waits for a response but none comes. I see his eyes look in the rearview mirror but Gunther Schlitz has already opened his briefcase. Inside, he has a sleek, thin computer, which he has flipped open. His briefcase has become a workstation. It has taken him no longer than the straight shot down his driveway to get into his work flow.

We drive south, and get on the highway and head into the city. It's not what I had hoped but there's no chance to stop and get out and hobble home. I can't complain. I am curled into the corner of the backseat, Gunther Schlitz works with admirable concentration, The Lug says absolutely not a word and I watch the landscape slide by. When we hit the bottleneck entering the city, The Lug stays calm and cool. I wish I had a blood pressure cuff, I don't think his pressure ever goes up or down. He's a study in equanimity.

Gunther Schlitz, however, starts getting agitated. "Twenty Liberty Street." The Lug nods. We wind our way down to the congested tip of the city, to a tall building with a big silver 20 on it.

"I really have no idea how long this will take. It might take five minutes or it could take five hours. I'll text you."

The Lug nods placidly; he's a good sport. The Lug makes a right, another right and a left, always signaling lane changes and turns. I'm not sure where he's taking us but I know we are not going home. There's a small square area of grass, a park of sorts, and a whole line up of shiny cars with drivers. There's a food truck that says "Café, Tacos, Tortillas!" and a picnic table where a few men sit and smoke. This must be where the chauffeurs and high-priced drivers hang out while waiting to be called to retrieve their bosses, all who apparently shit money.

I have spent the last 24 hours trapped in different spaces and although it's much safer to wait in the car, the thought of spending five hours waiting Gunther Schlitz to summon us has no appeal. I maneuver myself into the front seat while The Lug expertly parallel parks the Town Car. When The Lug gets out, I am ready to move fast, but I have plenty of time to make my exit as he folds his suit jacket, lays it neatly on the front seat and takes the towel, tee shirt and book with him.

The day is a little cloudy but there's no humidity hanging in the air, so chances are good that these clouds will burn off. The Lug unfolds the towel and lays it on the grass. He unbuttons his dress shirt and strips it off. His girth is solid, but it does not have the muscular definition of Miguel's. His hatching belt looks almost dainty. One of the drivers smoking at the picnic table makes a wolf whistle. The Lug gives him a big smile.

The Lug gently un-Velcro es the hatching belt and lays it on top of his folded dress shirt. He touches the egg and gently turns it. All his actions are delicate but purposeful. The Lug puts on the old Upenn tee that he wore washing cars. He drops onto the towel and does 30 quick pushups. Then he rolls over and does 30 quick stomach crunches. He repeats this over and over, only stopping to check his texts. He does this for probably 20 minutes. Then he lies down on the towel, gently places the hatching belt and his phone against his skin, under his tee, puts his arms behind his head and falls into a deep sleep. And even though it's broad daylight, and even though we're in a public space, I gently lay my ear on The Lug's chest and confirm his heart is beating strong and healthy.

I sit on a tiny corner of the towel and watch his chest rise and fall. I can't say I like The Lug but he has grown on me. I've never known a man with such dependable actions and precision in all quotidian tasks. I also kept to a dependable schedule and practiced precision in the operating room. But when I left the hospital, I certainly did not drive the speed limit or tidy my own space. I don't remember even thinking of those things. The Lug seems fully conscious and conscientious in all things he does. If fate had taken my children and dumped me in a foreign land, where I couldn't practice my profession but instead was a driver, I doubt I could navigate with The Lug's grace.

The afternoon passes. At one point The Lug gets a taco and a glass of water. He carefully sits upwind from the cigarette smoke at the picnic table with the other drivers. but His back is straight and he wipes his mouth with a little paper napkin. At 3:12, his phone dings and he gets a text, I'm assuming it's to retrieve Gunther Schlitz. The Lug carefully strips off the tee, folds it and the towel, buttons up his work shirt and we walk to the car. This time I climb into the passenger seat and The Lug hands me, well, actually, he sets on top of me, the folded towel, tee and book. The title of the book is *Bel Canto*. I've never heard of it and wish I could crack the cover and read the first page.

Off we go to 20 Liberty.

There's a NO PARKING pick-up zone in front and we glide into it and wait. After a few minutes, the security guard says we can't just sit there, so we do a loop around the block and come to rest again. We must do this ten times, like a fly returning to the same rump only to get swatted off. The Lug remains completely calm, only the security guard and myself are getting agitated. Finally, we glide up, Gunther-Schlitz-Who-Shits-Money is standing there. He gets in and mumbles, "Thanks."

Off we go. Naturally, we hit terrible rush hour traffic but The Lug doesn't seem to mind. He stays calm and focused and Gunther Schlitz barely looks up from the backseat, working on his computer and occasionally making a call. I can't even tell you how relieved I am when we finally take the exit to our town. It's been a long and boring day; my back feels much better, but I'm in a sour mood. Gunther Schlitz has wasted The Lug's and my time and has only confirmed what a self-centered human being he is.

I'm hoping we stop somewhere, anywhere, and I can get out and walk home... but we don't. The Lug actually drives up my street and I see my gentleman's farm from the road and Miguel in the front yard. If I could open the door with Spatula, I'd take my chances, open it wide and roll out. The Lug is only going 25 mph, the speed limit, which would be perfect for my plan. As if Gunther Schlitz Jr. can read my mind and wants to torture me further, he exclaims, "Can't you go a little faster, for Christ's sake!"

We keep going north up Round House Road to Schlitz's house. I've been thinking a lot about my next plan of action but haven't formalized my thoughts. My heart says to go home and be with Beth. My intuition says I should probably go up to Jessica's and check on both Margaret and Charlotte. A tiny bit of me wants to stay with The Lug and make his children smile. And lastly, the emotional part of me wants to make mischief for the despicable toad, who caused me undue stress and treats The Lug with such disregard.

When we pull into the garage, The Lug jumps out and opens the back door for Schlitz. He's rude and keeps typing while The Lug dutifully holds the door. I actually have time to crawl into the backseat, bad back and all, and exit the back door before Schlitz does. "Thank you, good sir," I say to The Lug, but he can't hear me.

Schlitz marches into his house and The Lug and I follow. The small Hispanic woman is standing in the kitchen, waiting for the microwave. Schlitz says to her, "How is he?" She says, "Bueno." And suddenly it hits me – this nurse or aide *lives* here. The only logical reason is that Gunther-Schlitz-Who-Shits-Money's father, the man I turned into a vegetable, whom I refer to as The Cabbage, is in this house.

The Lug hangs the Town Car keys on the hook and leaves. *Click* goes the door and I hear the rumble of the garage door closing. I wasn't sure what my plan was but suddenly my decision has been made for me.

I am committed to spending the night with Schlitz, and possibly The Cabbage, and I'm pleased. It won't be dull.

CHAPTER 45

I like the idea of being left in this massive house, to move about and study my nemesis at leisure. Although I'll miss The Lug's equanimity, I'll work better on my own, without his stabilizing influence. I'm operating in both our best interests, The Lug's and mine. I feel kindly towards The Lug and I start calling him Friedrich-the-Lug, out of kinship and respect.

Schlitz, however, is a consistently terrible person, worse than I imagined. He acted with pure spite against me and hurried me toward my catastrophic heart attack and from what I can tell, he's an ongoing pustule for Friedrich, infecting his already suffering psyche.

Schlitz walks through the cavernous, immaculate kitchen into an enormous grand hall that has two arched staircases running up either side, like a golden eagle's spread wings. It's a flip of a coin if one should call the layout antebellum or pure *nouveau riche*. The floor is cold, white marble and there's a round center table with a big bouquet of arranged flowers. Twenty five couples could waltz in the space that is as warm and inviting as a mausoleum.

Instead of going straight up the stairs (which I want to do), Schlitz walks across a monster living room, with no less than five sofas and a grand piano, into an imposing study. The study has built-in shelves along all the walls for books, but only the top shelves (where Schlitz would have to use the sliding library ladder to reach) have books. The rest of the shelves have masses of papers, some hastily stacked and others in folders. There's a navy leather recliner and an immense wooden desk with an ergonomic chair and four computer monitors. The impressive chair – that probably came with the desk – is cast to the side, piled with more papers. This is a working room, decorator be damned.

Schlitz sets his briefcase down in the very center of the desk, turns, and heads upstairs. I linger to explore the living room. The grand piano intrigues me, not because I play but because the top of the piano is covered with framed photos and I mean *covered*. A few in particular catch my attention. There's a black and white photo of a boy who could use more exercise holding a man's hand. The man has on a suit and a hat that look to be of the late '60s or early '70s. The boy stands straight and proud while the man smiles down on him. My guess is that it's young Schlitz Jr. and Schlitz Sr., aka The Cabbage.

Most of the photos mean nothing to me but I do recognize a few faces in some – surprisingly, the teenage brother and sister Friedrich and I drove to a party. Also the little girl we picked up at Madame Mimi's Ballet School. And the young boy who plays baseball. Now I get it – these are Junior's *children*. He's tucked one ex-wife on Old Creek and the second ex-wife on Breezy Point. He has his chauffeur, Friedrich-the-Lug, drive his kids on weekends; that way, he doesn't have to.

Friedrich probably does a better job anyway.

Thinking of my friend, delegated to the rooms over the garage, I head up the staircase on the right. This whole side of the house is some sort of master bedroom set-up. It's all ridiculously large, with his and her dressing rooms and his and her bathrooms. It would be very easy to avoid having any contact with your spouse at all. There's only a white terry cloth robe and simple slippers in her dressing room, like you'd find at any hotel. I shudder to think of the poor woman who slips them on. There is obviously no Wife #3 here.

I walk into the main bedroom, and what a bedroom it is! It makes Jessica's look small, it makes mine look like a college dorm room. There's a whole row of windows that look out onto the backyard and pool and the tennis court, like Jessica's, just much, much bigger. There are heavy draperies, two sofas with a coffee table between them, a huge canopy bed with mounds of silk pillows and tons of floor space to spare. All the decor feels like a set in a play, with lots of stage space for the actors to pace or even do cartwheels.

Schlitz comes out of the shower and walks into the bedroom with a towel wrapped around his sizable middle. The dark hair on his head is thinning but the hair on his chest is abundant. He lies down on the bed, picks up his phone and makes a call.

"Thanks for the idea," he says. "I like being early to the party." And with admirable efficiency, Schlitz hangs up, closes his eyes and starts to snore on cue, just like we learned to do in med. school.

After his power nap, we find ourselves in the kitchen, I am Schlitz's only companion as he eats a plate of food. When he chews, he makes noises and he taps his fork on his teeth, click, chew, click, chew. It's more than I can bare in the cavernous silence, so I politely excuse myself and wander off to his study.

I sit behind Schlitz's desk in his ergonomic chair (feels great on my back) and think how he makes money is so very different from how I made money. When I worked, often my labor was physical and required stamina. His work is purely mental. Schlitz is done eating and comes to sits in the navy recliner with a tumbler of amber alcohol and a cigar. He seems to be enjoying himself immensely. When his cigar is done, he stubs it out and we switch places. I sit in the navy recliner and he sits in the ergonomic chair behind the desk.

I'll give the man one word of credit: *concentration*. Gunther Schlitz Jr. is completely absorbed and focused in whatever he's doing. If Schlitz's desk was an operating table and a patient was bleeding on it, instead of the actual four computer screens and a pile of papers, he couldn't be more intent. Schlitz has great focus but that is the only compliment that will pass my lips. I'm sure he lacks the physical stamina needed to operate. The end.

241

The fact is, there isn't a body bleeding on the desk and after watching Schlitz shuffle papers, I get bored. I decide it's a good time to search for The Cabbage. I suspect he's tucked away. I planned to look for him during the night but now is as good a time as any.

I wander out to the enormous grand hall. I'd love to yell, "Helloooo!" and see if it echoes back, just to prove a point: it's too big. But instead of yelling, I head up the left staircase. Typically, in these *nouveau riche* set-ups, one side of the upstairs is organized into the adult wing and the other into the children's wing. There appear to be no children present, they all seem to reside with their respective mothers. My guess is: The Cabbage is planted in the children's wing.

I walk up the stairs, thankfully there's an arched doorway that requires no door and opens into a large open space that was probably designated the *playroom*. There's a flat screen TV on the wall and six bean bags chairs scattered around. Purple shag carpet covers the floor, which is a nice contrast to the cold, white marble downstairs. There are four bedrooms, two decorated for boys and two for girls. There are also two bathrooms, one with blue tile for boys and one with pink tiles for girls. There's a small staircase at the end of the hall. I'm assuming that goes up to the third floor, where any nannies, cooks, etc., must have rooms. Or did.

In the last bedroom on the left, a boy's room, the nurse or home health aide sits in an upholstered rocking chair with her feet up on an ottoman. She's watching her phone with earbuds in. Every once in a while, she chuckles.

In a hospital bed, by the window is The Cabbage. He actually looks pretty good, clean shaven and a healthy, pink complexion. He looks better than before he was rolled into the OR and *much* better than when he was rolled out. There's a brown teddy bear nestled next to his head, he's hooked up to one bottle of IV fluids and a single oxygen line to his nose.

The Cabbage appears very... shall we say, *relaxed*. He definitely *looks* more peaceful than I *felt* the first year of my forced retirement, when sleep brought no respite, only demons. With powder blue walls and a wallpaper border of Humpty-Dumpty, plus the nurse or aide sitting in the rocker like a nanny, it's easy to believe The Cabbage is a very obedient baby. I remind myself that it is Schlitz Jr. I have a feud with, not this Cabbage Baby. So, in a moment of reconciliation, I lean close and whisper, "I slipped, I'm sorry."

The Cabbage's eyes fly open.

It startles the hell out of me! I drop Spatula. I have to bend down and pick her up with shaking hands. When I stand straight, The Cabbage's eyes are desperately scanning the room, looking for something... me? When his eyes lock onto me, he seems to relax. I'm horrified and fascinated. I see his lips try to form words. I move my ear closer; nothing comes out, just a little warm, moist breath.

The nurse or aide keeps watching her phone. She has no idea the patient is awake and interacting with me, his dead maestro surgeon. I'm not sure if The Cabbage is interactive with everyone or if he's chosen me to be his confidante.

Some clock gongs somewhere in the house and the sound carries through the empty hallways. The nurse or aide looks at her watch, pulls out her ear buds and stands up. The Cabbage's eyes snap closed as she comes to neatly tuck the sheets around him.

Schlitz Jr. appears at the doorway, he was soundless, coming up the stairs in his butter-soft leather slippers. He moves like a cat, the kind of cat that does *not* fall off a wall. He stands in the doorway and his gaze sweeps the room. He spends no more time looking at The Cabbage than the rocking chair, the oxygen tank or the teddy bear.

"How was he today?"

"Bueno, bueno... tranquilo."

Schlitz turns and leaves. The nurse or aide sighs, touches The Cabbage's forehead and moves to the door. She flicks off the light as she goes but there are little nightlights plugged in along the baseboards, like an airport runway. They circle the room, there's one in the hall and there are two glowing up the back staircase.

The nurse or aide heads up the back staircase and I'm left with The Cabbage in the dim room. Out of professional habit, I lay my hand on his heart; the beat is strong and regular. There's no doubt, I fixed his heart, only to deprive his brain of oxygen. Thanks to my excellent work, he could live like this for many years.

The Cabbage stares intently at me. We almost speak the same language, the language of the dead, but not quite; there's still a chasm that separates us. His left arm moves from under the sheet and he reaches up, I think he's going to touch my face but he pulls out the oxygen tube that sets in his nostrils. This won't kill him but makes him participate more actively in the exercising of breathing. But he's not done, he sets his jaw and stares at me.

I believe he's challenging me.

I've never been an intuitive person, understanding human thoughts and desires, but at this moment, I believe I have become an intuitive ghost. I believe The Cabbage is challenging me to finish what I botched. He doesn't want to go on living, a Cabbage Baby in a Humpty-Dumpty room with a nanny nurse or aide. It is undignified for the man who once stood so straight in the black and white photo on the piano. I can understand this.

So I do something that I've never done as a maestro surgeon. They never taught us how in med school, but a great maestro can always improvise. After a moment of thought, I take Spatula and flip the teddy bear over The Cabbage's face. Its two arms hug The Cabbage's temples and its bear crotch sets on top of The Cabbage's mouth. The fit couldn't be better. I lift the bear's rear slightly, and I can't be sure, but I think I see a smile on The Cabbage's lips. I take Spatula with ⅔ a wooden handle and I press her down on the teddy bear as hard as I can.

244

The Cabbage shows great restraint. He doesn't fling his left arm up to his face, instead, he clutches the sheets. In the face of "death by teddy bear", he is brave and cooperative. The whole ordeal lasts longer than necessary because of the fantastic job I did on his heart. My construct fights and pumps until the very end. In some ways it's me versus my own clever engineering.

Long after the brain gives up, the heart gives up and The Cabbage lies in peace. I flick my accomplice, the teddy bear, off his face and whisper, "Good night, sleep tight." I think this will be his final sleep. I wonder if The Cabbage will find himself a ghost like me. Or will his final stop be a plot of earth that's been waiting for 2 1/2 years to cradle him?

I congratulate Spatula on a job well done.

CHAPTER 46

There's a crack of moonlight shining through the heavy drapes, illuminating Schlitz, sleeping on one side of the bed, like he still has a wife beside him. I listen to him snore and wheeze. What Spatula and I (and teddy) did to The Cabbage was an act of mercy, but now we have a different intent. I believe it's called *murder*.

There's no murderous teddy bear to conveniently hug Schlitz to death but *there* is a silk pillow by his head. I take a deep breath, after all I've already done this once tonight, twice shouldn't be too difficult, and I flip its silkiness over Schlitz's face. Before I can even press down, he takes the pillow and flings it across the room, knocking Spatula out of my hand. The violence and determination that he throws the pillow surprises me. I have to drop to all fours and crawl around, feeling for Spatula. I'm thinking about Schlitz's one admirable quality: his laser focus. Right now, unknown to him, he's laser focused on staying alive.

I grope around and find Spatula. We'll try again.

The king-size pillow under Schlitz's head hangs over the side of the bed. The logical course of action is to maneuver it over his face. There will be nothing for him to throw. I fold it over from the right, easy enough, and Spatula presses down. It seems to be going okay but then Schlitz grunts and rolls onto his right side. Spatula and I are left pressing a downy pillow on Schlitz's ear. That never killed anyone.

Okay, I think, *You are a worthy adversary. Without the help of teddy bear, Spatula and I may have to concede defeat.* It's humbling.

But then the maestro in me roars back. It says, "Examine The Toad, maybe your work has been done for you."

246

I, the maestro, gently lay my hand on Schlitz's bloated chest. I immediately like what I feel, a fast and irregular heartbeat. Then I gently lay my ear where my hand was and I hear a terrifically mistreated and malfunctioning pump. I laugh, a glorious, gleeful laugh. I need to do nothing! He won't be around long. I'll probably hear the news that The Toad died while I'm sitting at a cafe in Paris with My Darling, Saucisson and Spatula.

Confident that *time*, touted as a cure-all but actually the ultimate killer, will do my work for me, Spatula and I go downstairs to Schlitz's study. I survey his monitors, his briefcase, a pile of papers, the top one printed with a line that isn't even English: 77&5%RrF8*nmcv7'. I look at the next sheet, same thing, but a little different. And the next. I'm not being very careful, truth be told, and I knock the top two sheets off the back of the desk. They slip down between the massive desk and the wall. There is no way I can reach them, even with Spatula.

I get comfortable in Schlitz's navy recliner, wish I had a glass of amber liquid, and wait for morning.

CHAPTER 47

Morning comes.

Schlitz comes down in his boxers and makes himself an espresso with the fancy espresso maker on the counter. He moves like an experienced barista, twists the handle, bangs the grounds, scoops new grounds, presses the button, a stream of perfect caffeine comes out.

I follow him up the right staircase back to the bedroom. He walks into his bathroom that's attached to his dressing room and steps into the shower. I'm enjoying the steam and the aroma from the espresso swirling together; it feels masculine and clubby.

As he steps out of the shower, the two of us hear a small stifled scream from the other side of the house. Schlitz grabs his robe and we hurry over to the children's wing. Only I know what the surprise will be.

The nanny nurse is standing in the hallway of the plush, purple playroom, wringing her hands.

Schlitz hurries past her into the powder blue room with the Humpty Dumpty border. I don't go. I know I finally completed the job I botched 2½ years ago. Schlitz hurries back, to the distraught nanny nurse and the cool, calm me.

"Well, don't just stand there, call 911!"

We both jump. Nanny nurse rushes off to find her phone. Schlitz hastens to his dressing room and gets dressed. I sit, like a sultan, in the middle of the canopied bed. It's entertaining to watch all this rushing for absolutely no reason. The Cabbage is going nowhere. He needs no care, has no demands.

Schlitz comes out of the dressing room, meticulously dressed for a day at the office, even his tie is neatly knotted with the tip landing at the top of the sizable belt that cinches his middle.

I hear distant sirens coming our way.

I move my place of observation to the grand hall. It's perfect to witness the drama unfolding and there's plenty of room to not be in the way. Friedrich is now in the house. Schlitz must have texted him that he was needed. He's acting as butler, opening the grand front door for the EMTs. "Up this staircase to the left," he says, like a calm usher.

Three of them hurry up the stairs and a few moments later, two descend. They shuffle out to the ambulance to get the gurney. I hear one guy say to the other, "Could this place be any bigger?" And the other EMT says, "You know the cancer wing is named after this dude, you have to give big bucks to get a fuckin' wing named after you."

Schlitz comes downstairs and stands next to Friedrich. They both wear suits, one is cheap and worn and the other expensive and new. I still don't fully understand how Friedrich, the Congolese OBGYN, came to be living here in the United States, demoted to Schlitz's driver. Perhaps I'll never fully know but my best guess is Dr. Patricia Musa might be the common thread.

As they carry The Cabbage down, like a debutante who swooned for the last time, Schlitz asks the EMT, "So what's the protocol here?" The EMT tells Schlitz that he should follow the ambulance to the hospital. He'll need to sign papers and they can guide him through the next steps.

"Okay, Friedrich?"

"Of course, sir," Friedrich replies. He already has Schlitz's briefcase and hands it to him.

Friedrich and Schlitz walk to the mudroom door leading to the garage. Friedrich gets the Town Car key off the hook and hits the button to open the first garage bay. As he opens the back door for

Schlitz, he says, "Excuse me, sir, I hurried over, I need to get my hatching belt."

Schlitz grunts and he and I get into the back seat. When Friedrich opens the door to his apartment, I catch a glimpse of the boy and girl peering out. I wish I could do a quick entertaining trick for them because I'm sure they are frightened by all the extra commotion and the sounds of the siren.

I sit back into the soft upholstery. I look forward to going home and seeing Beth. We've never been apart this long, at least not in the last 2½ years. Hurting my back has ended up being very fortuitous. Without the pain, I wouldn't have been inclined to stop at Schlitz's, find and finish The Cabbage. (Note, I don't say *murder*, because it really wasn't.) It was simply the act of a maestro finishing an imperfect composition.

Friedrich backs out, the garage door closes, we follow the ambulance down the drive and out the gate. We're already a little funeral procession with the ambulance acting as the hearse. Friedrich is driving, Schlitz has his briefcase, respectfully closed, sitting on his lap, and I'm comfortably on my way home. Everything is proceeding perfectly.

When we get to the hospital, the ambulance turns onto the emergency ramp and Schlitz says, "I'd rather get out at the front entrance." Friedrich obliges and asks, "Do I have time to put gas in the car?"

"Sure, this will take at least half an hour. I'll text you. "

The gas station is across from Bon Vivant, which places me even closer to home, so I just stay in the car but move into the front passenger's seat.

We drive to the gas station, Friedrich parks at the gas pump. I'm waiting to get out and walk home when Friedrich takes his phone and texts Beth, "Can I stop by?" She immediately responds with a thumbs-up emoji.

I am not happy *per se* with the casual contact between my wife and Friedrich-the-Lug but I'm thrilled with the door-to-door service.

When we pull up at my gentleman's farm, My Darling walks out wearing shorts, a light sweater, and holding a cup of coffee. Saucisson barks once and then wags his tail, looking at Friedrich, but then he sees me and wags even harder. He whines and I wish I could bend down and stroke him with Spatula but I obviously can't. I go and stand next to Beth, wishing I could hug her; we've been apart too long.

"What a pleasant surprise," she says. "Everything okay with the egg?"

"Oh, yes," Friedrich says, touching the bump at his waist. "The egg is fine, not much longer now."

They both smile.

"It's been a strange morning. The man I work for, his father died last night."

"Oh," Beth says. "I'm so sorry. Was it expected?"

"Yes, yes, he was incapacitated. It was only a matter of time. But before he was bedridden, Schlitz the Senior was a good man. He made me laugh when I had nothing to laugh about. His son is nothing like him."

Beth is standing very still. "What's the name of the man you work for?"

"Gunther Schlitz the Junior."

Beth shifts from one foot to the other. She looks uncomfortable. "My husband Tom, my late husband, operated on Schlitz Sr. It went poorly."

Friedrich looks genuinely sad. I'm not sure if he's sad for The Cabbage, or if he's sad for me, a fellow professional, or if he's sad for Beth, having such a clumsy husband, but the bottom line is he looks sad. "Those things happen," he says.

I never met Schlitz Sr. before surgery; our first meeting was while he was being rolled into the OR. I was quickly explaining the procedure I was going to perform and he interrupted me. He turned to the head cardiothoracic nurse, Patty, who has frizzled grey hair and hands like a man. "When they put me under, do you mind if I dream of you, sweetheart?"

She gave him a deep laugh. It came from a part of her that I didn't even know existed. Schlitz Sr. had given her a gift that I never had.

"Would you like to come in?" Beth asks.

"No, I need to head back. The Schlitz Junior will be done at the hospital. He's very…" Friedrich searches for the right word. He chooses *sad*. "He's very sad this morning."

I relish being home…

I love how the French doors stay open and I can easily walk out to the yard whenever I want. I love the predictability of Beth's movements. (Sometimes I know what she's going to do before she does!) I look forward to Little Leftie hatching and seeing my pond put to good use. I'm even beginning to love Saucisson, who's greed for life has been tamped down by the knowledge that nothing is going to be taken from him, only given.

The most interesting thing to happen after Friedrich leaves is that my amigo Miguel comes with a new door handle to install on the back door. This makes no sense. I stand over his shoulder and watch him unscrew the knob and plate. Nothing was wrong with the old door knob but Beth must have asked him to replace it.

The mystery is why she requested a door *lever* instead of a door *knob*. Every other door in the house is opened and closed with a door knob. There seemed to be nothing wrong with this door knob, it opened and closed fine. But Miguel shows up and installs a new antique brass door lever. He carefully removes the shiny old door knob, puts it in the lever box, tapes it shut and labels it "back door knob". He puts it down in the basement with our partial cans of Modern Eggshell paint. I wish I knew Beth's motivation.

I spend way too much of my day thinking about the door lever. My world has grown and I know there's so much more happening out there besides door levers. Is this why, by evening, I feel so discontent?

Have my expectations grown? I was so satisfied as a house ghost, waiting for my dwarf trees to bear fruit and making plans to move to Paris. What's become of me? Have I become a spy? A lover? An entertainer? An assassin? There's real life human drama happening out there and I want to know more, be more involved.

Am I becoming like Stick-Your-Nose-In-Everyone's-Business-Sandy, no longer content with my little corner of the world? Which reminds me, I wonder how she's doing.

I spend the night walking around the house. I go up and down the stairs, even though Saucisson snores in our bedroom. I gaze at My Darling Beth, the good duck mother, sleeping on her back, incubating the eggs while she sleeps. Then I walk downstairs, do nothing, walk back up, sit next to Saucisson and pet him with Spatula, even though he does not whine in pain. His tail does a thump, thump, thump, without him opening an eye.

I'm a man with ambition who has a lot to offer and I'm under-utilized, I need more.

I perch on my chair and devise a plan. Tomorrow, instead of sitting, waiting for life to come to me, I will go out and find life. I'll go on an odyssey of sorts. Why not? I'll improvise and make do with what I have and seek truth. I'm not talking huge distances, I'm talking about a trip to *Pequeña Fleur* to check on Miguel, a trip up Round House Road with a stop at Schlitz's to cheer up Friedrich's children, and lastly a stop at Jessica's to see if I can be helpful.

CHAPTER 48

In the morning, Beth texts Friedrich over and over and he doesn't answer.

I can tell she's annoyed, alarmed and hurt all at once.

How do I feel? I am not sure. But I know I *don't* feel smug, jubilant, or victorious. I'll make it part of my odyssey to walk first to Schlitz's with Spatula and see if Friedrich is okay.

I wish I could meet Schlitz on his own turf and beat him at his own game. Maybe I should have studied finance instead of French. It would be so satisfying to press Spatula's ⅔ handle on a computer key and watch his wealth disappear. I'm not sure if that's even possible but that's how they seem to do it in the movies.

I'm sitting on the front steps, thinking of financial espionage when a beat-up old Fiat drives into our driveway. It takes me a minute to register but then I recognize it as the Fiat that was parked in the fourth garage bay at Schlitz's house. Friedrich is behind the wheel and, even with the glare of the windshield, I can see he's *not* smiling.

Darling Beth comes out of the back door (with the new lever knob) as he unfolds from the tiny car. She and I walk toward the Fiat.

"Oh, Friedrich! I was worried about you. I kept texting. How's the egg?"

Friedrich doesn't respond. His face just sort of caves in upon itself followed by his substantial body. Friedrich begins to cry, correction, sob.

Beth stops in her tracks and I inhale sharply. This is something I've never seen, nor experienced. I'm not sure Beth has, either. You know that expression, "It would make a grown man cry?" I never knew what "it" was. Darling Beth regains her sensibilities quicker than I do. She hugs The Lug, not too tightly because of the eggs and I don't mind. This act of kindness makes Friedrich cry harder. I think about stroking him on the back with Spatula.

When Beth lets go, she touches his middle, "Where's your hatching belt, Friedrich?"

"Beth, Beth, I am so disappointed with myself."

"It's okay, it's okay. It was just an egg."

But this is like a slap to Friedrich. He pulls back from Beth. "It was not just an egg *to me*." He takes a deep breath, "I have to tell you, I'm not who you think I am, Beth Paradise. *I'm a murderer*."

I immediately think of his ghost children and frankly, I'm shocked.

Beth doesn't miss a beat. She absolutely refuses to take him literally. "Let me get Achilles's leash, we'll go on a walk. You need to tell me what happened. From the *beginning*."

So we go for a walk. I follow behind like an obedient child. Saucisson is always one step in the middle, torn if he should walk beside Beth or me. When we walk in front of Ray's house, we don't have to detour off the sidewalk because, as Beth mentions to Friedrich, "My neighbor hired my lawn guy." Kudos to Miguel, he has cut the bushes back so they're neat and orderly.

Friedrich takes a deep breath, pauses, and begins, "My name is Friedrich Ngoy. I was born in 1969 in the Democratic Republic of the Congo, formerly known as Zaire."

Boy, I think, *he really is starting at the beginning.*

But Friedrich seems to have this narrative memorized and this is how he chooses to tell it. Maybe this is the only way he can make any sense of it, or maybe this is the only way the words will come out. I am not being judgmental, it's just not where I would choose to begin explaining how I broke my duck egg.

"My village was beautiful and my parents were kind and loving. When they saw I had promise, they sent me to boarding school in the capital, Kinshasa, and I received the best education a boy could get. I hated the city but I knew I had a duty to do my very best. When I was done with secondary schooling, I went on to the Université de Kinshasa, undergraduate and then medical training. I am a doctor of obstetrics and gynecology. I met my wife in the hospital, she was a nurse."

When Friedrich says "wife", Beth suddenly drops her head. She looks embarrassed. Not only is Friedrich nine years younger, he's married and she's been brazenly encouraging him.

"We had two children, a boy named Augustan, after my father, and a girl named Laura. They were wonderful children, smart and kind." His voice trails off, like a dog chasing a memory.

"The Great African war broke out, or what we call The Second Congolese War, a war for independence. Most of you Americans don't even know about it. Six million dead and no one even recalls reading about it." It sounds like he's being judgmental, but then he adds, "And you know, in retrospect, you can read all you want and even *I* can't make sense of it. The military killed, the police killed, the militias killed. Do you know corporations hired their own mercenaries? Dupont and Cargill paid killers to protect what they thought was theirs. Anyone could be a killer or be killed."

Beth says, "That's terrible."

"I was working in the capital and I sent my wife and children to my parents' village. It seemed safer, a little village not worth fighting over, just some fields and shops. But one of these groups, perhaps the Cargill army, perhaps our own army, who knows, raided the village and killed as many people as they could."

Beth stops. Friedrich stops. Saucisson stops. I stop. It is too difficult to listen *and* walk.

"They killed my children." Now he looks down, "I'm not sure about my wife, but I looked and looked and we never found her. My parents were in another village visiting friends when it took place. They were okay but both died within a year. I'm sure it was the guilt of being alive. And yet, here I am, still alive, strong as an ox." He laughs bitterly.

I think of the two ghost children. I think, *Poor Augustan and little Laura.*

"I did what I could for the survivors but my heart was no longer in my work. It was like watching the same terrible movie with the same terrible ending day after day. I thought about killing myself but that would have been too easy. Where's the suffering in that?"

He takes Beth's arm and says, "Let's walk, it's easier to talk. I don't want you looking at me."

So the three of us, each of us in our own thoughts with our own terrible images, keep walking. Even Saucisson's spirits seem dampened.

"I was at my lowest point when a group of doctors from this town arrived at my hospital. Patricia Musa was the doctor who organized the mission. We became friends and she eventually made it possible for me to come here. She found me a sponsor who gave me a job. She was the first person to save my life. She saved me when I didn't want to be saved."

This story is old, by my calculations about 15 years, but it's still vivid to Friedrich and very hard to listen to.

Beth, who's usually very good in social situations, has no words. Finally, she says, "I'm so sorry. I had no idea. It's funny, but my husband almost went on that mission... you would have had a chance to meet him. He had such potential..."

She doesn't add any qualifiers like, "He was chief of the department and needed to be here." Or, "Our kids were young and it was dangerous." And what is this about *potential*? The truth is, I didn't want to go and do half-ass work in primitive conditions. It wasn't the way I liked to work. But when you parse through all the pompous perfectionism, the truth was: I didn't care enough and Beth and I both knew it.

We've arrived back home after our lovely two-mile promenade among trees and singing birds while listening to a hellish tale. It's discordant, to say the least. Seeing the beat-up, robin's-egg-blue Fiat makes me remember the egg. The egg that started all this, or shall I say the *lack* of the egg. I want to say, "So Friedrich, this brings us to the egg…"

"Come in, I'll make you dinner," Beth says.

Friedrich looks hesitant.

"Come on, I was actually going to cook."

We all go in. He sees our big country kitchen with its attached family room and French doors opening to the back. He walks through the French doors and gazes at the pond. "Ah, the pond where my little duck was going to live."

"Sit, talk to me while I cook."

She offers him my stool, the stool I prefer at the kitchen island. "Would you like a beer? Or a glass of wine? I'm going to have wine."

"Wine, please. I never drink it because I love it. I'm afraid I'll drink the whole bottle."

It's a moment of levity; we all chuckle. Beth gets out a top-notch bottle of white *Fevre Chablis Les Clos Grand Cru* from Burgundy, France. Friedrich picks up the bottle and reads it with the accent of a sommelier. When Beth takes out a wine opener, he takes it from her and opens the bottle with the skill of a surgeon.

Beth smiles, puts out two glasses, and he pours. They do a light cheers and I wish terribly that I could have a glass, too. Beth pulls out some vegetables and garlic cloves, puts them on the cutting board and says, "Okay, now tell me about the egg."

I pivot in my seat and give Friedrich my full attention.

"So, as I said, I work for Schlitz the Junior. He came up with some insane idea in which I'm a thief." He swirls the wine.

Beth looks at him quizzically.

"The morning his father was found dead, I think he went a little crazy. I went into his study to get his briefcase and he thinks I stole his crypto passwords." Friedrich takes a gulp of his wine, refills his glass and takes another gulp. Friedrich-the-Lug is not one to be rushed with his story telling.

"Why on earth would he think such a thing?"

"He had each one written on a sheet of paper and now he can't find two of the pieces of paper. I've heard of this crypto currency but I don't understand it. I definitely didn't steal his passwords."

"Of course you didn't, that's ridiculous. But what happened to the egg?"

"Well, after searching for the missing papers without success, he summons me. I have... had an apartment above the garage. He's a little drunk, not very, but I'm sure a little. I assume he is going to have me drive him somewhere, but instead, he asks to see the egg. This makes me happy, there's been so much sadness this day. I take my hatching belt off, to show him and am planning to share the video with him. He seems interested. He picks up the egg, but then he makes his crazy accusation of stealing and drops my egg on the counter..."

Beth and I gasp. It's needlessly cruel. The duckling tucked in the egg had nothing to do with the alleged theft, which was no theft at all but my fault.

"My duckling was perfect. She was perfectly formed. She just needed a little time."

Beth walks over and rubs his shoulders and back. Friedrich starts to cry again. "I thought I had used all my tears up so long ago, but they grew back for this little duck."

I genuinely feel sorry for Friedrich and more than slightly responsible. Someday, the desk will be moved, to clean behind it, and Gunther Schlitz Jr. will know the mistake he made.

"He fired me. I would have quit anyway but still, I've never been fired. After all, I *was* a doctor of obstetrics and gynecology and *now* I am a driver. Where's the bottom?"

Beth sits down on the stool where I'm seated. She perches on my lap and it feels good. Her butt is warm and I wrap my arms around her. "What are you going to do?"

"Well, first of all, I didn't answer your texts because I was so ashamed. I failed in my duties to protect my egg and second, I needed to figure out where I was going to live."

Beth and I breathe in and out together. We are perfectly synchronized.

"Do you know Miss Sydney, at Bon Vivant?"

Beth nods.

"She owns that big old house on the corner of Park and Maple. She has it subdivided into efficiencies and one bedrooms. Ben, in prepared foods, wants to retire and she's hiring me and I'm renting an efficiency."

Beth claps her hands, "That's so wonderful, Friedrich!" She leans forward and almost falls off my lap to hug him.

Beth lifts up her cream cashmere, which is so light it's like gossamer threads. She touches each of the hatching belts and picks mine, Little Leftie.

"Here, take this belt. We only have a couple more days. I don't want you to miss the experience of hatching. Tom wouldn't mind."

But Tom *does* mind!

She carefully un-Velcros Little Leftie and offers it to Friedrich with two hands, like it's a sacred chalice.

Friedrich accepts it and straps it on. "It will be safe, I promise."

And that's that. In a blink of an eye, Little Leftie is taken from me and given to him.

That night, when Friedrich leaves, he bends and gives Beth the lightest kiss on the cheek. It could be a kiss someone gives to their grandma. It's perfectly innocuous and sexless but Beth blushes.

"Friedrich, could you go with me tomorrow to a Celebration of Life? My friend Sandy lost her son in a car accident. He played in a band. His band is going to play in her yard, there'll be tons of people. If you know Sandy, you know it will be big, loud and very cathartic. I'm so tired of being sad and going everywhere alone. I'd like to introduce you to some of my friends."

Friedrich doesn't hesitate, "Yes, it's a date." He opens the Fiat door. "I don't start work until Monday. I think he's having the funeral for Schlitz the Senior tomorrow but I am not welcome and I wouldn't risk showing up with my new baby." And he pats Little Leftie.

CHAPTER 49

Saturday dawns clear and sunny. I'm torn about attending the impending celebration of life. I want to keep an eye on Beth and Friedrich, but Beth is right, it's Sandy, and the ceremony of grief will devolve into some sort of wildness and I definitely feel vulnerable in crowds. But it's Saturday and Saturdays have proven to be unpredictable and fun and I enjoy them now.

My mood is dampened when Jessica texts Beth, "Can you come visit? The girls and I would love to see you."

Beth texts: "Yes, I can come tomorrow. Do you have a warm box ready for the ducklings? They should start pipping at any moment."

"Yes, we're all ready. We bought a baby pool."

"How's Margaret?"

"She's excited."

Everything sounds okay, even good, but I am suspicious that it's not.

I wish I could tell Beth, "We should go now. Let's drive up and check things out, we don't have to stay long."

But Beth seems intent on cleaning and "nesting". She goes down in the basement, gets a box and puts some old towels in it. She puts it on the counter under the lights that run under the cupboards. She turns on the lights and puts a thermometer in the box. The newly hatched ducklings must remain at 100 degrees with no drafts for 48 hours. Each day, they'll get stronger and temperature will become less of an issue. Beth's idea is good. The bulbs under the cupboards generate a lot of heat.

When Beth sits down to eat lunch, she removes her belt. She holds the egg to her ear and smiles. Even I, sitting one stool away, can hear the delicate tap-tap-tap. Pipping has started.

She immediately texts Friedrich, "Hold your egg to your ear, is it tapping?"

"YES!" he texts.

She texts Ray, "Hold the egg to your ear, is it tapping?"

Ray texts, "Yes!"

She texts Jessica, "Ask the girls to hold their eggs to their ears. Are they tapping?"

Jessica texts back, "All good! The girls are excited!"

Beth checks the temperature in the box, it's 100, perfect for the ducklings.

Friedrich arrives at 4:00 in his beat-up Fiat. He has on his same pointy shoes, the same threadbare suit, but is wearing a bright orange collared shirt. He grins and says, "It's the new me."

Beth laughs. She brings him into the house and shows him the box setup. Friedrich approves.

Beth pats Saucisson and tells him to be a good dog. I'm torn still, but the thought of staying behind is too depressing. I'm going to the celebration, which by its nature should be sad, but the communal nature of grieving will be cathartic.

Beth says, "Let's take my car," and the three of us go out to the garage.

"Please allow me to drive. I am an excellent driver."

I can certainly vouch for that.

He holds Beth's door open with great courtesy. I'm able to climb in first as she thanks him. When we get to Sandy's, cars are lined up on both sides of the street. We have to park ten houses away and walk.

"I told you," says Beth, "it will be big. Sandy knows everyone and her kids have lots of friends. Everyone will want to support Sandy and her family and say goodbye to Jason."

Sandy's house has a large side yard, where her kids used to practice lacrosse and throw frisbees. A small stage is set up at one end, with large speakers. Sandy's veranda has tables of food and two bars. There's a large screen with a projector against one of the house walls. It has a film loop of home movies and pictures of Jason at all ages.

The band starts to tune up. What I assume is Jason's guitar is propped on a chair on stage. The band leader says into the microphone, "We're the Bubble Heads. We're Jason's band and brothers. Everything we play tonight is dedicated to Jason." The young man looks at the chair with Jason's guitar. His voice cracks. "We miss you, brother, it won't be the same without you."

I can hear the collective sniffle as the drummer taps 1-2-3 and the electric guitar whines.

The band keeps the music to a low roar. It's still early and I'm sure Sandy has told them to keep it a little tame until sunset. Then they can play whatever they want and let all the young people act out their rage, fear, sadness and hope.

Beth finds Sandy, introduces Friedrich and gives her condolences. Sandy is defiant in a hot pink dress. She will not let this loss destroy her. Larry looks a little more defeated.

When we walk away, Friedrich says, "That is a strong woman."

Beth agrees.

Many of the younger people have gotten drinks and are standing out on the lawn. Beth sees Emily and pulls Friedrich over. "Emily!" She introduces Friedrich and then my amigo Miguel walks up. "Miguel!" Beth says.

"*Hola, Señora* Beth!" Emily puts her arm around his waist. My amigo and Drunk Emily are obviously an item, as they say.

"How did you meet, besides in my driveway?" Beth asks.

Emily smiles. "AA, I went back to AA. Miguel attends, too."

My amigo is a recovered alcoholic, who knew?

"Miguel, I gave your egg to Ray, my neighbor."

"It's good, Señora Beth. When he hired me to trim his bushes, he told me he'd keep his duckling with yours. We'll have plenty of duck babies, I'll help you take care of them."

"Speaking of babies, how's Fernanda?" Beth turns to Friedrich, "Fernanda is Miguel's daughter, she's a lovely girl, she's due soon."

"Fernanda has chosen her own path. Going back to AA has helped me understand." He smiles at Emily. "God grant me the serenity to accept the things I cannot change." He looks at the stage. "I'll be there for her when she needs me."

My Darling Beth smiles. "I think there's a lesson in that for all of us, 'to accept the things we cannot change.'" She bestows the sweetest smile upon Friedrich.

I know I shouldn't admit it but this smile fills me with rage. It's the blessing of an angel and it should be bestowed on me, not him.

He smiles back. I grimace.

Then Ray walks up. He's wearing a flamboyant flowered shirt, which given everything I know, is appropriate. He lifts his shirt. "Still got a bun in the oven! But he's tapping to get out!"

The band stops playing and takes a break. Sandy, Larry and their three surviving children walk up to the microphone. Sandy speaks for the group, "We just want to thank everyone for coming. We know Jason would love this, he'd be happy to see all his friends here having a good time. He'd be happy to hear his band play and see his favorite guitar. We miss him terribly, his life on this earth was too short." She looks at Larry and her three children, they all wipe their eyes. "It's a reminder to us all that life is precious. We have to seize the opportunities when they arise and love each other fiercely."

When Sandy says, "fiercely," her voice quivers and the family of five falls in upon itself in a group hug. There's not a dry eye. Friedrich, who never knew Jason, cries freely. Beth comforts him, knowing now that he and Jason's parents share something she does not.

I, obviously, can't help but compare this celebration of life to my own. It's the same cast of characters, plus about 200 more. Despite the loud music, I like it better than mine. I like the plentitude and the movies and pictures showing Jason as a boy, a son, a brother, a musician, a traveler. He seemed to have lived a full life in a short time. I think of Evie and her full days. She would approve of this celebration, too.

Then I think of Angel Margaret. What will happen to Sophia and Charlotte? How will they be able to understand death? Then I think of beautiful Jessica. She's much better off without Kline but she'll be alone and isolated in her grief. I'm sure she'll mourn and keep loving Margaret fiercely.

What if Margaret becomes a ghost, alone in that big house? Will she find a tool like Spatula? Who'll teach her the tricks of the trade? What's safe and how to enjoy oneself in this new form? It would be frightening to be a child and find yourself in my position.

Terrible, in fact.

CHAPTER 50

Beth, Friedrich and I stay at Jason's Celebration of Life for a few hours. The band will play late into the night. I'm sure Sandy warned the neighbors when she invited them and no one would dare complain about the noise, considering the circumstances.

When we walk back to our car, Friedrich opens the passenger door for Beth. I can easily climb in first. What's that quip? "If a man holds the car door for his wife, he either has a new car or a new wife." Friedrich may be on his way to having both.

We head home. Beth doesn't have to coerce Friedrich to come in, it's assumed they'll spend the evening together. Saucisson doesn't bother barking, in fact, he gives me a low growl before wagging his tail. Somehow, despite my wishes, despite my interference, Friedrich and Beth have found each other. They've inexplicably become a couple.

My Darling could have done worse. Friedrich was a worthy opponent, be it oblivious, during our epic 30-day struggle. In retrospect, perhaps I concentrated my energies on the wrong person; maybe my real nemesis was Beth and her desire to move on with life. But how does one combat the will to live? I feel it so strongly now within myself. How can I deny My Darling the only thing I can't give her?

They have each had a glass of wine at the celebration and a few appetizers. Beth, much to my surprise, opens a bottle of wine and without asking Friedrich, she pours two glasses. She makes two small plates of food with leftovers from the night before and microwaves each of them, putting it all on a tray with silverware and napkins.

"Friedrich, the TV's in my room. Let's lie on my bed, turn on an old movie and watch our babies hatch."

It is such a bold move on her part, so unlike her. Frankly, I am dumbfounded, speechless. Wine, nibbles in bed and an old movie is my favorite way to spend a Saturday night. Friedrich smiles. It's a simple smile that says, "Yes, you've won. I am ready to leave my misery behind, love and be loved."

Beth adjusts the nesting box on the counter and turns on the lights under the cupboard that will warm it.

Friedrich and Saucisson are standing behind Beth, ready to obediently follow her upstairs. I've reclaimed my choice stool at the island.

"Friedrich, please hit that switch," Beth says, nodding her head toward the light switch on the wall while looking directly at me, sitting at the island. "I'll come down *later* and *lock up.*"

Friedrich hits the switch.

The lights over my head go out and I am left sitting in the dim kitchen with the soft glow from the lights above the counter. For the first time in my life I feel abandoned and at a total loss. A man without a plan, rudderless, with no compass. I think about how Beth said I had *such potential* and ponder what that means. Was there something I didn't attain?

I'm sitting quietly when I hear a muffled noise. At first I think it's coming from upstairs, perhaps from the TV but it's not. I hear some scratching and then very clearly peeping. I get up and look in the nesting box. Nothing. They have their eggs upstairs with them. But that's where it seems to be coming from. Then I remember the warming drawer, which is located right below where the nesting box is sitting. Using the old rubber end, I take Spatula and pull it open.

Inside the drawer is a perfect duckling. It's even cuter than I expected, with a little black tiger stripe across its eye. I decide it's a "she" for no reason. She's sitting on the pink tea towel, half dry, with the egg fragments around her, looking very proud. When she sees me, she peeps loudly, imprinting. She can't help it, it's nature. She loves me, no strings attached, and I love her.

I pet her gently with Spatula and marvel at her tiny black beak. I'm wondering if I should transfer her into the nesting box, using Spatula (wouldn't Beth be surprised!) or if I should just let her rest in the drawer, leaving it open a crack so Beth hears the peeps and finds her. I am running through all the options while stroking her, when suddenly, it all comes so clear to me. The plan was there all the time, Beth had already laid it out. I just wasn't ready to see it. I hadn't pipped my way out of my own shell.

I whisper to the duckling, "I love you so much but it's time for me to go. I'm sorry to leave you but you will be in good hands."

I decide to transfer the little miracle into the hatching box. She will be my last gift to My Darling and I chuckle, thinking of Beth's surprise, finding her placed in the warm box. I wish I could put a little bow around her neck. What a wonder that would be! I get the tiny, downy ball placed on trusty Spatula and begin the precarious move. My hand is so steady, it is still a marvel, even to me. But low and behold, the duckling isn't an inanimate object, she isn't a clamp, forceps or scalpel, and definitely not a cup of coffee. She jumps! She jumps off Spatula, bounces off the counter and lands on the floor. I inhale sharply.

And here is the tragedy.

Saucisson must have heard the peeps. He carried his fat little body down the steps and I was so enchanted with finding my tiny miracle, I didn't even notice him sitting attentively at my feet.

When the tiny miracle bounces off the counter and onto the floor, Saucisson has no idea what this thing coming down is, but he is ready. He grabs the miracle, bites down and let's go. It's not the tidbit he expected. I scream but there is no one to hear my anguish. I smack him hard across the nose with Spatula, although it is after the fact and there was no malice in his actions. His greed for life robbed my downy miracle of her life. Saucisson yelps and runs back upstairs.

My tiny miracle isn't a mess, she's unmoving, lifeless. If I could examine her closely, I might not even find a puncture wound, she might have died from a broken neck. All I know is that I can't leave her here, on the kitchen floor. This is not the parting gift I want to leave My Darling. Definitely not. So I gently scoop her up with Spatula.

It's time to leave 22 Woodhill Road, my home, my gentleman's farm. I no longer belong here and neither does she, this tiny tragedy. So balancing her carefully on trusty Spatula, I head to the back door. I stare at the new lever and I know without a shadow of a doubt why Beth had it installed. I also know why she said she'd "lock up later." My Darling Beth was one step ahead of me the whole time.

I lay the tiny tragedy down and use Spatula to push down and pull the door towards me. Once I'm out the door, I carefully reach back in and shuffle the tiny tragedy back onto Spatula. I will give her a proper burial somewhere, maybe under a pile of leaves. I don't bother pulling the door closed, Beth will check the doors and lock up later.

As I walk down my driveway, I take note of where my catastrophic heart attack struck me down, beginning this journey. I'm confident that I'm a different man from who I was on that snowy day. I'm determined to live my life to its full potential.

I walk over to my favorite dwarf peach tree, which has a small pile of leaves and mulch under it. I kiss the tiny tragedy on her marvelous beak and think, *I'm so sorry we can't do this journey together.* I gently lay her down and brush some leaves and mulch over her. My heart is heavy, so heavy.

Then I cross the street and start down the sidewalk. I think I can hear the heavy bass from Jason's celebration of life pounding out a beat, "Thud, thud, thud." Is that possible? Could the band be so loud that I can hear it a mile away? Ray's lights are shining brightly. I imagine my buddy inside, watching his duckling pip out of its shell. Maybe he's switched into his floral lady's nightgown. Maybe he's texting Beth about the progress. It makes me ache for my tiny tragedy that imprinted on me. When I get to the end of Woodhill and start to make my way north up Round House, I realize that the heavy thud, thud, thud can't possibly be the band at Sandy's.

The thud, thud, thud is my heart.

I am so absorbed in listening to this new sound within me that I almost miss hearing the tiny peep, peep, peep behind me. It's my duckling! My heart has become so true that I've been able to bring the tiny miracle back in a ghostly form.

I pick her up. (So much easier to hold than balance on Spatual!) I kiss her marvelous beak, name her Peeper and easily hold her as I walk. She settles into the security of my steady, cupped hands.

After an hour or so, I find myself approaching Gunther-Schlitz-Who-Shits-Money's house. The road has a slight rise, so I can see over his wall in the near distance. I only see a few lights on and wonder what Schlitz is doing. Is he sitting alone in his imposing study trying to remember his passwords? I wonder how the massive house feels with no Cabbage, no nanny nurse, no Friedrich? Will he hire a new driver? Or will he just perch in his opulent splendor all alone?

But whoa!

I clutch Peeper to me a little tighter. I see a dark form huddled against the stone post where the gate is attached. My first thought is, "The Cabbage!" but the form is too small, too close to the ground. I approach, carefully, with Peeper shielded in my hands and Spatula tucked under my arm.

It's Augustin and Little Laura! When The Lug didn't come back, they must have wandered out of the estate and found themselves locked outside the gate, helpless without a spatula . They're huddled, squatting side by side, against the stone post.

Heidi Matonis

When they see me, Augustin smiles and Little Laura shrinks back. I hold out my hands with Peeper, showing Laura how to make a nest with her small hands. I carefully place Peeper in the cup of Laura's hands and she smiles happily. I untuck Spatula from under my arm, give her a flip in the air and then hand her to Augustin. Because it's dark, I let him hold Spatula like a baton and wave her about. Then I take his hand and he takes Little Laura's elbow and I say, "*Allé avec moi, Augustin et Petite Laura.*"

Little Laura giggles, probably because my accent is so good.

Augustin says, "Okay, mister!"

With my little troupe, I head north to Jessica's. There's so much I want to communicate with Augustin and Little Laura. I want to tell them how they'll be safe and cared for by me. How they'll have plenty of room to play. How their human siblings are sweet and rambunctious and their human mother beautiful and kind. I want to tell them about Angel Margaret and how she might be joining our ghost family.

I vow to show my ghost children how to float on their backs in the pool, while Peeper paddles around us, and we listen to the wren sing at sunset. Then I'll show them how to lie on the lawn and I'll point out constellations. I'll leave them to grow, like the lush grass outside the wall. I won't cut or trim them, I'll just let them flourish and accept them as perfect.

And then there's Jessica. I will not provide, protect, assume, ignore, objectify, lecture, diminish, manage nor control. I'll just love her.

I imagine, later this summer, maybe in the fall, we'll all be downtown, strolling along main street, and we'll meet my amigo Miguel. He and Emily will be walking with Fernanda between them, a happy family. Then we'll run into Beth and Friedrich. I'll clasp Friedrich on the shoulder, kiss him on each cheek and say, "*Bonjour, mon ami!*"

I'm sure Beth will hug Jessica and each of the girls, Sophie, Charlotte, and maybe Margaret. Because miracles do happen. Ask any heart surgeon. Or any hatching-belt wearer. They'll talk about the ducks. Will they fly north? No one knows. Peeper won't. She'll never grow adult feathers. She'll always be a great joy to Little Laura, and perhaps Margaret, and stay with us, our tiny miracle.

As the imagined chatting between the two women winds down, and Beth and Friedrich turn to leave, I'll take Spatula from Augustin and tap Beth on her derrière. Augustin will probably laugh, he's like that, amused by slapstick. Beth will twist and see Spatula, with her yellow rubber and ⅔ handle floating in the air behind her. And Beth will know that I, the maestro, finally reached my potential and found a way to fix my own shitty heart.

Le Fin

Made in the USA
Middletown, DE
03 June 2023

31678728R00170